Reviews

"Compelling story of a man and his journey from the stoops of Brooklyn to the heights of Manhattan… I couldn't put the book down!"
— Steve F.

*"Wonderful, heart wrenching account of a piece of history.
My congratulations to this author. Thanks for writing your story."*
— Stella A.

"I loved it!"
— Judy C.

"Riveting, couldn't wait for the next chapter."
— Richard M.

"Courageous author, publicizing his personal experiences."
— Sam S.

Acknowledgments

Johanna, my wife who gently provided the push for me to write this memoir. My best friend, Sam Singer who started me on the correct journey into the bar business after hearing it was what I wanted to do. John Shanker and Herb Fisher my partners. Bill, Stanley, Allen and Dennis who gently guided me into gay culture as I began my apprenticeship in a new environment. Seymour Seiden who taught me the New York bar business and whose expertise was an integral part of its success. A great partner and friend, I miss him dearly. Ken Gaston, his talent for publicity was crucial for the initial success of Rounds. Gerald Richland, the talent designer who was able to work with the demanding Seymour. Paul Spinnelli who treated me to endless hours of laughter as we palled together. Walter Lucy and the close relationship he generously extended to me and everyone he came in contact with. Bruce Nid a trust worthy employee and a true friend to this day. John Sorrelli has been a true friend the longest of anyone. Always there for me. His exceptional wood work made Rounds envious. My associate in construction, Sal Fiori who was able to transform a rundown bar/restaurant into a thing of elegance as he interpreted Gerry's plans. Toni's kitchen talent enabled us to present fine cuisine as he managed the staff and vendors. Michael Davie, another trusted hard working host.

Edwin Dom who Belgium background gave the host's position European charm.

Steve and Maria Finkle who guided me towards Jon and Bridget who edited my manuscript.

All the exceptional customers who patronized Rounds and made it the place to be, the famous and the working boys, sadly most have succumbed to the HIV virus.

The exceptional staff : security on the door, bar tenders, waiters, bus boys, cooks, porters and finally the very talented piano players who made Rounds a special place where single lonely patrons could relate to: Mickey, Enid, Berry, Susan Tug and others whom I no longer remember.

Thanks To All From The Bottom Of My Heart

Charles M Scaglione Sr.

Introduction

Chas an ex construction executive wants to learn the bar business in order to be self employed and also be able to enjoy his passion in his free time working with his cowboy friends in northern Nevada. Through associates he meets and bonds with Seymour an ex school teacher with business savvy and mob connections famous for opening the Sanctuary, a popular discotheque in a converted German Baptist church on west 49th street in Manhattan years earlier. He became known as the "Velvet Mafioso". Its popularity drew huge crowds. Police would cordon off the street to maintain safety until it closed years later.

Ken is a well known small time producer in New York City and a friend of Seymour. He has an affable personality and a strong desire to be the star in his "Casablanca". He finds a closed restaurant on East 53rd St. in Manhattan and suggests the trio open a restaurant. "My mailing list will fill the place", Ken boasts.

The partners struggle with their differences, however they manage to raise the funds to design, build, promote and staff the piano bar known as ROUNDS with the sexiest male help anywhere. Ken's promotion draws the rich and famous to feast, drink and cruise the help.

Being an owner in the popular ROUNDS gives Chas power wealth and sex. He compromises his core values of a life he always dreamt about. He eventually realizes he has been trapped, swimming in shark invested waters.

1   Chas resigns from an executive position in the high-rise building business at thirty-six years old. After eighteen years in that business, he is burned out and looking for a new, exciting career.

He enjoys some vacation time each year at his friend's ranches in Nevada and California. The rest of his vacation time is spent with his wife and children at the shore.

Going into a small business for himself seems to be the way he will be able to support his family, and enjoy his hobby during his free time. He and his wife raise three children in New Jersey suburbs.

At six-foot-three-inches tall, lean, with dark brown hair and a deep voice, he has an intimidating affect on some people.

The only person he respects to discuss his plans with is Sam Singer, a self made business man. He's tall, slim, handsome with wavy hair, and has a dynamic personality. He is Chas' best friend and mentor. He phones his friend.

"Sam, it's Chas. How are you doing?"

"Good, Chas, what's up with you? Long time with no news from you," Sam replies.

"Yeah, I know, I've been out west at my friend's ranches the last six weeks, helping him," Chas explains. "I need to meet with you, to run questions by you."

"Want to meet for lunch, Chas?"

"It's what I had in mind Sam," Chas replies. "How about tomorrow, at that dump by your shop?"

"One it is," Sam says. "See you then. Bye"

At a noisy, crowded, smoke-filled diner occupied by factory workers in Queens, New York, Chas waits for Sam.

He is excited, hoping Sam will be happy he found a new vocation; as he waits for Sam he thinks: *Sam's business acumen will provide the answer I need. The food odors are making my empty stomach gurgle. I hate when people's tardiness keeps me hungry.*

"Sorry I'm late. I couldn't get off the phone," Sam says. "It's good to see you."

He sits down opposite Chas and both men shake hands.

"Good to see you," Chas replies. "It's okay, Sam, you're a busy man with all the men under you. First, how are Irma and the kids?"

"Everyone is well, thanks for asking," Sam mentions. "I never know where you are—you move around so much. You sounded excited on the phone. What's up, my friend?"

"From now on, Sam, being in business for myself is how I plan to make a living—away from the skyscraper market, with all its scheduling and budget-constraint pressures. I thought a bar would be something I could handle, and enjoy working.

I contacted a business broker. We looked at three different bars with different price tags and formats of operation in Nevada."

"Here are the menus," she mentions. "The specials are on the back. I'll be back for your order. Ray, bring water to this table, dear."

"A bar, way out there?" Sam scoffs. "What's wrong with the east coast? There are plenty of rural areas here, too."

2

"You can't compare the majestic western terrain with the east coast." Chas replies "It's two different cultures and terrains."

"You ready to order, gentlemen?"

Chas is frustrated with the interruption, and they order.

"I'll take the cheeseburger special, medium," Chas snarls.

"The same for me but no fries and a cop of *hot* coffee please. Thanks," Sam says.

"Are you sure leaving the big money and excitement in construction is what you want?" Sam whispers.

Chas turns away from Sam and thinks: *I hoped he, of all people, would understand.*

"I want my business close to my friend's ranches," Chas quips. "In my free time I will work with my cowboy friends. Living near the ranches will give me the life I want."

"Well, my friend, if you do what you want, not what you are forced to do, it's okay," Sam advises. "Give it careful thought. This is a big move, my friend"

"Sitting on my dads' lap, listening to the Lone Ranger on radio at four, got to me," Chas recounts. "As a kid I spent years watching cowboy movies on TV. I guess I never outgrew my fantasy."

The waitress brings the food.

"Two cheeseburgers with fries and cold slaw," she grumbles. "I'll check back in a few minutes."

The noise of dirty dishes, silverware and glasses clanging as they're thrown into the bus tub by the staff tells Chas he picked the wrong place to discuss a delicate situation. And unhappy with the dialogue from Sam, he shifts his weight in the chair repeatedly, anxious to leave.

"Sam, the worst thing to happen as I become old, is looking back and regretting my life. I need to ensure when I look back, that I made the right choices."

"I am in the air-conditioning ductwork business," Sam mentions. "I know nothing of buying a bar or owning one."

Listening to Sam, Chas thinks:

Shit, he's missing the point. I know he can't answer bar questions. Tell me how to negotiate a small business deal.

"If you want feedback about bars, talk to my ex-foreman," Sam suggests. "Bill and you got along well, you both socialized on the job a bit."

"I remember Bill," Chas growls. "Let's get the hell out of here. The smell is nauseating me. I don't see that damn waitress. I want her to take the check."

"The union didn't appreciate how hard Bill pushed the men," Sam mentions. "He also wanted to get out of New York City and away from the union's coercive tactics. Being his own boss appealed to him, too."

"Yeah, Sam, I know all that shit!" Chas snarls, and thinks: *Now he'll bore me with gay fucking history. Boy what a Pandora's Box I opened.*

"In the mid-60's, life was dangerous for a gay man going to underground bars at night," Sam whispers. "Working at a machismo construction job could be dangerous if coworkers discovered Bill is gay.

"For the last ten years, he has lived in San Juan, Puerto Rico. Gays are treated better there than here. Now he owns three gay bars in Old San Juan. We should call Bill now. You know what they say: 'Any Port in a Storm?'"

"Okay, Sam, these are stormy times, in New York City?" Chas replies, and thinks: *What has that shit to do with a California or Nevada bar business? I want to get away from all this crap. Here, I feel fenced-in. I don't enjoy a quality life here, I just exist. I sure as hell don't want to live in the fucking tropics. I just told him. Wasn't he listening? Shit, this sucks.*

"I'll pay the check," Chas growls. "Let's go to your office and call Bill."

As he watches Sam dial the phone, Chas has second thoughts: *My best friend is doing everything he can possibly do.*

Chas and Sam Singer

There is no simple answer that Sam or anyone can give me.

Bill gets on the phone and describes his operation in great detail. Sam and Chas listen on the speakerphone, and are impressed with Bill's explanation. Bill knows he and Chas have the same diligent work ethic.

"Chas, learn the bar-discothèque business as my partner in Puerto Rico, in my straight bar. I am running three clubs and renovating a forty-room hotel on the beach in San Juan. I'm desperate for a partner."

Thinking about his options: *Bill is the only person he will get honest answers from. He decides to meet with him. The answers to Chas' questions will be costly either way that he decides to go.*

Buying a place from a stranger may lose his money and self-respect. If, on the other hand, it is profitable, he will have his way of life.

Buying with Bill is financially secure; however the time he lives in San Juan he will be miserable. He knows the west; now he shall experience the tropics.

"I'll catch the first plane and see you in San Juan."

"Great. I look forward to seeing you. Bye."

"Sam, I don't think coming to see you is a good idea," Chas mocks. "You solve one dilemma and create another. My goal is to move to Nevada, not Puerto Rico. Okay, Sam, 'Any Fucking Port in a Storm.'"

2 Three days later, Chas arrives in San Juan. During the ride from the airport, he looks at low-cost housing along the highway; wash hangs on ropes across small balconies, small children wearing shorts play on swings, and tease barking dogs, salsa music blasts from inside dwellings which are on the other side of a high chain-link fence separating the housing from the highway.

The sun is bright and the air cleaner than home; however, he thinks: *What am I doing in a third-world country?* The taxi's air-conditioning system struggles to maintain cooling.

The economical hotel reminds him of old black-and-white Bogart films, shot in third-world countries.

The taxi stops in front of the hotel and Chas gets out.

"*Muchas gracias*," Chas says, and pays his taxi fare.

The small lobby has ceiling fans which rotate slowly, keeping the air-conditioning moving. The lighting is dim, and the lobby, too, looks like an old Bogart film.

His mood has deteriorated since he got off the plane. Puerto Rico is not where he wants to be, under any circumstances.

He signs in, takes his key and walks up three flights of stairs, carrying one suitcase as he avoids the elevator. The window air-conditioner's noise barely drowns out the busy street noise.

He picks up the phone and dials Bill.

"It's Chas. I just checked in."

"Hi, it's been too long."

"Yeah, Bill, we have lots of catching up to do. What time will you pick me up?"

"Be in front of the hotel at 8 PM."

"Okay, see you later."

They both hang up.

Chas requests a low floor on purpose. He distrusts elevators and reluctantly uses them if no other option exists. On lower floors he uses the stairs.

He lies on the bed staring at the ceiling, starts the tape in his memory recalling the incident which causes his "erroneous" anxiety:

My eight-year-old cousin Ludwig plays a prank on me when I am four years old. Ludwig takes me for my first ride in an elevator. As soon as it begins moving, Ludwig opens the manual gate slightly causing the elevator to stop, as the outer door remains closed.

"WE'RE STUCK," Ludwig shouts. "YOU WON'T SEE YOUR MOTHER EVER AGAIN!"

"OH. NO. I DON'T WANT TO DIE IN THIS THING," I implore. "PLEASE CALL MY MOMMY TO COME AND GET ME." I am screaming and crying. "LUDWIG, MAKE IT OPEN." I grab Ludwig's hand: "PLEASE MAKE IT OPEN, PLEASE."

"What a baby," He laughs. "LET ME GO YOU BABY, I don't like babies."

Hearing my screams, a tenant demands Ludwig close the gate to allow the elevator to travel. He does, and the elevator goes and stops at the second floor. She opens the door and gate, freeing me from my perceived tomb. She takes Ludwig and me next door, and tells both shocked parents what happened. I'm shaking and crying.

The long plane flight to Puerto Rico and the booze Chas drank on the plane is taking its effect. A nap will refresh him for tonight's introduction to gay nightlife. He sleeps for an hour.

He has many "firsts" in his life. He wonders what Providence has in store for him now. After a nap, he showers, dresses, and goes to the street to wait for Bill.

The first time Sam goes to Old San Juan, he tells Chas what he saw. Chas recalls Sam's words:

The men that live in Old San Juan have a sinister look on their faces. Almost all wear a thin black mustache as they lurk in the shadows; gay men at The Abbey wear eye shadow and color their lips.

Sam, his wife Irma, and three teenagers visit Bill in Puerto Rico at *The Abbey*.

Proud of his accomplishments; Bill tells his guests the history leading to *The Abbey*.

"I begin in Puerto Rico as a starving construction contractor. The clothing store owners on the first floor hire me to build a bar where we are standing, here, on the second floor. Not long after I begin construction, they go bankrupt, and I take over their lease. I complete *The Abbey* using money I borrow from my nervous father's retirement savings.

Before *The Abbey*, gay bars in Old San Juan were dumps. *The Abbey* is the first bar to provide customers with standards similar to New York City. I copy *The Sanctuary*'s design for *The Abbey*. *The Sanctuary* was a Baptist church on, West 43rd Street in Manhattan, populated only by gays.

The most famous straight people try to get in. A few make it. Ms. Seymour is the creator and operator of the new discothèque. He is an old queen, whom I know, known as the "Velvet Mafioso" in New York City. He's believed to be connected to organized crime.

It is so popular that every fag within a hundred-mile radius tries to get in on weekends. The police have to cordon off Ninth and Tenth Avenues to maintain safety. Faggots and lesbians come out of the church from midnight 'til sunrise."

Sam is amazed at what Bill tells him. The five straight people have seldom been close to gay men—now they are surrounded by gays in the infamous *Abbey*.

Sam returns from *The Abbey* and tells Chas the story. Chas remembers Sam's words as he waits for Bill:

"Chas, you never saw anything like it! We watch men with shirts off, wearing eye shadow trying to swallow each other's tongue while dancing close and sniffing Amyl nitrite (poppers). Used poppers litter the dance floor. Air saturated with the chemical odor makes us high, too. The sound system is rivaled only by the strobe lighting as it exaggerates the dancer's gestures."

Chas waits on the crowded sidewalk, a steady stream of people with their sickening aroma of sweet perfume or alcohol aftershave pass, permeating the cool, fresh evening air.

Bill is on time, and the two shake hands.

"Good to see you again, Chas. I invited two good friends to join us tonight, Allen Kalenburg, and Stanley Pasafaro, my manager at *The Abbey*.

"Okay," Chas replies. Annoyed, he gets in the car and thinks:

I won't be able to talk business with Bill, with his friends along. I came to learn as much as I can, as fast as I absorb the bar business from Bill, not to socialize with strangers. What a waste of my time, after the long trip. Can't he go to dinner without his cronies?

Bill has rugged good looks. His hair is light brown, combed with a part down the middle. He grew a mustache since Chas last saw him. Underneath his silk shirt and tight pants, he maintains a muscular body. His raspy voice is partly due to chain smoking. The dashboard of his car is littered with crumpled empty cigarette packs; inside the car it wreaks of nicotine and stale cigarette smoke.

"Sam is proud of your accomplishments," Chas advises. "You must have some Jewish in your thick Polish head."

"Actually I do, it's in the form of Allen. He and his lover, Peter, own residential buildings. Peter lives in Brooklyn Heights all year, where he runs the business.

"I rely on Ally's business acumen when I am faced with a perplexing business decision. Allen resides in a two-story mansion, two blocks away from *The Abbey*," Bill laughs. "It's a short way for him to drag his prey from *The Abbey* to his lair at home."

"Stanley is the youngest. He leaves the Bronx, a Jewish mother and an Italian father to come here for a new life. Allen always teases Stanley by saying, 'Too bad you have a Jewish ass and an Italian head; if it was reversed, Bill would work for you.'"

"I met Stanley operating the hotdog stand he owns, as I am building *The Abbey*. He hears I am opening the quintessential gay bar in Old San Juan and begs to be the manager. I agree, but warn him that honesty and loyalties are paramount if our relationship is going to survive. Our relationship has been good for the last three years."

San Francisco Street is one of two main streets that run through Old San Juan. Bill parks the car in front of the San Francisco Inn guest house. An exercise room occupies the main level. On the second floor is the restaurant. The guest rooms are on the last two floors above that in the four-hundred-year-old building. The décor for the small restaurant is impressive. The ceiling replicates a night sky filled with blinking stars. The walls have murals consistent with the old city's historic look.

"Welcome, Bill," said Jon.

Jon is the owner and host, his lover is co-owner and cook. Jon is dressed casually and wears a clean white apron around his waist to protect his pants.

His black hair is combed tight to his head, and he wears a smile on his round face.

"We are expecting Allen and Stanley," Bill says.

He sits down next to Chas and lays down a big ring of work keys on the table.

"Bill, would you like a drink to start?" Jon asks.

"Yes, two very dry Bombay Gin, up, with olives on the side."

Bill and Chas are catching up on the time they spent building a forty-story building in New York City years earlier.

Left to Right: Stanley, Bill and Allen

A voice interrupts them.

"Good evening, gentlemen," Stanley greets.

He and Allen sit down across from Bill and Chas. Chas shakes both men's hands.

"Pleasure to meet the people behind Bill's recent story," Chas laughs. "It's a compliment Bill paid you two, I swear."

Allen is short. Except for his potbelly, he's medium-built, and his shirt is worn out of his pants to hide its protrusion. He's in his late forties, with black hair, a mustache and Vandyke to achieve a sinister look to intimidate young prey at *The Abbey*.

Stanley is in his mid-twenties, six feet tall, well-built, handsome, black hair, and sports no cultivated facial hair. He is kind, generous, and will go out of his way to help people.

Jon brings Allen and Stanley their drinks, and rattles off dinner specials before leaving the table.

"Stanley's been anxious to meet you, Chas, I have been reassuring her that you're not here to drive a wedge between Bill (his meal ticket) and him," Allen scoffs. "I'm kidding, just kidding, Stanley. Don't turn so red, you'll look like a tourist who took in too much sun."

"Ignore her, Chas. Allen uses her ass exclusively for sex; that's why shit comes out of her mouth."

Bill stretches his arms upward, as if speaking to God.

"Forgive them. They know not what they do."

Stanley is angry and changes posture several times, avoiding eye contact with Chas.

He feels betrayed by Allen for divulging personal matters that they discuss in confidence.

Bill puts his left hand on Chas' shoulder, and looks him in the eyes.

"Welcome to the land of fruits and nuts," Bill derides.

"Ready to order," Jon asks.

"Yes," Bill whispers. "Chas, the steak is great."

The New York strip is as good as any he had in New York

City. They finish with dinner and stand on the sidewalk talking.

"Chas, come see my house," Allen suggests. "Bill and Stanley will be a half hour getting *The Abbey* open."

"Don't let that bitch talk you into trying her handcuffs on," Stanley scolds.

Stanley and Bill cross the street and head to work.

Allen and Chas walk along old dark streets consisting five-hundred-year-old three-story residential stone buildings, flag-stone sidewalks, and narrow cobblestone roads built in the 1500s for horses that carried Conquistadores.

Once through the door, Allen guides the way through the atrium, lush with many kinds of plants which surround an ornate working fountain. Room by room, Allen names each huge piece of artwork that takes up much of the two-story wall space. Whether canvas or tapestry, its age, its artist, and of course, its value. Allen rattles all of it off effortlessly. The house reminds Chas of a museum.

Finally the boring tour given by the energetic braggart Allen is over.

"It's time to leave. I'm curious what unsuspecting prey awaits me at *The Abbey*, as the natives say."

Thinking he hadn't impressed Chas, Allen feels the need to pontificate.

"You can consider the time you spend learning the bar busi-ness in this decadent city as your degree in operating a night club. The operation is the same, whether it's straight or gay."

"I'm here to talk with Bill about the bar business," Chas derides, "not to buy into his empire. You assume too much."

They reach *The Abbey*. Allen looks in the small window in the entrance door. Security personnel one flight up approves Allen to enter the restricted club, a buzzer releases the locked door, and they enter.

They ascend the plush red carpeted stairs with walls covered in red velvet paper. The entire area is illuminated by a huge ornate crystal chandelier. Chas thinks:

At this point, Sam hadn't exaggerated about The Abbey.

Allen introduces Chas to the security personnel.

"Meet my lover from New York City, Chas," Allen quips. "This is the best security crew on the island."

"In your dreams, Mary," José scoffs. "Good try, Allen. No one with class wants an obnoxious queen like you for a lover. Chas has class we can tell."

"Thanks," Chas says.

José has a shaved shiny head and wears a round gold earring in one ear. He motions to a second staff member to open the heavy wood door to let them enter. He's accompanied by other intimidating well-dressed young, attractive gay men. They all wear the popular short-sleeve formal white shirt common to the island.

Chas thinks: *Must be the "in look"; the shirts look like a fancy version of the shirt his barber wears.* Two have curly black hair; each one has a mustache. Feeling nervous, Chas continues toward the door, which is held open for him.

It's only 10:30, and the place is packed. The entire floor vibrates in unison with the dancers' active movements.

"It's exactly as Sam described this place, Allen," Chas says. "In order to hear over the music, I have to put my ear an inch away from your mouth. Walking toward the bar takes effort because the pulsating strobe lights affect my focus and balance."

Allen and Chas manage to reach their drinks, in spite of the customers standing three deep at the bar. Bill finally joins them.

"This is the place that made it for me Chas," Bill brags. "The place I have in mind for you is *Otello's*. It's mostly a straight club. Let's walk to see it."

Chas is feeling uncomfortable in his first gay bar, and is happy to leave. As they walk Bill tells Chas how *Otello's* got its name.

"After seeing the corridor in the vacant space with Arabian

brick archways, the motif has to be Moorish. Shakespeare's *Othello* comes to mind.

"I changed the spelling from the English *Othello* to a Latin version.

"The promotion of *Otello*'s targets an upper class of young Puerto Rican girls, most of whom don't drink. They love to dance to a great sound system and current hits played by my popular disc jockey.

The first weeks of business two years ago, parents brought their daughters to ensure the place remains up-scale. Their dates are respectable gay boys, old enough to drink and not interested in sex with them. A minimum cover fee is needed. The boys will buy alcohol but the girls won't drink unless they pay for it in an admission ticket. Girls are school-age or holding down a job. We're open Friday and Saturday and a few hours Sunday night."

"I'm amazed how quiet the city is," Chas mentions. "Few people are on the streets. A policeman is at each intersection, though. I remember what Sam described," Chas recounts.

"Ominous men with thin black mustaches lurk in the dark shadows."

"That's Sam," Bill laughs.

As they approach the entrance to *Otello*'s, Chas notices the lights from the club represent the only illumination on the entire block except for occasional streetlights. The club's lighting acts as *the light at the end of the tunnel.*

The white Moorish arch is well lit and obvious on the dark street.

Four white steps lead to the club's entrance foyer. An attractive young brunette sits behind a small desk selling admission tickets.

Norma is wearing a tight dress, cut in front, showing a respectable amount of cleavage. The shape of her attractive legs with sexy high heels and ankle straps are visible under the desk.

To her right stands Buddy, a formidable native with a body of steel. He is tall, with curly hair, wearing a tight shirt and pants.

An obvious bulge at his crotch indicates he's well-endowed and advertising to potential customers. A happy look is on his pleasant face as he flirts with the girls.

Buddy speaks only four English words: "Telephone for you, mister," which means go inside, possible trouble. It indicates he senses a potential problem and wants to handle it alone. He does this for your protection.

Norma is a typical youngster, born and raised in New York City, before her family returned to Puerto Rico.

A Ne-O-Rican is the local's terminology for a New York Puerto Rican.

Along the building, young people patiently wait their turn to buy a ticket and enter the popular discothèque.

"Welcome to *Otello's*," Norma greets.

Buddy extends his arm to shake both Bill's and Chas' hand, and smiles.

"Hi, Norma, this is Chas. We worked together years ago."

"Hello, Chas, it's a pleasure to meet you."

"The pleasure is mine, Norma."

Inside, Moroccan hanging lamps subtly illuminate the club. The dark red wall fabric causes Chas to recall fabric tents he'd seen in Arabian movies as a young boy. Kings traveled across the desert on camels, with their harems, wealth, and a contingent of warriors.

The beautiful young female patrons are dressed in tight-fitting chic outfits. Their hair and makeup are exemplary. Watching the girls dance, he notices as the strobe light above the dance floor goes on, at times it almost penetrates their shear dresses. Most of the boys wear formal jackets.

As he watches the girls and listens to the tantalizing disco music, he thinks: *being the owner of this club will certainly make life interesting, but never shit where you eat...* a motto he tries to keep in mind.

"Bill, sorry I didn't greet you and your friend when you

entered. I was dealing with her highness, Jesús in the DJ booth," Carlos laughs. "Hi, I'm the club's manager; pleased to meet you, Chas."

"Pleased to meet you."

Carlos is a tall, elegant native, about twenty-two, wearing a white dinner jacket and tie. He speaks fluent English. As Bill and Carlos excuse themselves, the bartender extended his hand to Chas.

"Hi, I am Denis how long will you be in town?"

"I'm Chas. A few days to a week."

Denis could be taken for Bill's younger and smaller brother.

"I have days off; I can show you around," Denis advises. "Are you planning to move here?"

"Maybe, but right now, my kids have six months 'til summer recess. If Bill and I become partners, I'll rent a furnished apartment. I don't know whether the family will relocate here."

"Excuse me Chas, your wife is on the phone," Carlos says. "You may take it in my office."

"Thanks Carlos. Hello, Mari, what's up?"

"Nothing's *up*. I thought you'd call when you arrived. Is that too much to ask for?"

"No, I've been on the go since I landed."

"I hear music, I thought the number I dialed was to Bill's office. What type of patron goes there?"

"*Otello*'s is supposed to be the straight club. The girls are straight; their escorts are gay. The remaining males, I have no clue."

"Call me tomorrow," Mari demands. "Don't forget. Bye."

"Thanks for the use of your phone and office, Carlos."

"My pleasure, Chas. Any time you need it, it's there."

"Denis, let's have another drink," Bill says.

He returns the empty glass to the bar.

"Bill, why is the security staff in the men's room?" Chas inquires.

"Marijuana is a big *No-No* down here. Heavy fines are levied, even a loss of the liquor license if convicted. The seating area at the dance floor is watched too, by Dwayne, who you were talking with. We run a tight ship—no short cuts."

It was a long physically- and mentally-challenging day topped off by a caustic reprimand from Mari. Drained of energy, Chas takes leave of his host.

"Thanks for dinner, the booze, and especially the tours," Chas mentions. "I know you want to get back to *The Abbey*, Bill. Have a good night. I'll get a cab after I finish this drink and stop drooling over the jail bait."

They shake hands and Bill leaves.

"Chas what hotel you staying at?" Denis inquires.

"The Tanama in Condado. Why?"

"My lover Rolando and I have a three-bedroom apartment a few steps from the beach. You can spend the rest of your time with us. Rolando has an executive position with the phone company. He works five days a week, I'm free to show you the sites. If you like it with us, you'll have a place if you return. Here's my number; call if you need any help."

Chas thanks Denis and leaves.

Next morning he sits alone at the *Atlantic Beach Hotel*'s outdoor bar, staring at the ocean. The white surf makes soft music accompanied by palm tree leaves as they brush against each other; both are keeping tempo with the gentle breeze off the warm ocean.

"*You're a New York Girl*" is playing on the juke box. The song reminds him when he worked in the city during a simpler and happier time.

Black coffee clears his head as saltwater air clears his lungs of chemicals inhaled last night. The sound of waves hitting the beach has a soothing effect on him. It's peaceful, concentrating on the ocean.

He learned a lot last night, and is tempted after seeing

Otello's potential. Every step he takes creates more questions to resolve. Naïvely, he hopes this experience will enable him to proceed on his own in Nevada.

He is reluctant to leave his quiet place, and talk with Mari again after her attitude last night. He *faces the music* and calls her.

"You must be having a good time in the tropics," Mari quips. "Based on your description of *Otello*'s last night, I never should have let you talk me out of joining you."

"We discussed it. I'm here on business only. There is no one to leave the kids with. I had no idea what I'd find here, Mari. This gay thing is new to me. They seem pleasant and friendly, but can I deal with their personalities on a constant basis, and over a long period of time?"

"You managed to find a bar with young straight women, so what's the problem?" Mari scolds. "I'm sure your time will be well occupied with them."

"Why the jealousy and anger? You do this all the time. Bill says now's the time he needs a partner for *Otello*'s."

"Oh really, and what do you say, my dear husband?"

"I need time to think all this through, Mari. Now you are upset because of young girls? I don't understand you. Have you ever caught me cheating on you?"

"I never *caught* you," Mari mocks. "I suspected you more times than I care to remember. Well, you take your sweet time figuring out whatever. We're millionaires!

"Why do you quit a good job to play cowboy? ...to own a bar in nowhere land? I'll never understand. Now you're considering a new scheme involving jail bait. I can't keep track of this nonsense. What does your quack doctor think? I think you lost your mind. Have a great fucking time. Bye."

Mari's comments bring anger and frustration to the pit of Chas' stomach as he slams the receiver into its cradle. Now he has more things to add to his already cumbersome list of questions that only he can answer. He thinks:

Maybe she is right. Maybe I should give the whole thing up. Why the hell did I call her? I had to call. Who do I think I am kidding? Fuck me. Mari always pulls the guilt trip on me. I ignore her most of the time. She hadn't honed her skill as well as my mother had.

He thinks: *Mother was an expert when she wanted me to supplement my dad's earning power. Her manipulation sent me out working at eleven years old during the time after school, Saturday, and summer recess. I broke my ass delivering heavy bags of groceries. Fuck these women.*

Denis is in the process of opening the bar as Chas returns.

"Good morning," Denis quips. "Did you get any sleep? You look like shit."

"Hi. I feel worse. Give me a scotch on the rocks, please."

"What happened?" Denis asks. "Last night you looked fine."

"I just got off the phone with my wife."

"That'll do it. Rolando always pisses me off. I don't know why I stay with him?"

"I'm trying to keep it together with Mari, too," Chas snarls. "I tried taking her to group therapy.

"She thinks no one should share our problems. I see a therapist to understand what's going on—without her—she won't join me. She needs therapy, said my doctor.

"I'm frustrated dealing with her shit.

"Give me another scotch, please, this glass has a hole at the bottom.

"The main reason I quit my job was to get us all to a simpler lifestyle, where I have time for the family. Running multimillion-dollar projects, I am burned out when I get home. Weekends, and two weeks vacation a year never allows my batteries to charge.

"Where is the quality of life?"

"Chas, check out of the hotel," Denis recommends. "Stay with us for the remainder of your visit. You won't be alone, staring at a ceiling. You'll have someone to bounce ideas off. Here is my key. It's number 25 Valentine Street. No one is home. Go check it out."

Chas takes the suggestion, and checks out the apartment. The booze and getting stuff off his chest makes him relax.

He's surprised what a clean, airy, spacious apartment it is. His private bedroom faces the ocean. The open windows with security bars allow the room to fill with wave rhythm sounds and the water's sweet aroma. Intoxicated, he falls on the bed and naps for two hours.

Bill and he will review *Otello*'s financials at *The Abbey* later this morning. Bill keeps records for both clubs in a fireproof safe there.

Chas arrives at *The Abbey*, rings the bell and looks in the small glass window. The buzzer sounds, and he opens the door.

"Good morning, Chas, come up. *Otello*'s records are in my office."

They begin with the first day's figures, two years ago. Every page has columns for: door sales, service register, and bar register sales recorded to date. Costs relating to building and furnishing the club are listed in a separate file, which is reviewed, too.

The figures prove Bill's price is fair. Chas estimates in three years, fifty percent of the profits will return his investment. If he stays longer, every dollar received will be profit. Chas' salary is additional to percentage. Bill receives only his percentage.

"That's everything to show you," Bill brags. "It's easy work."

"Friday and Saturday night, the club's open until sun-up the following day. Sunday night there's few customers. I do payroll and pay the kids, and after I calculate the sales figures, I take the profit. We close by 1 AM Monday morning. Monday at noon I make all the deposits at the bank. Carlos does the liquor ordering, and buys the supplies on Wednesday. That's it."

"Thanks for the run-down, Bill. It's helpful in making my decision. I need a little time to think things over. Meantime, I shall see you at dinner tonight. Bye."

After a few days, it is time to return home. Chas stops at the beach bar to see Denis.

"Denis, let's have a good-bye drink for now. It's been great staying with you."

"The pleasure is mine," Denis laughs. "We don't get straight men to stay more than an hour."

"Everyone is sincere and has a sense of humor," Chas mentions. "Those traits are important to me. In a short time, I've been impressed by what I see and hear.

"I shall be in touch. Take care." Chas walks away thinking:

Mari is being selfish and unwise to ask me to go back and do what I hate. I'm thinking about all our happiness. Maybe my approach is wrong; I don't know. Still, I'd rather make a mistake as an act of commission than one of omission. If I do what she wants, I will resent her and possibly my kids as well. Our relationship will deteriorate further. I won't allow that to happen. A man has to do what a man has to do.

3 Chas spends some time with the family explaining why he is buying *Otello's*. He calls Sam, Bill Erdelyi (Willie), and other close friends. They are interested to know his decision.

"Hi, Joan, is Sam in? I just returned from Puerto Rico."

"Yes he is, Chas; hold on. He's anxious to hear what happened. Take care."

"Chas, how did it go?"

"I return in a few days to my new career with teacher Bill. I think the price is okay. We'll see what the new receipts show. I want to say thanks for all your help. Bye for now, and the next year or so. Take care and give my best to Irma."

"You take care, my friend. Don't be a stranger, and let's hear from you," Sam says. "On your trips north, we'll get together. Bye."

"Bye, Sam."

Next he calls Willie in Detroit.

"Willie, how are you doing buddy?" Chas greets. "You must be freezing your balls off by the lake."

"They fell off, frozen solid," Willie laughs. "I heard them hit the wood floor in my apartment, and roll under the bed. You at least are warm though?"

Left to Right: Willie and Bill at Lake Powell.

"No shit, Willie—I thought your voice was a few octaves higher. Actually, I'm home getting ready to go back. I made the deal, came to say bye to Mari and the kids for the time being, and get my stuff.

"Seems we won't be seeing each other for a while. I'll miss you, man. You're the best—with humor I enjoy. Tell Scotty we'll ride my horse together again as soon as I return. He shouldn't give up on me. He's young; he can wait a while. I promise we'll ride again.

"Chas, after this project we're returning to New Jersey. Things will be normal again for us. You need to remember the words from *West Side Story*."

"What words, Willie?"

"I'll sing them to you*: There's a place for us, somewhere a place for us, take my hand and I'll lead you there, somewhere, somehow…* Bye, Chas."

"Bye, Willie."

Willie loves classical music as well as show-tunes. A radio on his desk at work is constantly on, playing music at a low volume so as not to disturb others.

Saying goodbye to his best friends makes Chas sad, knowing he will not see them for a while.

He returns to Puerto Rico two weeks later. As he waits at the carousel in the San Juan airport, he hears a familiar voice.

"Your plane arrived early. It's good to see you again. I missed you," Denis greets. "I'll grab your bag. I thought you'd have three bags that size."

"The last time I was here I realized all my clothes are the pits, as you'd say. I need tight silk shirts and tight pants without pockets.

"I shall live with two queens and run a fag joint. One needs to dress the part. As I do my cowboy thing, I'm authentic, except for my New York accent. Majoring in Gay World 101, Disco 101 at the University of Fruits and Nuts, I need to look the part."

"Chas, you already pass looks, personality, and intelligence," Denis lauds.

"Remember, don't judge me when I dress faggot," Chas laughs. "I'm still a straight wannabe cowboy. Sissy talk won't cut it, *pardner*."

"Oh, I love when you talk butch to me," Denis laughs." Don't talk that way to Rolando; I'll get jealous."

The two are having a good laugh as they drive to the apartment.

In a short time, Chas is accepted by his gay associates and vice-versa. No one is insulted as he sometimes uses gay terminology.

Unpacking bottles of scotch and gin, he places them on the kitchen counter, and pours three drinks over ice cubes. With three glasses, he hands a scotch to Denis, and a gin to Rolando.

Taking his scotch to the couch to catch up on the latest with his roommates; he notices magazines on the coffee table with pictures of semi-nude woman on the cover.

Pointing to the magazines, Chas looks at Denis.

"You shouldn't have, I don't use them."

"They are for the straight boys (tricks), not you," Rolando laughs. "Kids use the pictures to get their cock hard."

"Keep talking, Rolando," Chas says.

"Okay, sometimes looking at pictures of nude women makes them hard, other times they prefer their girl friend get them hard. Watching me or Denis nude won't get a macho kid hard.

"A kid, once hard will even stick his cock in a live chicken. You've seen a dead chicken after it's been fucked to death by a pervert, on the beach, haven't you?"

"I haven't so far," Chas responds, "If I do, I'll remember what you said, Rolando. You may leave out further details on my account, please."

"She gets nude, does seductive poses and talks dirty. I'm undressed, get on my knees and elbows, wearing my woman's wig. I beg him in my female tone to fuck me.

"After I have my orgasm, he pulls out and fucks her. Depending on the kid, we can do sex a few times. Talking about this is making me horny."

"Don't look at me," Chas quips.

Rolando turns toward Denis.

"It's your cock I want, dear."

"That's exactly what you shall have," Denis brags. "Listening to you describe sex with José gave me a hard-on. Follow me dear, and *get* those clothes *off,* bitch."

Rolando begins taking his shirt off as the two rush to their bedroom.

Chas heard enough. As he makes a hasty exit, he hears Denis say, "Excuse us, Chas."

"That is thoughtful of Chas to give us our privacy," Rolando mutters. "Telling him about sex with the straight kids made me hard—look, it wants your mouth, dear."

Denis and Rolando are nude and Denis is sucking off Rolando. After a few minutes Roland is sucking Denis' cock, both men are hard and excited.

"Let's go missionary, Denis," Rolando says.

"Love to dear, you turn me on when you're butch," Denis advises.

Denis is on his back with his legs spread, pointing to the ceiling. Rolando gets between Denis' legs as Denis raps them around Rolando's waist. They kiss passionately as Rolando inserts his cock into Denis' rectum.

"Baby, you got the best cock that my ass has had," Denis praises.

As Rolando pumps, Denis is masturbating. When Denis is ready to come he tells Rolando.

"I'm ready, babe—let that wad go."

"Uhhh!" Rolando groans.

Denis' cum hits Rolando's chest, which Rolando rubs over his chest with his fingers which he puts in Denis' mouth. Denis licks the fingers clean.

Outside, the temperature is a cool eighty degrees; the ocean breeze makes the humidity seem low. The air smells saltwater sweet. As he walks to the beach bar, Chas thinks: *Gay Lifestyle 101 is interesting.*

Arriving at the beach bar, he notices it's always cocktail time, regardless of the time of day. The bar entices people by being outside overlooking the ocean. ...Also a beach that caters to locals wanting to connect with wealthy tourists. A hotel guest turns toward him.

"Hi, I'm Marv."

"I'm Chas. Hi."

"I'm always amazed at the different culture down here," Marv scoffs." The only time I mix with lesbians is at this bar. Everything's so liberal here, not like New York where we have separate bars. In popular discos, however, we'll mix. We even mix with straight people who are allowed in some clubs.

Here the butch lesbian is smashed by 5 PM and becomes horny. Her feminine lover prefers to socialize with the crowded, and have sex later. An argument ensues. Look at those two at the rail."

"What about them?" Chas scoffs.

"The Fem is hot, I'd even fuck her," Marv quips. "The Butch is a dog. I wouldn't let her suck my cock. Well—maybe—if I keep my eyes closed. We men talk, kiss, hug, and grab each other's ass, then have sex. The difference between us and gay women is obvious, don't you think?"

"No, tell me," Chas quips.

"We fags are similar to straight women, and dykes are similar to belligerent straight men," Marv explains. "If you want a simple life, stick with fags."

"Know-it-alls" bore Chas. As soon as Marv pauses, he takes the opportunity to leave.

"Good meeting you. I'd love to stay and chat more, but my

lover has dinner waiting. Have a fun vacation."

Figuring sex was finished at the apartment and Denis is preparing dinner, he returns to the apartment. His stomach is growling for food.

"I cook Norwegian food the way my mother taught me, growing up in Iowa," Denis boasts. "You will enjoy the food. It's different from Italian, Chinese or American cuisine you eat in New York.

"The wine is poured, and a candle lit in your honor. The table is set using Rolando's grandmother's china in honor of your return. The food is ready for me to serve. Hey, Rolando, are you joining us?"

"I'm blow-drying my hair. Give me two minutes."

Rolando finishes his hair and sits at the table.

"And now," Denis boasts, "I want to toast my friend Chas' success in his new career."

With their glasses raised, Denis proposes a toast.

"He's a great fellow, deserving of success in his new venture. Here, here!"

After a delicious meal, Chas thanks his two new roommates for their generosity. He leaves the apartment to sit on the beach and think.

The ocean is black; only the white surf can be seen now. The night sky is full of stars, a cool breeze off the ocean fills his lungs with sweet air rejuvenating his tired body.

Tomorrow, Bill and he will sign legal papers giving him fifty percent of the stock in the *Otello Corporation*.

He thinks: *Is this the thing to do? Yes. Is Bill honest? Yes. I saw honesty in Bill in the past—he hasn't changed. Bill's successful record in the business is obvious. By reviewing the books, I'm satisfied. I shall do better in an established business. Attempting this with a total stranger or on my own is no longer an option. Unfortunately, Nevada will have to wait until I master the complexity of the business.*

He satisfies his conscience and turns the tape in his head off.

Major learning about the disco business will commence as soon as the document is signed, transferring fifty percent of the shares to Chas.

Now he retires to his room to sleep. A long day in a new vocation and lifestyle will begin after breakfast tomorrow.

They meet at the lawyers at 11 AM the following morning, and finish the signing at noon.

"Congratulations, Chas, glad you chose to be my partner," Bill lauds.

Chas and Bill shake hands, walk from the lawyer's office in Old San Juan through the crowds of people from the cruise ships who clog the narrow sidewalk. Tourists are window-shopping for jewelry, and anything else they can buy duty free; or spend money on presents to impress someone back home.

The sun is high in the noon sky, temperature in the high ninety's; high humidity makes their shirts begin to stick to their perspiring bodies.

The car and taxi traffic accommodating all the tourists creates uncomfortable noise levels. Engines spew clouds of dark exhaust fumes into the hot humid still air.

Holding their breath at times, they hurry by, walking mostly in the street, dodging moving vehicles to avoid hoards of shoppers on the narrow sidewalks. As their lungs cry for oxygen, they are forced breathe again.

At the club it is cooler, quiet, and the air is breathable.

Finally they're at *Otello's*. Opening four locks on the gates and main huge wood doors gets them inside.

Using the bright work lights, Bill shows Chas all the control panels necessary to operate the club during business and day hours.

Two hours later, they're finished. Bill relocks *Otello's*, gives a set of keys to Chas; they both leave the old city.

The next day, Chas returns and meets Carlos, and they stock the club.

As they finish stocking the club, Bill comes by.

"Chas, will you join us? We are all invited by Seymour to join him for lunch at *The Hilton Hotel*. Seymour, Allen and I go back to *The Sanctuary* days.

"Sure."

They walk to Allen's house, dodging the noon-hour crowd.

"I hate it here during the day," Chas grumbles. "I never would buy into the club if it meant a day operation."

"It's a small price to pay, a few hours work during daytime hours, for the return you'll get back, Chas."

Reaching Allen's house, the housekeeper opens the door, and tells Bill in Spanish where he can find Allen. Sitting in his study, shirtless, with a thin cigar in his mouth, he's talking to Peter in Brooklyn. Even with air-conditioning, Allen's hairy potbelly and head are sweating as he wipes his brow repeatedly. The conversation ends, and Allen turns toward Bill to complain.

"I don't know what she'd do if I wasn't available to advise her, every time a tenant has a problem paying rent. That's why we have a big strong dumb house boy. If he takes Roberto with his baseball bat along during rent collection, there will be no problem. My lover is such a sissy."

"Well, maybe if you spent the same time working as Peter does, he wouldn't need to ask you questions. You should be there doing your job along with Peter."

Allen ignores Bill's comment. With a look of indifference on his face, he turns to Chas.

"A bunch of us girls are taking you to lunch to celebrate the *Otello's* deal. My older sister Seymour will finance lunch with a hot credit card she is using on this trip. She also wants to meet the big handsome straight jerk that Bill conned into buying a dying club. I'm kidding—about the club—don't faint on me, Chas."

"Alley, at this point in my short career in Gayism 101, I believe gay men are women, gay women are men. Nothing would faze me, unless you said we were not having booze at lunch today."

A few beeps from a car horn outside indicates that Stanley is waiting to drive them the short distance to San Juan. As soon as they enter the hotel, Allen inquires of the desk clerk the whereabouts of Dr. William—the name on the hot credit card Seymour is using on this vacation.

"He and his son are waiting for you in the main dining room. Turn right at the elevators—you can't miss it."

The four of them head to the dining room, toward Seymour's table. On the way:

"She brought George, that skinny bisexual with the big cock, on this trip? That will cramp her style if she sees something else she wants to fuck her," Allen mocks. "Let's not pick on the bi-fag. You know how protective my older sister gets when it comes to her lover. You better watch your Italian head, Stanley. She dislikes the mob Italians she has for partners. You won't get credit for being fifty percent Jewish."

"Allen, go fuck yourself." Stanley snarls.

"Look what the wind blew in, George."

Allen, Stanley, and Bill each kiss Seymour's cheek, and say hello to George.

Seymour turns his attention to Chas. With a palm down, he extends his hand toward Chas, as a royal woman does, so a man can kiss the back of her hand. Chas grabs the hand, turns it upright, and shakes it.

"Thanks for allowing me to join your party."

"Thank you! It's not often I have the pleasure to dine with two handsome straight men."

"We are not sure of Chas anymore," Allen scoffs. "He's taken to fags easily. It just isn't done to the best of my knowledge."

"How would you know about straight men, Mary?" Seymour quips. "The last straight man you knew was your father, who was probably a closet queen."

Everyone laughs, including a red-faced Allen. The waiter asks if they want drinks; everyone except George orders alcohol.

"George is an avid soccer player who watches what he puts into his mouth... when it concerns food and drink," Seymour quips.

He has a grin on his face, as he looks at a shy George.

George is in his mid-twenties, thin, average height, average looking, of Latin parents, bisexual, and possesses a well-endowed penis.

Seymour is an ex-grade-school civics teacher and ex-perfume dealer. He's in his early sixties, bald, five-feet-six-inches tall, medium-build, and wearing glasses.

With his day wig on, which is a little darker than the night wig, he reminds Chas of an old woman wearing her spectacles and needing a shave. His personality indicates he is obnoxious most of the time, friendly on rare occasions.

"Do you like it in the tropics, Chas?" Seymour asks.

"It's okay. The tropics are pleasant this time of year. It's below freezing and snowing up north. Living on an island is too restrictive. I prefer the West where I can work cattle with my cowboy friends."

"Are you crazy? You're not the Marlboro Man, are you?" Seymour scolds. "Do you want to die with your boots on?"

"How I die is of no concern; how I *live* is important. Life is not a dress rehearsal."

"Me, I want to die having the best orgasm ever with George in my bed," Seymour brags.

"Allen tells me you and Ms. Bill worked at building tall buildings, at a time Ms. Bill thought she was macho. Now you, a straight man, come to this island of fags to work in the fag business? Something doesn't jive."

"Mary, your wig is cutting off the circulation to your feeble brain," Bill scoffs. "I always knew that I was unlike Saul, your sister and partner in crime."

"I had to work in a real business, with real men. I couldn't be a sissy like you, teaching naïve children, as you hid behind a false façade of respect as a teacher; or Saul's charade as a perfume dealer.

"If I made the slightest gesture as subtle as a limp wrist, they'd throw me off the fucking building.

"Saul thought he could mess with his mobster partner who pushed drugs for him. The mobster accepted Saul as a fag, until Saul came on to him. First he put all of Saul's valuables in a large plastic garbage bag. Then he threw Saul out of his tenth floor window for assuming he could treat him as a fag."

"Please," Chas pleads. "I'm here, not for the lifestyle. Bill is someone I trust and respect to teach me the bar business."

"Here is my number, Chas. Call me the next time you're in New York," Seymour grumbles. "I have two bars in Greenwich Village. I'll show you my straight clubs. That's if anybody is totally straight anymore."

After lunch, Seymour, Allen, Bill, and Stanley all kissed each other good-bye. Chas, Seymour and George shake hands.

Once they are in the car heading to Old San Juan, Seymour is derided by Bill.

"She has some fucking nerve referring to me as Ms. Bill," Bill growls. "I came out when I was in my mid-twenties, after sex with lots of women. She was born a fag, never had her little dick in a woman."

"Look at it this way, our sister is a homely little man," Allen scoffs. "She's always reminded of it, because she surrounds herself with good-looking gay men—taller, more talented, and better looking."

They arrive in the old city; Bill and Chas are dropped off first, in front of *Otello*'s. Chas notices that in Puerto Rico, every door, window and patio is enclosed with locked gates. The outside gate to the club is locked. The huge wood entrance door is open, allowing fresh air in, indicating that an employee is inside

Left to Right foreground: Guest, Seymour, Chas, Fred.
Background: Tony

working. After unlocking the gate, they enter and relock the gate before going further.

"I will introduce you to our maintenance man, Raphael," Bill says. "You can't leave anything to chance on this island. Robbery is the fourth most popular pastime, after sex, music and wine. That is why we are conscious of locking up."

Chas is introduced to Raphael as the new Partner who will run the club instead of Bill.

Raphael is medium-build and height; a native, schooled in refrigeration maintenance and electronics, as well as other things necessary to maintain the club.

After the cordial, brief introduction, Bill and Chas leave the club. Outside it is the hottest part of the day. It is time to find shelter from the bright sun and high humidity.

"I am going back to my crypt," Bill mentions. "I'm referring to my dark, cool bedroom as a crypt during the midday hours. We operate on Dracula's schedule, by working at night."

They will emerge later, as darkness prevails over their tiny island, when temperatures drop substantially. At 8 PM, Allen and Stanley meet them for their ritualistic dinner get-together at a fish restaurant in Old San Juan. The follow morning, Bill calls Chas at home.

"Are you free for lunch?"

"Sure. What's up?"

"My… uh… *tenant* and partner, Eddy, is a dress designer who has his shop in a building I own. I need to alter the space so it's desirable for his showcase. He's been after me to make this change. He's pissed I haven't gone to see what he needs. He wants to meet you. Do you mind?"

"Not at all, pick me up."

"I'll get to you in twenty minutes. Thanks."

The ride from San Juan to Old San Juan takes about twenty minutes, depending on the traffic through residential neighborhoods. Bill tells Chas about Eddy's relationship with him.

"I know nothing about men's clothes, let alone women's clothes. Eddy likes shopping for my clothes; I hate to shop. He has clothes he bought me that I need to get or he'll be pissed more."

Along the route, the road gets close to the shore and offers a beautiful closeup view as the sound of waves crash against the rocks. Seeing the ocean often is one bright side of living on the tiny island. They reach Eddy's shop in fifteen minutes.

As is commonly done in Puerto Rico—especially in the old city where roads are narrow, preventing street parking—cars park with two wheels on sidewalks, and two wheels in the road, leaving enough room for pedestrians and cars to pass. Bill parks and he and Chas go into the shop to see Eddy.

"So honored to see you are able to fit me into your busy schedule, William. This must be Chas. I've heard so much about you, I feel as though I know you."

"Bill has told me a lot about you," Chas whispers. "How handsome and talented his... a partner is."

"Oh, really?" Eddy quips.

A startled Eddy looks at a surprised Bill, wondering how Chas figured they are lovers instead of only partners. Eddy knows Bill does not advertise their relationship.

"That is good to hear," Eddy quips. "I wish he'd say that to me."

Eddy has a mischievous grin on his face, giving off a provocative glow.

"Uh, can we get to what you want changed Eddy?" Bill grumbles.

"You are always in a rush. You just walked in. Now you want to run out. Go look at the wall I marked with an X on the third floor. Can it come out? I need more open space."

Chas watches the short, handsome, yet effeminate young man with black, straight, shiny hair, turn and give him the once-over, and looks him in the eye.

"Chas, I don't want to seem rude. Who dresses you in the morning? You can't wear shirts with horizontal stripes—or for that matter, any stripes. You need to wear solid colors—white and dark only. Wear no sissy pastels, stripes, plaids or designs; they are childish. Classical straight men should exude subdued elegance."

"Thanks for the advice and compliment, Eddy. I will rectify my wardrobe immediately."

"Okay, Eddy, I'll have Raphael remove the wall tomorrow. Anything else? We have business in San Juan."

"No. Take this package. It's been here two weeks. You need to throw out that tacky shirt, and others you have. Wear the ones in the package. It's my pleasure meeting you, Chas."

"The pleasure is mine, Eddy. I hope to see you again."

On the way home, Bill is thankful the visit with Eddy is over. He didn't want to deal with Eddy on his own.

"Thanks, Chas, for making me look good with Eddy. He's a nice kid, but sometimes she's a pushy queen. Tonight, you start running *Otello*'s. We need to eat early in order for you to watch the help set up before we open at ten."

They arrive at the club at 9:30 and everyone is hustling. The work lights are on. The mystique happens as the cabaret lights go on, the work lights go off, and the DJ starts playing music.

"It's showtime, people; the kids are lined up outside," Carlos shouts. "Buddy, let them in." Bill and Chas observe the help as they do their jobs. If Chas has a question or suggestion, he talks to Carlos or Bill. Things go smoothly, and in no time the place is packed. Bill leaves for *The Abbey*. Chas notices Carlos setting up a reserved seating area.

"Carlos, who are the reserved seats for?"

"We have a famous female singer in Puerto Rico. She is performing at *The Hilton*, and after she finishes she comes here. These kids are big fans of hers. They consider her a star. Her name is Edie Chacon."

Getting a drink at the bar, Chas asks Denis about Edie.

"Oh that bitch, she's no star, she's a fag hag. She sings some nights at the cabaret the two old queens own. If I didn't know better, I'd tell you they helped lay the original cobblestones for building the roads in the old city."

"That old?" Chas laughs.

"You can't miss those three, Chas. With their hooker between them they look like withered bookends supporting a witch with too much makeup."

When Edie and her escorts come in, Carlos treats them like royalty. He gets a bottle of champagne in an ice bucket, and puts it on a cocktail table in the seating area next to the dance floor. Chas has Carlos introduce him to the popular trio. Mickey tells him about his and Paul's experience in Old San Juan twenty-five years earlier. He figures he'd play cat and mouse with them. Chas sits in the middle of the group next to Edie.

"It is such a pleasure to meet famous people on my first night as the owner," Chas mentions.

"Oh, the pleasure is ours. We welcome you to our historic city," Angel lauds. "Your last name is Italian, yes? You are from where?"

"I am American, born in Brooklyn."

"What a small world, that is where Paul and his gorgeous brother Mickey are from." Edie just sits drinking champagne, smiling, getting kisses on the cheek, and returning cheek-to-cheek smooches, preventing her lip-gloss from smudging her admirers.

Each time the voluptuous woman bends forward to take her glass of champagne from the low table, her tits are totally exposed, except for her nipples.

"The men you mention are my senior cousins," Chas replies. "Paul, the older of the two, is a neighborhood mobster. That tit bar he ran next to your club was a front for the mob. Mobsters in trouble with other mobs would hide out with Paul 'til the heat was off.

Mickey visits Paul on occasion to bring money back to New York. You're right about Mickey being very handsome. I fell in love with the picture of him smiling and wearing his bombardier jacket, white scarf, and googles pushed up on his leather flight cap, when I was four. My mother kept a candle lit near his picture 'til he came home from the war."

Most of what Chas said about the mob is false, but he uses it to intimidate the three, as Paul and Mickey did years earlier. What good is having an Italian surname if you can't exploit deadbeats?

"That is so amazing, we are so glad to meet Paul's relative," Francis whispers. "Oh, I think we better hustle or Edie will miss her entrance at our club. Thanks for the champagne. You must come see us one night."

"Thanks, I will do that," Chas warns, "as long as you compliment me and my guests with champagne, as I have done for you."

"We will, we most certainly will," Angel mumbled. "Please, you must come to our club. We look forward to your visit. Please come and bring your guests."

"Wasn't it exciting," Carlos boasts, "having a star in our club?"

"Carlos you need to know my feeling on this matter," Chas scolds. "The girl patrons scrape up four dollars to get in, bum a ride here, and bum a ride home. They are the only stars in this place.

"Edie, the lush and her two zombies are freeloaders. They don't spend a dime. You are never to give away the profits. I'm surprised a sophisticated gentleman like you falls for that con job. Good night; I'll see you tomorrow."

The following morning, Bill finds on his desk Carlos' resignation written on note paper splattered with dried tear stains. Carlos is melodramatic to the end.

A few weeks later, Rolando brakes off his relationship with

Denis, and moves out of the apartment. His reason for breaking up, he says, is due to Denis' desire to be a philanderer. Denis is now free of Rolando, and opens the beach bar at the newly-renovated Atlantic beach hotel every morning and works 'til the 4 PM shift change.

Affluent gay men from all over the world come to this gay paradise, and Denis gets to hit on them as soon as they order a drink. The weather and ample supply of sex partners guarantees an excellent time. Chas is at the beach bar enjoying looking at the ocean; there isn't much else for him to do in this gay paradise. The breeze, with its fragrance of saltwater, fills his lungs, and music from the juke box lifts his spirits.

Denis is speaking low to a guest.

"Oh, him," Denis quips. "He's my husband, but don't let that stop you."

The guest finishes talking with Denis and walks over to Chas.

"Hi, my name is Marv. Your lover tells me you're Chas. Good to meet you. It's always great weather here. I used to vacation in Florida, at the Grove, but the weather there is not as reliable as here. I arrived this morning, and couldn't wait to see what's available at the bar. Denis says you and he are liberal, sex-wise?"

"Oh, we are. We don't have sex with each other. We prefer different partners."

"That is normal in gay relationships," Marv mentions.

"Denis likes black men with huge cocks to fuck him," Chas quips. "Me, I like little light-skin native sissies with tight ass holes. The reason is I was cursed with a small cock in spite of my height. I can't enjoy normal men. I tried getting fucked once but the pain was too much to endure. Being on top is the only way I do it."

"Well, I don't fit your profile," Marv mumbles. "Have a great day; it was interesting talking with you."

Denis comes to Chas after Marv goes to hustle someone else.

"I love to tease the queens that don't hit on me first," Denis laughs. "They want to shop around first. They learn quickly, I'm the best ass on this beach. After my shift, let's go to the movie."

"What's playing?"

"I don't know. Who cares what's playing?"

"*I* care, because I go to see something *I* want to see," Chas scolds. "You scour the balcony in search of a sex partner or partners. You're oblivious to the movie. Okay, I'm bored. We might as well go. Maybe I'll see something I'll like. I know you will enjoy whatever?"

The movie is over. Denis meets Chas in the lobby.

"What did we... I mean *you*... see?"

"*One Flew over the Cuckoo's Nest*," Chas mentions. "I can really relate to Jack Nicholson's character.

"I feel cooped up living on this Island. My close friends are weird. My customers are children from a foreign culture who speak another language.

"Nicholson's character is interred with crazy people who can't communicate.

"I'm interred with fruits and nuts. I've got to *get out*, too. I will figure a way out."

"It's a pleasant, cloudy, cool day to walk home," Denis whispers. "I will tell you my situation concerning *getting out*.

"I was twelve and became friends with a kid in my home class. We go to the movies, malt shops, and hang out together a lot.

"After a while he said he thinks I'm gay due to my mannerisms. I say I'm not sure. I like girls, but have no desire to kiss them or touch their breasts.

"We are passing a cornfield on our walk home from the malt shop. He suggests we take a shortcut. Halfway through the field he says let's see if you're gay. It won't bother him if I am, he says.

"He stops, takes down his pants and asks me to touch his cock. Surprised and excited, I reach over and touch it. It doesn't get hard, so he tells me to put it in my mouth. I am confused as my heart pounds with excitement.

"I get on my knees and open my mouth. He puts his cock in my mouth. It feels nice. He says to move my mouth back and forth on his cock. He has his hands guiding the movement of my head. The more I move my mouth the harder his cock gets. Mine gets so hard in my pants, it hurts. Then I hear him groan as his cock vibrates and his cum shoots into my mouth."

"Well," He snarls. "I guess you are a fucking faggot after all."

"He punches me over and over in my face. With each hit I see stars. I fall to the ground holding my broken nose and screaming. He kicks me repeatedly in my ribs, fracturing two of them."

"Shut up," He scoffs. "You cock-sucking fucking faggot."

"The pain causes me to black out; how long, I don't know. I come to, and at first I wonder what the bottom of the cornstalk is doing close to my eyes. I realize I am lying on the ground with my face in the dirt. I have trouble standing erect due to the severe pain at my slightest movement.

"Once on my feet, I have one hand on my bloody broken nose, and my other hand holds my ribcage. In a bent position with blood and dirt on my face, I drag my painful body to the street.

"A passing motorist stops and takes me to the emergency room. After examinations, I am admitted to the hospital.

"My parents are embarrassed to learn I'm gay, and engaging in sex out in the open."

"We'll have to move," Father shouts. "He can't go back to school in this town. He will be harassed and beaten daily. We have to *get you out* of here."

"For the rest of my life, I feel as though I am in the *Cuckoo's Nest*. I will not trust anybody. I'm afraid to go to gay bars for fear of being found out. Things made an about face when I came to this gay paradise."

Left to Right: Chas, Denis, Bill and some staff from Otello at a beach picnic.

"Denis, what a horrible experience at such a young, vulnerable age. My sympathy goes out to you."

"Look how depressing the movie made you, and you made me," Denis laughs. "See, if you came to in the balcony with me we'd be in a much happier mood. You straight people don't know how to enjoy life. You need to *let it all hang out.*"

"Denis, it's your night out of the kitchen—my treat. Let's have Cuban food across the street."

The restaurant has comfortable furniture. The smell of the food cooking entices their appetites, and they realize how hungry they are. They finish eating the tasty food, and Denis lights a cigarette as they enjoy after-dinner drinks and talking.

"Things are running better at the club since Ms. Carlos quit," Chas whispers. "I have something you may be interested in. With your background it's a no-brainer. Managing the club takes common sense. Even *I* can do it. You were supposed to laugh at that, Denis. Getting on with it, spending all my time in Puerto Rico, working only two-and-a-half nights is making me crazy."

"Ha! Get to the point, Chas."

"Okay, I propose that I manage the club the first and last weekends of each month. You manage the club the second and third weekends of that month. I'll end up with nineteen consecutive days off. I believe I've learned most of what there is to learn in *Otello's*. Additional time here will be wasted as far as learning the business.

"The time off this island I will spend with my family, and friends I'd like to see more of. One week in the fall and one week in the spring, I'll do cattle drives, pushing beeves with Vinton's crew through God's country.

"Looking for bars in New York City with Seymour will take most of my time when I'm there. I will be attending the *Big Apple University*, instead of *Fruits and Nuts University*.

"While I'm doing my thing, you will be paid out of my salary.

It will be equal or more than the tips you get bartending. It's a big relief to me if I don't have to be interred here for three years."

"Sounds like a good deal for both of us," Denis lauds. "It's a deal. I'm sorry you're displeased on my Island of Fruits and Nuts. I understand a guy with your active mind dislikes the slow pace here. I'll miss you, but we'll make up time when you are here. When do we start?"

"On Monday," Chas mentions. "It will give us time to go over details."

The following Monday, Chas and Denis go over procedures.

"Those are things to look for," Chas mentions. "Anything else you handle using your smart head. Man, you're a godsend, Denis."

Too bad you missed *Cuckoo's Nest*. Seeing the big Native American break-out gave me a high—same as I'm feeling now, after finalizing our arrangement."

Chas has lunch privately with Bill, and they go over the arrangement Chas and Denis made.

"It's okay by me, Chas, our deal is intact. How you run the club is your call. Denis is a good worker. We will see you on the weeks you are here. Take care."

The following two and a half years, Chas spends a lot of time with Seymour, looking at bars and restaurants for sale. Each time they get together, Chas learns something new from the shrewd Seymour.

In a meeting with a broker, Chas listens as Seymour explains what he dislikes about a deal. Listening to the conversation, Chas thinks: *He's learning these years what he wanted to glean from Sam at that infamous luncheon the two spent in a Queens Diner years earlier. There is no way his friend Sam could teach him in a short time what he needed to learn.* Seymour pokes Chas out of his thoughts.

"Chas, you hear this?" Seymour shouts. "The joint we passed across from Fat Tony is for sale."

"Not so fast," Jackie scolds. "Your friend Ken has a deposit on it. I gave him the keys, and a copy of the lease for legal review."

"That's why she's left messages for me," Seymour quips. "We'll take it, Jackie. I was there when it was a cabaret. It's a good store. I'll return her calls when I get home, and take care of things. Don't you worry, Jackie."

They leave Jackie's office, and each grabs a taxi home. Seymour and Chas are excited that they found a store. Now real work will begin.

4 Seymour and Ken agree to be partners. Chas calls Denis in Puerto Rico, and relays the details concerning the partnership with Seymour, Ken and the store on 53rd Street in Manhattan.

"Seymour and I have a great deal in New York.

"An acquaintance of Seymour's found *location-location-location*, the three most important things for a successful business. A closed bar on East 53rd Street, is in the Loop just east of Second Avenue. It's where gay hustlers hang out, night and day, waiting for johns to stop their cars and make a deal to have sex.

"You will love this area, Denis. Johns drive along 53rd Street, where gay bars stretch from First Avenue to Third Avenue. If a deal is made, the pair drive away. If not, the john does the loop again. Mind you, this is an up-scale neighborhood."

"I can't wait to visit you." Denis shouts.

"Yeah, that'll be great. I'll show you a real city. No having sex in the balcony, though. Ken Gersberg, a wannabe producer known as Ken Gaston, desires an up-scale restaurant using a famous chef. We know he is wrong. Ken knows nothing of running a restaurant; he thinks owning one will make him a star.

He needs successful people with deep pockets as investors. At present, he's relying on friends without a dime to spare. The restaurant business has the greatest percentage of failure of any business. Figures prove it. We'll spread the risk among partners; it's the smart thing to do."

"He's lucky to have two smart operators as you two," Denis cautions. "But he won't appreciate what you offer."

"Ken found the store and location Seymour and I wanted for two years. We won't blow it with a fancy restaurant. The street is a perfect location for a hustler bar. That is what it shall be. I'm going to Seymour's apartment this morning. I wanted to give you the news for now. Take care."

"Call as you know more, Chas. Bye."

Chas arrives at Seymour's apartment for their private talk. He rides the elevator and is stunned; it is the first time he isn't anxious. The pain of loneliness he endured in Puerto Rico without his family didn't kill him; instead, it made him stronger. He realizes that his trauma at four, erroneously connected elevators with separation from family. Feeling triumphant, he swaggers from the elevator, an enlightened, peaceful man. Seymour is waiting, with his head peering into the hallway.

"Come on in, Chas," Seymour whispers. "I just left the shower."

He wears no wig, only a towel around his waist. Droplets of water cling to his gray, hairy chest. Without his boots, his shortness is obvious. He returns to the bathroom to dry himself. The bathroom door is left partially open so they can talk.

"Chas, Ken's got three things in his favor. One: He has a deposit on a lease. Two: He's popular and liked by every fag in New York City. Three, and most important: He does successful promotions.

"Remember that restaurant with the fancy chef that we didn't buy?

"We told the owner that the money is in liquor, not food.

Every customer thinks they're critics for *The New York Times*. The chef knows he makes or breaks a restaurant. We'd be working for the chef, had we taken the deal.

"We'll get paperwork showing you as Ken's partner. With that completed, we'll persuade him that our way is best. The location is perfect for an up-scale cruise bar. We need to run a strong door to keep out the garbage types. We'll use everything. Proper dress code, ID, and no straight girls allowed. A girl tries to compete between two fag lovers. She fails, gets sloppy drunk and creates a scene. She has to be thrown out of the bar.

"This afternoon, we'll see inside and what we need, money-wise. Get a copy of the lease from Ken for our review. Okay?"

"Yes."

"Brian is an excellent attorney and respected at the Liquor Authority. You and Ken have clean records. Because of my relationship with my partners, I can't be on the liquor application, or even suspected of being a partner with you and Ken.

"There is some prejudice against Italians at the Authority. Italian mobsters as my ex-partners are suspected of undisclosed ownership in our clubs.

"We will have no problem. You have a Jewish partner. It helps with the bigots at the Authority. Some may hate Jews, but they know we're not mobsters. Ha!"

"We need a designer to draw up plans in order for us to get prices from subcontractors," Chas mentions. "Someone without a big ego and a big fee. He'll have to accept the revisions we make to his cherished designs. Are you just about ready to go meet the other princess?"

"Yes, and I'm not a princess, I'm an elegant queen," Seymour laughs.

"Excuse me, you elegant queen."

As Chas and Seymour exit the cab, Ken is unlocking the entrance door to 303/305 East 53rd Street. The two buildings have one door which leads to a common space on the first floor and basement.

"Ken, this is Chas, a previous partner, and ex-construction contractor," Seymour mumbles.

"Hi," the two each say, and shake hands.

Chas figures Seymour talks at times from the side of his mouth, thus mumbling, caused by a habit derived so only his mobster associate could hear him say something.

They enter the premises, and Seymour and Chas carefully examine the layout and condition of the premises as they walk and observe.

"This will make a perfect restaurant for what I want," Ken boasts.

As he struts throughout the store, his explanation of how the place is to be designed falls on deaf ears.

Ken is in his early thirties, gentle looking, medium build and height, with curly light brown hair. He generally dresses casually, wearing tennis shoes and jeans.

"Experience taught me to record the space I will renovate," Chas advises. "I'll speak into my recorder as if I were describing the area to a draftsman, who will sketch the space. You two excuse me," Chas begins.

"Twenty feet from the entrance door of 303, along the corridor is a men's room. Ten feet further down the corridor begins a thirty-foot-long bar along the left demising wall.

"Opposite where the bar is, is a four-foot-wide walk through the eighteen-inch-thick brick structural wall, which divides the two spaces and supports the three floors above. Put the meat rack on this wall; it's opposite the bar and is perfect for it.

"Continuing past the bar, the brick wall ends. A large open space flows into the 305 space, which has an old piano in it. At the end of the 303 space is a sliding pair of doors leading to a lounge with skylights in the roof of this one story section of the premises. At one time, it was an outdoor lounge.

"I continue by turning back in the direction I came from,

but in the 305 space; I am at the four-foot-wide walk through again which is the entrance to the dining room from the bar. I completed making a big U-turn.

"This area is the dining room. The kitchen is through an adjacent opening. I'm in the kitchen, and I open a door which leads directly to the sidewalk. A stair near the kitchen goes to the basement.

"The two spaces total about two-thousand square feet; however, the traffic flow is perfect for a cruise bar. People will cruise through the bar, over to the piano bar, on through the dining room, and into the lounge… and eventually, back to the beginning of the bar. This flow pattern is important to keep in mind while developing the drawings for a cruise bar.

"The purpose of parading around a club is to see and be seen. People go to bars to meet people, drink, and have a good time. As people move about, they have a better chance of meeting other people.

"The end. Contact me before sketching."

Chas and Seymour know they have a jewel of a space. Ken will have to see it their way, but not now. After he finishes recording, Chas tells Ken and Seymour what he thinks.

"This place is run down, guys, it needs extensive amounts of work," Chas warns. "My construction experience will save us from opportunistic subcontractors."

"How much do you think it'll cost, Chas?" Ken asks.

"The first thing to do is get plans drawn up of what we want," Chas replies. "We need an architect or designer to draw the plans. Next step is to get prices from subcontractors. If the cost is in our budget, we proceed. If not, we revise the plans until they match our budget.

"My guesstimate is it won't happen for under a hundred-fifty grand. If we keep the cost down, the minimum we'll contribute is fifty grand each."

"I have a good friend who does all my stage sets: Jerry

Richland," Ken suggests. "I'll call Jerry and set up an appointment for tomorrow night. Okay?"

"Okay, but I'm not sure this is for a set designer, Ken," Chas mentions." I'll know for sure after we speak with Jerry."

"You got fifty large, Ken?" Seymour quips.

"I have a lot of offers of money from friends who will invest in *my* project," Ken boasts. "I'll come up with my end, don't worry about me."

"I'm not worried, not a bit," Seymour derides.

He smirks at Chas, who understands the meaning of his look. Seymour and Chas are prepared to do the venture without Ken if need be.

The following night, Jerry talks with Seymour and Chas at *The Mayfair Restaurant* on First Avenue and 53rd Street.

Jerry is average-looking, gentle, also in his thirties, with a little paunch and minor baldness. This project will be a major step in his career. The egotists, Seymour and Jerry, must work in harmony for the project to succeed. As they talk, Chas realizes Jerry will be perfect working with Seymour and himself.

"Working as a set designer," Jerry brags, "my designs are exceptional at making artificial light appear natural. The space is two steps below the sidewalk. Only the front entrance has minimal natural light. I can design an elegant club using lighting features."

Jerry shifts nervously in his seat, and beads of sweat are wiped off his brow as he speaks.

"We gather you are available to start immediately if we accept you?" Chas asks.

"Sure, as soon as I get the word to start," Jerry advises. "Thank you, guys, for considering me for your project. Bye."

"Bye, Jerry," Chas says.

"Well, what do you think of Jerry?" Seymour inquires.

"I think he'll be fine as long as you don't treat him like shit. He's a temperamental queen. All designers are, and so are you."

"You can't screw with his ego," Chas scolds. "Be fair. We need his talent; he's priced right. The big-shot designers want four times what he's asking."

Brian Kenny formed the corporate papers, made minor changes to the lease, and quickly submitted all the paperwork to the New York State Liquor Authority.

Three weeks later, after minor plan revisions, Seymour and Chas receive the final plans from Jerry.

"Jerry, you designed a great set of plans," Chas praises. "Seymour and I are pleased.

"The only item we owners have to contend with is the time needed to fabricate the finished woodwork items you and Seymour used to give the place a soft, rich, cozy look.

"My dear friend of eighteen years, John Sorrelli, owns *Creative Woodworking*, and works for New York City's biggest builders. John always comes through for me. He will now."

A few days later, with Jerry and his plans, Chas drives to *Creative*'s shop in Brooklyn.

They enter the main office.

"Wow, Chas, look at these walls covered in beautiful and rare paneling from floor to ceiling," Jerry lauds. "I never saw such beautiful woodwork before."

"Hi, Teresa, how have you been?" Chas says. "John is expecting us."

"I've been okay. Thanks for asking. Yes, he knows you're scheduled this morning. He's excited to see you. It's been a long time."

John quickly comes from his office with Joe, his younger brother and partner. The three embrace each other.

"It's good to see you again, big guy," John lauds.

John and Joe are short, attractive men in their late fifties, with graying hair. Both have big generous hearts and affable personalities. Dressing in suits and ties reflects their executive positions in the firm.

"Good to see you, John, it's been three long years," Chas replies. "You two never age, you both look great. Meet our designer, Jerry."

John, Joe, and Jerry shake hands.

"What great paneling you two have. I'm astounded. I never saw such beautiful wood before," Jerry lauds.

In the huge conference room, they spread out the drawings. Jerry explains what he wants. *Creative* knows exactly what to do. This small project is child's play for them.

"Jerry, as the commercial says...*we're in good hands*," Chas laughs.

"Chas, you haven't lost your schmoozing personality," Joe remarks. "We'll jump right on making the shop drawings for Jerry's approval."

Joe is in charge of the production staff and is critiquing Jerry's plans as they sit on comfortable swivel chairs around a huge oak conference table in a lavish paneled room.

"We have done a lot of work for Chas, Jerry, so we already know the answer to the question, When do you need it? *Yesterday* is always his answer," Joe advises. "I guess it's even sooner now that it's his personal project."

"Come with me, Jerry," Joe boasts. "I'll give you the tour all first-time designers get of the drafting department, the formidable shop equipment and I'll introduce you to your expediter, John, Jr.

Jerry has never witnessed anything similar to this operation before. He is impressed, and curious about everything he sees. Joe is happy to answer all of Jerry's questions. When the tour is over, Jerry returns to Teresa's office.

"Are you hungry, Jerry? We are close to *Lindy's* famous restaurant," Chas advises. "Right after I talk with John, we'll go there and I'll treat you to lunch."

"Sure, I am having such a great time. What a nice group of people to have as friends and business associates. You're very lucky to have these people in your life. I'm going to enjoy every minute I work with them. I have so much to learn, and such nice teachers, too. I know how fortunate we are. As you said, with built-in cabinetry, woodworking can be a major obstacle to a job. You're correct, a seasoned company like *Creative* run by John Sir, Joe, and John, Jr., we are in excellent hands and need not be concerned," Jerry lauds.

Jerry is learning fast, Chas realizes.

"You're right, Jerry. Excuse me a minute. John, may we talk in your office?"

"Sure, kid."

"John, you need to know my situation. The main problem at hand is Ken's inability to come up with his end of the money. He is the key to promoting the place.

"Construction is well underway. Sal Fiori, whom you know, is doing all the rough carpentry. He's building the plywood and the anchor system for the floating couch.

"Construction money is low. I guarantee you will be paid. I will ask Sam and his friends to loan Ken what he needs. With my guarantee, they will do it. Ken has to promote the newly-named *Rounds*. His extensive mailing list is surpassing our expectations. It's where I'm at. I want to keep you, my dear friend, informed. Thanks for listening, John, and taking my project on short notice."

"I love ya, big guy. I'm not worried about you; glad I can be of service. God bless you," John mentions.

The two men hug and go their own way.

"Jerry, you ready for lunch? Let's get in the car."

As soon as they begin driving, Jerry has the urge to pry into Chas' sex life.

"Chas, as a handsome man owning a popular disco in Puerto Rico, you must have a ball fucking the Latin woman?"

"Not really, Jerry, the kids that come to the club are sexy jail bait. Even if they are the proper age, I still don't shit where I eat.

I also don't want to be in a situation where I can't avoid her, because I have to be at the club."

"Have you ever had anal sex with women? I know you don't have it with men. Seymour said you're straight to the core."

"No, Jerry, I don't want to pull out with shit on my dick."

"Chas, that's nonsense. I can't believe you said that. Boy, straight people are uninformed about anal sex. No offence to you.

"The rectum is clean of shit. A cock doesn't come in contact with shit during anal sex. The way the cock goes in is the way it comes out, only not as hard.

The sphincter is very sensitive. Try sticking your tongue there when you're with your next sex partner, or put a finger in her ass. She will come from that alone. Straight people don't relax enough to enjoy anal penetration."

"No offence taken, Jerry—you're fired," Chas scoffs. "Just kidding Jerry, you can breathe again. Gotcha."

"What about oral sex?" Jerry quips. "Don't tell me you don't do that either."

"Of course I do, Jerry. Are you writing a book about naïve straights? I'm responsible for stimulating my partner and myself. I'm dating this hot babe with a great body. I'll try her ass next time. She doesn't like me to eat her, though; I can't get close. She loves to blow me. I don't understand why she won't let my tongue at the beaver."

"Ask her why," Jerry advises. "Some women do stink because they don't douche. Tell her to douche because eating her is as enjoyable to you as blowing you is to her. That should get you to the beaver."

"Jerry, I feel as though a professor of sex education proved how ignorant I am about anal sex and women. Thanks for a half-hour person-to-person crammed course. All my future sex partners thank you.

Also, thanks for being subtle as you hit on me. I hate guys

who come right out and say, Let's fuck."

"Chas, how could you say that; I'm not that type of girl," Jerry laughs. "Even though, you're my type of man."

He appreciates the knowledge he got from Jerry, making him a better lover. It's important he be good at what he enjoys.

One month later, *Creative* makes a major delivery to the site. The same afternoon, Mari comes to the city to see a matinee on Broadway. Chas has an appointment to meet her after the show at his new friend's restaurant, down the street from *Rounds*. Now he is reviewing construction schedules with Sal.

"Our renovation is almost complete," Sal advises, "except for suede wall covering, the recessed, narrow, tinted mirrors that create a paneling effect to break the long unbroken line of the dining room wall. Jerry's panels of slices of dark mirror, vertically recessed every four feet, is a great feature, Boss. The cabinetry is waiting installation after the place is further along."

"Great, but now I need to meet Mari. She came to the city to see a show. Have a good night, Sal."

Mari joins him at the bar in Lantana, an Italian restaurant on Second Avenue near 53rd Street.

"How was the show?" Chas asks.

"You wouldn't enjoy it. It was a musical."

Tommy, the owner, comes to the table.

"What can I get the lady to drink?" he asks.

"A Black Russian, and please call me Mari," she answers.

"I've just got to tell you, Mari, how excited we in the neighborhood are to get a high-class piano bar, thanks to Chas and his partners," Tommy lauds. "A bar that caters to various age groups is great. I'll enjoy patronizing such an exciting place along with handsome boys."

Tommy is thin, short, with thinning black hair. He has a gentle, warm personality.

After a good dinner, Mari wants Chas to show her the work progress at *Rounds*.

Mari and granddaughter, Nicole

"Chas, I would like to see the store you refer to as a bar, while talking with your sweetheart Seymour, from the house phone."

"Tommy, thanks for the great food," Chas lauds.

They leave, turn the corner and walk west on 53rd Street to a locked door at *Rounds*.

"Mari, wait, let me find the damn key to unlock the door."

He finds his key, and they enter the dusty site. The smell of construction debris and stale body odor is noticeable in the dusty air.

"Be careful, there is debris everywhere, and I need to relock the door before we go further," Chas warns. "What was that reference about my sweetheart Seymour?

"Don't be angry," Mari mentions. "Sometimes I feel you care more for him than you care for me. You haven't gone to the other side, have you?"

"Are you crazy? He's my business partner. Talking and spending time together is the same as going to work," Chas scolds. "Don't we fuck enough?"

"Yes, when you're around—which isn't often."

"You want me to stay home and fuck you," Chas scolds, "or put food on the table?"

"Forget it, just forget it. Sorry I made you angry. My period is a day away."

"Don't blame your attitude on that crap," Chas snarls.

They avoid stepping on material and debris, as Chas holds Mari's hand, guiding his tall, thin, beautiful hazel-eyed brunette wife through the dimly-lit space.

Creative's uninstalled cabinets occupy the floor space near the bar. Mari seems aroused at the sight of phallic symbols in the form of a tool left on the bar, like a ten-inch-long by one-inch-in-diameter drill bit that lies on top of a the bar. Masculine sweat odors from Sal's crew are still in the air adding to her arousal.

Without warning, Mari turns to Chas, puts her arms around his neck, smiles and says," Fuck me, right now, right here."

A surprised but extremely obliging Chas helps Mari get her skirt and panties off. The caustic answers he used with Mari turn him on, too. The cleanest spot to place Mari's bare bottom is on *Creative*'s bar cabinet, still wrapped in clean shipping paper. One cabinet is the right height for Mari to sit on. As Chas stands, she spreads her legs apart. Her legs wrap around his waist, enabling his angry powerful strokes to consummate passionate sex. After their brief but enjoyable make-up sex, Mari takes a cab to the bus terminal where she gets transportation home.

Chas has a meeting later with Seymour, Ken and Sam, concerning money for Ken's investment; he will drive home after the meeting.

Sam and John meet with Chas and Seymour and agree to put up the money to cover Ken's portion. They stipulate that Seymour and Chas are responsible if Ken defaults.

In the cab ride back to midtown, Chas tells Seymour of his and Mari's escapade in *Rounds*.

As far as Seymour is concerned, the incident of spontaneous sex in the club is the christening which guarantees *Rounds'* success and fortune.

The following morning Chas goes to the site to do his daily inspection.

Sal is a short, friendly fellow with thick, gray curly hair, which Seymour would kill to possess. Sal is competent either working with tools or supervising all the tradesmen.

"Good morning, Sal, things are really humming. I'm glad to see the cabinets being installed," Chas laughs. "I was worried that a careless workman would use one to stand on."

The following week, Chas and Sal are appraising the construction progress.

"With the back bar cabinets in place, the bar is almost finished," Sal advises. "Next item to be installed is the marble bar top and *Creative*'s eight-inch oval oak bar armrest. Mike Kenney will be installing the tinted mirrors between the wall panels. The six-inch brass pole at the service bar and the rest of the brass railings, he'll install tomorrow. We'll make the opening on Tuesday the 24th of April, as the invitations say."

"With your special workman's gift for handling all sorts of tools, things turned out great," Chas lauds. "Thanks, from the bottom of my heart."

The following days, Jerry, Seymour, Chas and Sal oversee every item as it arrives at the site. The dark solid carpet is installed. Two-foot square oak wood tables with a clear protective finish are placed in the dining room. The cushioned bar stools and dining room cushioned chairs are set in place, too.

All sorts of dishes, glasses, silverware, dry goods, meat, fish, and vegetables are delivered. Most important, the soda and beer system, bottled wine, bottles of alcohol—the money maker—are set on the bar's back shelves, and the balance is stocked under lock and key.

Still to be delivered are the cushions for the floating couch and other gut-wrenching items, which should have been installed by now. Their absence makes for uneasiness with those concerned.

The birthday of *Rounds* has finally arrived, on April 24th, 1979.

The delivery time of 6 PM is not accepted by one of her three parents.

Ken never got his white tennis shoes dirty visiting Mother Renovation during her difficult pregnancy which was nurtured by Dr. Sal; he is displeased with the birthing progress.

Chas and Seymour, however, with the aid of Sal, Jerry, all the waiters, bartenders, cooks, busboys, and porters are all busy assisting Mother Renovation's timely birth. The contractor is finally installing the floating couch cushions, the last installation that's needed for an on time delivery.

Jerry and Chas are cutting and installing plastic panels which hide the overhead bulbs that light the top of the floating couch.

Chas temporarily lowers the overhead hi-hat lights and turns on the over and below lights that give the illusion the coach is free-standing.

"*Wow*" is the unanimous response to Jerry's ingenious design, which makes the couch appear to float.

At 4:30 PM, one-and-a-half hours prior to the scheduled birth, Ken arrives and is disappointed Mother is still in labor. Wearing a blue Armani suit, white shirt and tie, hair professionally cut and combed, he makes an announcement.

"I'm not opening *my* restaurant tonight. I have friends outside, who can't enter an unfinished restaurant at the time the invitation states they can. I've never been so embarrassed."

Every one of the midwives assisting with the birth hears Ken and ignores him, except Chas. Quietly, but forcibly, he gets his face up close with Ken's.

"Who do you think you are?" Chas scolds. "You, of all people, mister wannabe producer in show business, knows the curtain goes up when the invitation says the show will begin. The invitation says 6 PM. Don't try to rush the delivery by even a minute.

Now, go take your deadbeat, no-money-to-invest friends to some bar, and buy drinks for them until we open. Do it, Ken. Don't make me have to slap you in front of the staff."

None of the midwives lose a beat during the lecture that Ken receives from Chas.

An hour later the staff is lighting candles on the dining room tables. They are making sure that the set-up of the silverware on each table is correct. A pinkish cloth napkin shaped as a leaf is inserted into each water goblet. Two-foot gladiolas are put in ornate vases, then placed around the dining room on low partitions that separate seating sections and create cozy seating areas.

"Mary! Not there—over here—this way," Jerry growls. "What fag can't figure how to arrange flowers?"

Tony, the restaurant manager, is giving a last-minute dress

rehearsal in the proper methods of serving bottled wine at the table. The staff are handsome, out-of-work "wannabe" dancers, actors, musicians, artists, writers, and young people looking to support themselves 'til... ?

Mickey's at the piano, checking his equipment and his vocal cords.

Seymour gives the final touch, as he lowers the dimmer switches for all the lights after the work lights are off. The lighting enhances the cozy, sexy, and seductive ambiance of *Rounds*. Natural suede for the walls, natural fabric, and five-inch-thick cushions on the floating couch, with plush, dark solid carpet on the floor creates a soft, elegant atmosphere to the club. Importantly, the dark mirrors reflect a favorable skin tone to the vain patron as he views himself in the mirrors constantly. He thinks: *"Mirror, Mirror on the wall, who's the fairest... ?"*

The beautiful ambiance is seen for the first time as baby *Rounds* is delivered precisely at 6 PM. Her anxious customers quickly enter as the entrance door is unlocked.

Rounds rear dining area

5 Seymour and Chas realize Ken succeeded in promoting *Rounds* to a resounding debut. They return a short time later, cleaned, dressed, and in proper attire to a packed club. The limousines, Mercedes and Porsches adorn hundreds of feet of adjacent curb space at *Rounds*.

Sal returns to ensure all is running well mechanically and assists Nick, the doorman, in handling the crowd properly. Carding and dress-code are not common practices used by owners in bars and restaurants; however, the people allowed in either add to or detract from the club's ambiance.

Rounds was designed and built using expensive materials, thus creating an elegant club. Customers congruent with its ambiance are allowed in. Most have invitations; many only hear of the opening and are admitted, provided they meet the club's standards.

Gay men normally are not prone to acts of violence. They expect the proprietor to ensure their well-being while patronizing their business establishment.

Rounds is located in an affluent neighborhood where many famous people such as Truman Copote and Henry Kissinger, to name a few, reside; however *The Loop* draws unsavory characters

Rounds entry

as well. New York City's five boroughs and surrounding areas encompass a fifty-mile radius that provides millions of people access to Manhattan's nightlife. A strong door code keeps the undesirable culture from entering *Rounds*.

Once Seymour and Chas get as close to the bar as the crowd will allow, Chas orders drinks and uses his long reach to retrieve them, squeezing between David Geffen, the famous record producer, and another customer. "Excuse me, David," Chas says.

He reaches for the drinks that Kenny, the young handsome bartender, gives him.

"It's okay," David lauds. "Congratulations to the three of you. The place is beautiful—the help, too."

David likes the handsome nineteen-year-old bartender, as do other patrons. David is wearing an expensive jacket and a white silk skirt which complements his tanned handsome face and black hair. Seymour knows the boys he hires have to be attractive to please the discerning customers the club is geared to attract.

As they continue moving along the bar, Seymour sees other famous people he knows intimately and greets each one with affection.

"Thanks for joining us, Steve, Calvin," Seymour cheers. "It's a pleasure to have celebrities in our club."

Steve Rubel, the owner of the most popular disco in the country, *Studio 54*, and Calvin Klein, the renowned designer, both extend their hands and shake Seymour's.

"Good luck, Seymour," Steve praises. "It is an elegant bar you guys built."

"I wish you, Chas and Ken, much success," Calvin says.

Steve is short and prefers to dress casual. Calvin is always fashionable wherever the tall good-looking clothing designer goes.

Jimmy Mary, a successful middle-aged gay bar owner/ neighbor, advises Timmy, the service bartender:

"It's a custom in the bar business for owners of other bars to wish the new owners good fortune by buying the bar rounds of drinks."

He puts two new hundred-dollar bills on the bar and tells the crowd:

"Drinks are on Jimmy Mary!"

The generous bar owner of *The Cowboys and Cowgirls* down the street keeps doing it. Hundred-dollar bills kept the service register ringing for the next two rounds of drinks.

Jimmy is average height, thin, and has a complexion acquired from liquor. He grew up in this neighborhood, the son of hardworking Irish parents, long before the Yuppies moved in.

Chas receives a handshake from Jim.

"Good luck, kid," Jim praises. "This bar is what 53rd Street needs—class."

Two *piss elegant* queens, further down the bar, dressed in tuxedos, looking quite elegant, complain to Seymour.

"There is too much *fish* in this bar."

They refer to sophisticated women standing nearby, guests of other gay men. Some women prefer company of gay men to straight men. Thus the term *fag hags*. *Fish* is a derogatory term implying vaginas smell as fish.

"You're jealous, Mary," Seymour derides. "The women have too much class to be with you two fags."

It's a concern of Chas and Seymour, as Ken charges his second bottle of expensive champagne to *Rounds*. He's financing his friend Steven's thirty-fourth birthday.

What a schmuck, Chas thinks, watching Ken guzzle expensive champagne. Smart business sense; Steve will pay the tab, but Ken thinks he's a star.

Steve's the same height as Ken, good looking, and wearing straight blond hair to the collar of his tuxedo. A large diamond ring adorns his right pinky finger.

"Chas, have a drink with us," Ken cheers.

"Sure, but I'll stick with scotch," Chas quips. "I can't afford giving away champagne.

Sitting left to right: Tommy, Guest, Walter, Ed, Guest. Standing: Camille.

Happy Birthday, Steve. We have two celebrations to look forward to: our anniversary and your birthday, if Ken can afford it."

As the waiter brings slices of Steve's cake to the table, Seymour comes to the table; he never misses a chance to hit on handsome young men.

"What do we have here, a party?" Seymour bemoans. "And I wasn't invited?"

"Steve, this is my other partner, Seymour," Ken advises.

"My security tells me they won't let the straight young boy and girl you're traveling with in," Seymour warns. "How well do you know those kids?"

"I picked them up in the Hay Market bar on Eight Avenue. It's my birthday. I want to celebrate it with someone. I hate being alone, especially tonight. Look at the present my parents sent from Florida," Steve brags."I wanted a Rolex watch to complement my other jewelry"

"Better get used to loneliness my friend," Seymour advises. "Loneliness is a big part of gay life. You are safer alone. I know, I'm old enough to be your mother, Mary. The bar where you chose to pick up those two was a very poor choice on your part."

"Thanks for the champagne, guys," Steve replies. "I need to attend to my guests outside."

"Don't thank us," Seymour scolds. "It's coming out of Ken's end."

"What? It's a special occasion. I don't believe my ears, Seymour."

"I warned you, Ken. You may buy friends booze. You can't give food away, bottled wine, especially our most expensive champagne. You're not a single proprietor; there are three of us to share equally in debt as well as profit. We each pay our own debt."

"That sucks. What's the point of owning my own bar?"

"The point is showing a profit, and as I just said, you don't own this store. We three, the people you borrowed from, own *Rounds*. Chas will deduct the cost of the champagne from your pay this week."

A gentle tap on Chas' back causes him to turn around.

"Chas, excuse us," Tommy mentions. "Meet Walter Lucy, an ex-IBM executive who accepted retirement. He's considering the priesthood again. This handsome devil is Brian Burns, the feature actor on the daily soap, *The Doctors*."

Brian is a tall blond and quite the ladies man on TV. In real life, he prefers boys. Walter is medium height, has gentle looks, graying hair, and a complexion that is prevalent to people who drink excessively. He exhibits a sincere attitude. Brian shakes Chas' hand. In a joking, tough-guy manner, he says:

"So you're the mob guy in this fag joint."

"You need to drop the resentment toward Italian surnames," Chas quips. "Besides, if I am a mobster, I still have my degree from the University of Fruits and Nuts. I majored in Gayism 101 through 103, and I graduated with honors."

"Because I'm an actor, I enjoy different roles where I imitate people's ethnicity; no offence intended," Brian mentions. "We're tired of eating at *Tommy*'s, the prime rib at that table looks enticing. Is there an open table for three?"

"Brian, never shit a shitter," Chas derides. "The prime rib is a great choice. Because I like you, my owner's table, dubbed the "Spy" table, is yours. From this table, Seymour and I see everyone who walks to the bar, into the dining room and hangs at the piano.

"You three old-timers can cruise the joint while sitting on your asses. If you happen to snag a boy, you'll have energy to expend on sex, but not here. Boys are the reason you're here.

"Thanks for coming, I hope to see again. Now, excuse me, I need to check the rest of the club."

Mickey is doing great on tips—nothing less than a five-dollar bill is in his tip bowl. The queens love show-tunes; *Annie* is big. They request it often. Chas hears these words in his head, even when another song is sung.

"Hey, Mick, I'll give you a five every time I *don't* hear, *tomorrow, tomorrow…*" Chas implores.

As he walks through the bar Chas notices people blocking the entrance corridor.

He learned in Puerto Rico to check the toilet often. The narrow corridor leading from the bar has a men's room door located midway between the bar and the entrance door. It opens into a small adequate toilet area.

It's packed with frustrated people waiting to use the men's room.

He enters the men's room to see what the delay is.

Noticing four legs in the only stall with a commode indicates sex is going on. A door provides privacy for one occupant. Two occupants are unacceptable.

He places one foot on the adjacent urinal and raises his body above the partition to see the culprits. Sitting on the toilet with his pants at his ankles, Chas sees the handsome young porno star who was at the bar during lunch. Sitting on the porno star's erected cock is the middle-aged business man with his pants around his ankles. He was having drinks with the star during lunch; now he is riding up and down on the eight-inch shaft as it goes in and out of his rectum.

"You two get the fuck out!" Chas scolds.

Walking behind the two shocked ex-patrons, he escorts them outside. People waiting to use the toilet appreciate an owner who resolves the problem.

Word of this incident will travel throughout the gay community. Round disallows indecent behavior. Chas is glad to set the record straight. Some gays, he'd learned, will engage in sex anywhere, any time.

"Nick those two assholes are eighty-sixed. You need to monitor the men's room often—it's part of your job," Chas bemoans. "Now I need a break from the smoke and noise in here. I'm going outside to chase the trash from the front door—it's also part of your job as door man, my boy."

As soon as he gets outside, he says in a firm tone:

"People, loitering is a crime. If you don't disperse, the police will be called."

Nick is in his twenties, over six feet tall weighing two-hundred-seventy-five pounds, and formidable in appearance. He prefers talking to fighting. Only Chas and the staff know this.

Chas hears a few disparaging remarks as the loiterers leave.

The quiet and cool morning air outside is what he needs. It is 1:30 in the morning, and *Rounds* is still filled with people. He's thankful and happy for their success.

As he enjoys a much-deserved break, leaning against an awning support at the curb, a car pulls alongside him. Two men, in suits, get out of the car to question him.

"Do you know who Ken is?"

"I do, he is my partner."

"We need to ask him a few questions about a customer of yours," one detective says as he presents his badge.

"Do you know a Steven Cohen?"

"Yes, I met him tonight. He's my partner's friend," Chas replies. "Would you like to come inside and speak with Ken? He's still here."

"Will it be a problem to bring him outside? It's a private matter."

"Not at all; I'll be right back."

Chas goes inside *Rounds*.

He and Ken return. The police ask to see identification from both men. The information from both driver's licenses is written on a small note pad a detective takes from his inside jacket pocket as his holstered revolver on his belt becomes visible to Chas.

"Your friend Steve had a *Rounds* business card in his pocket, and your name is on it, Ken.

"He was murdered in his apartment tonight," the detective said. "His head was blown off by a .357 bullet." Ken is almost ready to faint. "The gun is registered in his name. He had no cash on his person, or in the apartment.

"There was no jewelry on him or in the apartment, and his Porsche is also missing. The neighbors say they heard arguing amongst three people. Was he with anyone while he was here?"

"The people he was with were not allowed in this bar. One was a young Hispanic male, and the other, a Caucasian girl," Chas explains. "We cater to gay men only. My doorman may be able to give you a better description."

Chas waves to Nick to come outside and talk with the detectives.

Nick told the police what little he saw at the time the kids were waiting for Steve in his Porsche.

"Thanks for your time, gentlemen. Here are our cards. If you think of something else, please call us," the detective said, and drove off.

The day was twenty-hours long. He is too tired to fully comprehend what he heard; it was time to go to his apartment. With talk recently of separating, Mari had prompted him to rent a two-bedroom apartment at 300 East 54th Street, a new high-rise building around the corner from *Rounds*. It is his home away from family now.

Seymour joined him outside while he waited for a passing taxi to take him home.

"Ken is distraught over the news," Seymour moans. "This shit is commonplace in gay life. Nothing we can do about it."

"We did well, Seymour. I'll do the receipts, and we'll know how much tomorrow morning when I pick up the drop bag."

As soon as Seymour is safely on his way, Chas goes home.

The staff, under the watch full eye of Nick, the doorman, will close. Leon, a Korean porter will arrive at 4 AM to begin his chores just as the bar staff closes.

Having staff at the premises twenty-four-seven is a good security measure. The cleaning work gets done and the place is protected from fire and flood, all at the same time. The alarm system adds extra security. The day bartender comes on duty at 10 AM, and the door is unlocked.

Seymour's experience in the bar business convinced him that Orientals are the most dependable and honest workers for bars and restaurants. The kitchen and cleaning staff are proving Seymour correct.

The next morning, the noise from the Second Avenue traffic, as well as traffic off the 59th Street Bridge heading south, makes it impossible for Chas to sleep longer.

"*Convenience to Rounds has its price,*" Chas grumbles.

During noisy moments, Chas pictures a popular movie he enjoyed years earlier. It's Jack Lemon and Ann Bancroft in the movie, *Prisoner of Second Avenue*. In one scene, Jack is ranting to his wife:

"*Life in this city is unbearable. Last night while we were out, thieves broke in and stole our TV. The tenant above makes noise all night. The constant traffic noise on Second Avenue is making me lose my mind. Garbage trucks banging metal cans at 4 AM. Police and fire truck sirens. Taxi-cab horns blaring twenty-four-seven. We are prisoners of Second Avenue.*"

The rest of Lemon's dialogue, he forgot. Now *he* is the Prisoner of Second Avenue.

"How true fiction in the movies really is," he says, amusing himself, as he dresses to go to the bank on the southwest corner of 53rd and Third.

As he walks toward the bank, he notices the old four-story buildings which represented a neighborhood of people who knew each other, is rapidly disappearing. This area is destined to provide room to build two high-rise office buildings for the thirsty rejuvenated real-estate market, and luxury high-rise residential buildings for yuppies. Gentrification is taking its toll on the old friendly neighborhood.

For now, a small area houses a mom-and-pop convenience store. He purchases a container of black coffee, a bagel for himself, and a can of soda for Ms. Brochette. She controls the basement vault area with small private rooms. Chas will reconcile the cash received from *Rounds* inside a room. Once inside the bank, Chas waves to Bill Brown, the manager. His office door is always open; affording him the ability to see and monitor the banking activity on the first floor.

"Hey, Chas, how's it going?" Bill greets.

"Fine, Bill, how about you?"

"Good, thanks, Chas."

Bill, a stout, short, pleasant-looking man in his mid-thirties, is always accommodating.

The locked dropped canvas bag containing the previous day's receipts is given to him by the commercial teller once he signs a receipt. The bank's Night Deposit functions as a twenty-four-hour vault; securing *Rounds'* earned cash receipts around the clock. With the locked bag, he proceeds downstairs to the vault.

"Good morning," Chas greets. "Here's the soda you like."

"Thanks, and good morning to you," She replies.

Ms. Brochette, a matronly woman, comes from behind her desk to use her key and Chas' key to retrieve his safety-deposit box. With his box, he enters a vacant room to start counting the cash. He takes only the cash needed for the day's expenses to *Rounds*. The remaining cash stays in his box in the vault. He completes the figures in ninety minutes.

He walks to *Rounds*, enjoying the cool April morning weather. He's happy he no longer has to scurry with hordes of people going to work in the skyscrapers he'd built and worked from. Most of the faces he looks at wear a serious, pensive expression; few are jolly. Seymour will be as pleased as him, when he learns how well *Rounds* did, which was three times what was expected. If these standards are maintained, they are off to a great run. Smart and hard work must be the rule to follow.

Until he is sure Mark, the day bartender, is reliable to report to work on-time, every time he's scheduled to work, he constantly checks on him. He wants no surprises even though only the bar is open for the few daytime patrons.

Outside *Rounds*, Leon is painstakingly polishing the brass poles which support the awning and the brass handle on the glass and dark aluminum entrance door. Inside, Leon still has the six-inch brass tubular banisters, the lounge tables, and miscellaneous other pieces to polish. Brass is used to achieve an elegant appearance, to intimidate people without class, and to impress people *with* class.

"Mark, how is it going?" Chas asks.

"We'll be open at noon," Mark moans. "I read about the murder in the paper this morning. How gruesome for the building manager to find someone with his head blown off."

Mark is a studious-looking young part-time college student and enjoys talking for the sake of talking. He's perfect in a bar that caters to lonely day customers drinking away their lives.

"Put a Johnny Black on the bar, Mark. I shall tell you of my personal experience," Chas bemoans. "Yeah, how gruesome, how fucking gruesome it is. That scene never leaves one's mind. It's ready to replay at the slightest provocation.

* * *

"I and a friend Jeffery are thirteen years young. He is my bookworm, a short, inventive friend with red hair, who wears large, thick glasses on his small face. He lives in a six-story building which has elevator service near where I live in a two-story building. One afternoon, after school, Jeffrey explained to me an idea he had.

"We don't have to worry about getting caught smoking anymore," he cheers. "We ride on top of the elevator in my building."

"Are you out of your fucking mind," I reply. "We'll be crushed when the elevator gets to the top."

"No, we won't," Jeffery boasts. "I already took the ride yesterday and I'm still alive. Let's take the stairs to the third floor, I'll show you how it's done. Once we get to the third floor, I'll press the call button, and the unoccupied cab will arrive at the third floor."

I watch Jeffery open the hall door and enter the cab after it arrives at the third floor, he presses the second floor button and comes out while holding the hall door open with his foot.

He holds his copper house key with his handkerchief and on tip-toes reaches up to touch the contact switch recessed in the wall; this is where the closed hall door closes a circuit, telling the elevator it's safe to move. It descends as long as the key is held against the switch by Jeffery.

We wait for the top of the elevator to be level with our floor while keeping the hall door open as we peer into the foreboding chasm which is created by a descending elevator. When it is level, he removes the key thus opening the circuit, the elevator stops moving.

We get on, sit on the steel beam which connects to the cables and elevator cab before the door closes, the elevator moves again.

"You get all this technical shit, Mark? A yes or no answer will do."

"Yes."

"Good, it's a pain to describe this to a non-mechanical person, but all we did is override the circuitry which runs the elevator with a copper key," Chas recounts. "At this time I was afraid to ride *in* one, but not *on* one.

"Being in the shaft is exciting. At the second floor, a passenger gets in and goes to the sixth floor. I almost shit my pants because the space at the top is confining, and I was feeling claustrophobic. I hope we won't be there too long. Hearing clicking sounds from a control box near us told us that a call button was pressed and the elevator descends to the first floor.

"As we travel in the shaft, I notice how foreboding a place it is, with its gray masonry walls on which huge roaches travel. The whole place stinks of grease and metal rubbing against metal. The steel we sit on is extremely dusty.

"We'll get a big kick eavesdropping when women talk personal stuff," Jeffery boasts. "Tormenting my retarded thirty-year-old neighbor is my main passion, though. A voice with no visible body will be frightening. Garson will think the cab is haunted. It will be so funny to see his scared reaction."

"Jeffrey's wish came true. Garson lives with his parents on the sixth floor. He enters the elevator at the lobby. Excited, Jeffery put his head between the shaft wall and the elevator cab recess, allowing him to see passengers riding the elevator without being seen by them."

"Garson," Jeffery mocks. "The elevator cable is breaking and you will fall into the basement and die."

"Garson's reaction to the prank is uncontrollable loud screaming, and banging against the walls and gate. I have to cover my ears, from the loud sound. Jeffery however neglects to consider that as the elevator travels in one direction, the counterweight system travels in the opposite direction. As we go up, it comes down. Jeffery is reveling as he watches the antics of the frightened Garson screaming. The cab and counter weight are passing each other between the second and third floor level.

I hear the sound of his skull being crushed. I can still hear it to this day, Mark. Blood is hitting the side of my face. I hear one loud brief scream by Jeffrey. Instinctively, I grab hold my friend's mutilated body to keep him from falling off the cab and into the pit at the bottom of the shaft, sixty feet below.

Jeffrey, it will be okay, I shout. I got you, don't worry, I won't let you fall, I promise. I promise. He is dead, but I don't know it.

At the sixth floor, a screaming Garson is relieved as he runs out of the elevator into his startled parent's arms. I am screaming for help; his parents can't see me but they figure out where I am. They keep the elevator door propped open preventing it from moving with the two of us on top until help comes.

I'm in a state of panic as the feeling of claustrophobia is intensified. I beg to be removed from confinement with my dead friend's mutilated body oozing blood on me.

The building Super comes to my rescue—not a minute too soon—by lowering the elevator top level with the sixth floor. I faint as I look at my dead friend's mutilated bloody body next to me.

I regain consciousness lying on the cold terrazzo hallway floor, which stunk of being washed recently with a strong commercial cleanser. A rolled-up bloody towel is under my head. Someone used it to wipe Jeffery's blood from my arms and head. I can see medics and police removing my friend in a body bag. We are taken to Kings County Hospital; me to the emergency room, Jeffery to the morgue. A couple of hours later, I wake up from the sedative the doctor gave me. Now I face a scared, angry and delusional mother in the emergency room.

My mother is a tall, stout woman in her mid-forties. She walked to the hospital, a few long city blocks away from our apartment, dragging my two younger exhausted siblings behind her.

My head and arms were cleaned again of the blood, but my clothes remained soiled. I hear her voice as soon as she sees me. She brought clothes for me to change into."

"Are you crazy?" She scolds. "You won't ride in them, but you ride on the top. Whose crazy idea was this? Don't tell me it was yours. Wait 'til your father hears this. You'll really be dead. God forbid me. Jesus! Mary! And Joseph! What am I going to do with you?"

"Don't worry, Ma," I mutter. "It won't happen again."

My brother and sister look at me with concern in their eyes at the sight of my blood soaked clothes. They are assuming it is my blood. Seeing the worried state my mother is in, the attending doctor gave her a mild sedative to take to settle her rattled nerves. My father learns of the accident at dinner."

"Chas, promise me you will never do a dangerous thing again," my father growls.

"I promised, Dad."

"Was my encounter gruesome enough for you, Mark?"

"Holy shit," Mark cries. "You are some lucky guy."

"Thanks, Mark. I didn't need to reiterate the incident. Thanks to you, I did.

"My phone number is taped to the register. If you need me, call. I'll see you later."

* * *

After telling Mark the story, Chas goes to his apartment, sits on a lounge chair on the balcony, facing the afternoon sun. He hopes its warmth will clear his mind of what he recalled. The sun feels warm on him, along with the peaceful effect Johnny Walker Black produced. He is ready to rest now. The street noise is a small price to endure for eliminating a daily commute to New Jersey.

Now it's time for earplugs, a white-noise sound machine on high, closed windows, closed balcony door, closed blinds, and a cozy bed. His Crypt awaits him.

He made arrangements with Mari and the kids to visit every Tuesday and Thursday, after school. If the kids want to spend the weekend in New York, there is room for them to sleep at his apartment. On Sunday afternoon, they can see Broadway shows in spite of the limited rest he receives from working from Saturday night well into Sunday morning.

Tomorrow is Thursday he shall spend from 3 PM to 8 PM with them at an indoor mall in New Jersey. They can shop, have dinner, and spend quality time together. After returning them home, he returns to Manhattan and work.

The ringing phone, two hours later, returned Chas to the here and now.

"Hello," Chas mumbles.

"How did we do in sales last night?" Seymour asks.

"More than we estimated. I'll show you the figures tonight at dinner," Chas remarks. "I'm tired of *The Mayfair*. Where else can we go?"

"We'll meet at *Rounds* for drinks at eight, and check out the store. I'll make sure the morons are doing their job correctly.

"After, we'll give the queens at *Uncle Charlie*'s, and Ms. Katz something to dish (talk) about as we have dinner. Some of those fags told Ken I could not produce a successful restaurant. Vengeance will be mine.

"Did you read the paper yet? It's a shame what happened to Steven," Seymour repeats. "You heard me warn him."

"I don't read horror stories," Chas scoffs. "Talking to Mark earlier was enough to last me a long time."

"Well, get used to this sort of thing, it's part of gay lifestyle," Seymour warns. "The lonely life most fags lead causes them to have sex with strangers, or someone they know. Any time, any place, as long as they appease their sex craving. This lifestyle asks for trouble, bodily harm, or death."

"I know that too from living with Denis," Chas replies. "We went to the movies in the afternoon. I sat downstairs as Denis goes to the balcony and engages in giving head and getting head with strangers. After the movie, we team up in the lobby. On the way home, I tell the entire movie to Denis. He is prepared in case Rolando asks him questions about the flick.

"If there is another bartender on duty with him at the beach bar, he suddenly disappears," Chas advises. "He is gone for an hour having sex with someone. He returns after sex and sits with me at the bar describing the details of his brief interlude. Denis liked getting fucked by big cocks; he is a 'size queen.'

"At our apartment, I keep my room always double-locked at

night. Traffic in the apartment is the heaviest at night with different sex partners coming and going. I am fond of him and worried often. I want assurance he survives the encounters.

"He certainly educated me well. I miss him, but not for his lifestyle."

At the bar that night, Seymour and Chas are discussing how to get Ken out of the habit of giving away the store's resources.

"This kid has no business acumen," Seymour growls. "You have to set boundaries for this moron. He's afraid of you."

"I wonder why," Chas quips.

"Well," Seymour recounts, "I'm her sister, you are the big, bad, straight Mafioso, he thinks. No sane fag or a straight dude is going to risk your ire."

"You need not play with my ass, Mary," Chas quips. "I already worked out a system we will use, if it meets with your approval, your highness.

"He knows we owe a lot of money to the contractors and his benefactors.

"Until the debt is paid, we'll take a fair salary. In addition, we sign tabs for all comps, regarding food and wine, and the costs will be credited to our allowance.

"Drinks can be on the house, as long as they appear on a comp bar check to prevent shenanigans by the waiters. There will be a maximum allowance of two hundred bucks a week for each of us. He can't accept personal checks from customers; end of discussion.

"After our debt is paid, a new system may be introduced for approval by the three of us."

Later, Seymour and Chas go to *Uncle Charlie's* restaurant.

The owner, Lou Katz, isn't in. The manager recognizes Seymour and seats them immediately. He hands them menus.

"Lou said to buy you guys a drink, on him, and wish you two much success."

"Thanks." Seymour and Chas say.

They order lamb chops, a favorite they prefer at this restaurant. As they wait for their food, Chas notices a bragger's glow on Seymour's face.

"It's good to be a star again," Seymour boasts.

Anxiously, Chas waits for Seymour's rebuttal to his next statement.

"Yes, a bullshit star," Chas laughs. "Don't forget who brought you back to stardom. Ken is responsible for finding the store and getting Jerry on board."

Laughing, almost choking on his drink, Seymour looks at Chas and replies.

"Fuck, you, Mary. We made that broken-down package a star. She owes it all to us, Sam Singer, John Shanker, Herb Fisher and John Sorrelli's quality workmanship."

The food is enjoyable. They pay the check and tip the waiter well, as all bar restaurant owners do to waiters in other places. They leave the restaurant, and get a cab.

Fun time is over, and their baby *Rounds* is waiting for her parents. She requires lots of attention during this early time in her life.

The two owners lavish her with it. They know that if she is to grow and be healthy, constant TLC has to be a big part of her diet.

As soon as they enter *Rounds*, Nick, the doorman, has something to tell Chas. He stops to listen to Nick.

"You received a call from a woman named Brunhilda. She gave me this number for you. She said it's urgent, and hung up."

Brunhilda is Willie's wife. Anxious to learn why *she* called instead of Willie, he goes straight to his basement office and calls her.

"Hi, Bruny. What's wrong?" Chas exclaims.

"Sorry to bother you. You've been away these few years so we haven't been in touch. Willie is behaving weird lately. He finished the job in Detroit six months ago, and we came to Pittsburgh. He joined another company here. At home, he sweats often, wiping his brow and staring at a wall or ceiling without saying a thing."

"Please put him on the phone," Chas implores."

"Chas, hello," Willie whispers. "I screwed up at work. I'm scared. I can't talk now. Bye."

"See what I mean," Bruny pleads. "What can I do? He refuses to see a doctor; he's depressed and needs medicine. He didn't even talk to you, his best friend."

"I'll catch the next plane, and we'll learn what he needs," Chas replies. "It's been three years. Me in Puerto Rico and you guys in Detroit. As soon as I have a flight, I'll call, and you can give me your address, okay?"

"Thanks, Chas, it's a load off my mind knowing you're coming."

"Bye, Bruny. Give Scott my regards."

Chas calls the airline, gets a flight for the following morning, calls Bruny, gets her address and gives her his schedule.

He is concerned for his dear friend and ex-boss from the days they built skyscrapers as part of a team. Sitting at the end of the bar, he recalls his construction schooling, a method he will teach Nick.

Building up Nick's morale, is foremost in making him a top doorman. The right personality is essential when you need to tell a person they are not acceptable to enter your establishment. Being either soft or tough in his delivery and Nick will have a problem with most people.

Chas' experience, as a leader over the last twenty years, convinces him Nick has the mettle. Nick is worth Chas' time and energy to groom him into a good doorman.

In the beginning of his high-rise construction career, Chas figured a method of how to make an arrogant, rigid, seasoned foreman do what he wants. He convinces them what he wants is their idea, not his, and they comply with his suggestion.

Their compliance is paramount for him to be successful. New York City's building business demands he have a strong character to be successful.

Every chance Chas has, he shall tutor Nick in his methods of manipulating rigid people.

The following morning, Chas does his chores and leaves for Pittsburgh. Upon arrival at the airport, he rents a car and drives to visit Willie. His friend's behavior is contrary to his usual affable demeanor, and Chas hopes it's a problem which can be easily remedied. He arrives at Willie's house at 2 PM.

"Chas, it's good to see you," Bruny greets. "Come in; he's in the living room. Bill, Chas is here."

Chas looks at his friend sitting and wiping his forehead in the cool room.

"Man, it's great to see you," Chas exclaims. "It's been too long. What's bothering you?"

"I haven't cut the grass in the yard," Willie moans. "The landlord will be angry."

"What, you're worried about that?" Chas replies. "We'll go cut it now."

"That's part of my problem," Willie whispers. "I forgot to include some plans which relate to the buying of the heating and cooling system. We awarded the contract, now I have to tell my boss it's not a complete buyout."

"Look, man, that's no big deal," Chas advises. "The problem is, why are you in a state of depression and severe anxiety? You need to see a doctor. I used a drug, Atavan, when I had anxiety once. It will fix the problem pronto."

"We know no doctor here," Willie moans.

"You, me and Bruny will go the emergency room at a hospital," Chas suggests. "A doctor will give you a once-over and determine what you need. Right, Bruny?"

"Yes, that's what I've been asking him to do."

"Willie, I came all this way to see and help you," Chas implores. "The least you can do is come to the hospital for a few minutes so they can help you get well again."

Willie stands up and looks at Bruny.

"Do you know where the hospital is?"

"Yes, get in the car and we'll leave right now," Bruny remarks.

"What about Scott?" Willie moans. "We won't be home when he comes from school."

"He has a key," Bruny explains. "Let's go, please; stop worrying about everything."

At the hospital, Willie waits as Chas and Bruny keep him occupied with small-talk until he sees a doctor. Bruny explains to the doctor what her husband is suffering with. A brief examination confirms Willie's anxiety, and medicine is prescribed. On the way home they pick it up at the pharmacy. At home, Bruny hands Willie his pills and a glass of water.

"Thanks for coming here and getting him to see a doctor," Bruny says.

"No problem," Chas mentions. "I wanted to get here and visit, now that I'm in New York, but I've been busy opening the club. That's behind me. I'll be able to visit more often now."

After taking his medicine Willie takes much needed sleep before dinner.

"Chas, I'm glad you came," Scott exclaims. "I want to ride a horse with you again. Now that I'm seven, you can teach me to ride a horse by myself."

"It's a deal," Chas says. "As soon as you guys get the time to vacation, we'll do it. Now I have to get back to work in New York.

"Willie, promise you'll take your meds, and as soon as you are feeling better, you'll hook up with a personal psychologist."

"I promise," Willie responds.

Rounds

Chas returns to New York City and has a drink with Seymour at their table in *Rounds*, then goes to the office to make sure there are no important notes in his cubbyhole. Finding none, he returns to check on the dining room service.

Seymour goes to cruise the bar area and the meat rack area located along the entire wall opposite the bar. The meat rack is a favorite area where non-spender's like to hang out until they manage to hustle a drink from a passing patron or one with a drink standing next to him.

Seymour asks anyone without a drink:

"Where is your drink, Mary?"

"Oh," he says, "I don't drink alcohol."

"That's fine," Seymour quips. "We also serve juice, soda, and water for only one-fifty a glass. Either buy something, or you will have to leave, *now*."

This is standard procedure that Chas, Seymour, and the staff use to make deadbeats buy drinks. If a customer has a drink, Seymour will chat, while appraising the physical attributes the person possesses in his pants.

"So, Mary, how much meat you got?" Seymour derides. "From where I'm standing I don't see much meat in your basket."

"Of course I have meat," he laughs. "Ten inches is more than I need to make a living with my cock."

"Do you make house calls?" Seymour quips.

"Yes," he recounts. "It's three-hundred an hour and five-hundred for two hours. What ever is your pleasure?"

"That much?" Seymour scoffs. "Are you crazy, Mary? I just want to rent you, not buy you. I have my own cock. If it was big enough and I was double-jointed I'd fuck and blow myself. You should give me a discount since I own this joint. If I have you eighty-sixed from *Rounds*, you'll lose income derived from meeting johns in my joint."

"You're blackmailing me, Seymour. You don't give drink discounts to hustlers."

"Mary, take my offer or stay out."

"You leave a hardworking girl no option. Here is my card; call me at your convenience. I'll do it for whatever you want to spend, Seymour."

"Smart boy. You still need to put a glass in your hand. That prick of a partner is watching us."

"I was only flirting and being social with the paying customer," Seymour claims. "Not trying to score."

"Yeah, right," Chas laughs. "If we didn't have strong rules governing behavior, you'd shove your hand down their pants."

Each time Chas catches Seymour appearing to deal, he teases him with the same lecture.

Meanwhile, Chas sits on the couch, at the spy table. From his vantage point, he judges the performance of the service bartender, and of the cocktail waiters working the piano bar and back lounge.

His concentration is interrupted as he notices he is being watched. A handsome figure of a man is looking his way as he sips from his drinking straw. He is about five-feet-eight-inches tall with black hair, a trim Latin-style mustache and extremely handsome. Tight clothes exhibit a well-proportioned muscular body. He walks toward Chas.

6 "You must be Chas. I'm Paul Spinelli. Sorry I couldn't make the Grand Opening. I do masonry construction. We had to work overtime to meet the schedule—you remember the deadline situation? I learned from Sal, you used to do construction."

"Sit down, Paul; welcome," Chas replies. "Yes, I remember it well."

"I stopped by a few times during *Rounds'* construction phase," Paul explains. "You weren't around. Your foreman was friendly and answered my questions. It's how I know you're straight and like hunting birds and horse riding. He said he hunted with you on occasion.

"Before I came out of the closet, I liked to deer hunt with the guys I worked with. I always wanted to try bird hunting, though. What's it like on a preserve? How do you hunt this time of year?"

"Paul, you reminded me of a hunting date I planned this weekend. I hunt in Pawling, New York. We have a private hunting preserve where we raise pheasants to shoot and we also fish for trout. We hunt pheasants using a handler and his dog."

"How does it work?" Paul asks.

"The birds are disoriented temporarily by the dog handler to prevent them from flying off too soon. Each bird is placed under some brush in different spots by the handler. It's done roughly ten minutes before we hunt. We go to a spot near the birds; they are oriented now.

"The dog is let loose by the handler. He picks up the birds scent, his tail goes up, he stops moving, and stands still, sniffing the bird. The dog keeps pointing at the bird hiding in the brush. He can't see it, he can only smell it.

The bird gets nervous and takes flight thinking it's been discovered. Sometimes this pause is shortened by the handler approaching the spot the dog is facing. The handler flushes the bird by kicking the brush. The bird jumps from the brush, crowing and vigorously flaps its wings to get airborne fast. The handler crouches, and we try to shoot the bird.

"I'm leaving late Friday night, after work to drive up, and sleep at the club. I'll have breakfast first thing in the morning, and be ready to hunt after dawn.

"Will you join me, Paul?"

"You're kidding," Paul exclaims. "I'd love to. That's very generous of you; we just met. You have a date, Chas. Thanks."

"I don't like hunting alone, Paul. My son is away at college; sometimes he joins me. Hunting, to me, is about the camaraderie of friends sharing what they find enjoyable. You can't enjoy someone unless you spend time to know him."

The following night, Seymour is told of Chas' forthcoming date with Paul, by the bartender. He didn't appreciate what he is told.

"Are you crazy, Mary?" Seymour scolds. "How am I going to keep these fags convinced you're straight, when you spend the night with Paul, a faggot?"

"Tell them I'm giving gay sex a try," Chas derides. "If I like it with Paul, I will come out of the closet, and fuck them.

"You're telling me a straight man and gay man can't be close friends? Paul and I can't spend quality time together without sex?

"The queens, who object to me and Paul being close, if we

get close, are jealous bigots.

"It surprises me that oppressed gay people, abused by igno-rant, biased straight people, don't appreciate our relationship. What relationship can you and I have? Should we be only busi-ness partners, instead of good friends?"

"You're right, of course, Chas, I am sorry. Have a great time; you deserve to."

Seymour turns his attention away from Chas and looks around the dining room.

"Andy Warhol is at table seven, I'll tell her not to draw on the cloth napkins," Seymour growls. "They cost money to launder after he finishes scribbling on them."

"Don't you dare insult a customer—and a famous artist at that!" Chas scolds. "Go over and thank him for coming to *Rounds*. Buy him a drink, you cheap old queen."

Andy notices Seymour approaching.

"Congratulations, this place is absolutely charming," Andy lauds. "For Jerry's first time engagement as a decorator, he did great."

"Andy, may I buy you a drink?"

"No thanks, Seymour," Andy replies. "I ordered drinks for you and your partner Chas on me, as a token of much success. This bar is just what the New York City gay community needs."

"Thanks for the drinks, and compliments," Seymour whis-pers. "Andy, enjoy your dinner, and please let me know if we can do anything for you."

As soon as Seymour leaves Andy, two admirers quickly sit to watch the famous artist draw on the cloth napkins. They are expecting the artist to treat them to drinks and food, too, which he does.

Dr. Eduardo Gonzales is sitting and talking with Chas, wait-ing for his favorite patient and longtime friend, Seymour, to rejoin Chas. Eduardo is a thin, vibrant man with eyeglasses. His once-black hair is thinning out on top of his head, making him look a little older than fifty years old. He is blessed with a good sense of humor as well as an outstanding talent as a surgeon.

"Well, well, look what the wind finally blew in," Seymour scolds. "It's been almost a week since we opened. Where have you been, Mary?"

"Some of us earn a living at a real job as being your proctologist," Eduardo replies.

"Mary, you call getting five-thousand dollars an operation, a job?" Seymour derides. "I call it robbery. What's more, the last time you looked up my ass with that spy glass of yours, it hurt for days."

Smiling at Seymour, Eduardo responds to him.

"That spy glass you refer to," Eduardo quips, "is probably a third in diameter to the cocks you normally accommodate in that big ass of yours, you old size queen."

With a big grin on his face, Seymour counters.

"Not that you would know, but a cock is flexible," Seymour derides. "As I have my feet at his shoulders, George fucks me missionary style. He attains maximum penetration that way. I love it, and it doesn't hurt."

Laughingly, Eduardo suggests something different.

"Next visit," Eduardo derides. "We'll perform your examination missionary style, providing you don't try to kiss me in the process."

"It has been a pleasure meeting you, Doc," Chas says.

Chas heard more than enough, and he makes a hasty exit from the two jokers.

"Pleasure was all mine. Call me if you need service," Eduardo laughs.

The next night Chas comes up from his office and notices Walter Lucy at the bar, and walks over to join him for a drink.

"Hey, Father, how's it going?"

"Pretty good, I've been speaking to the monsignor at St. Joseph's, around the corner, about going back to the seminary."

"Be careful over there, Walter."

"Why, what's the problem?"

"Well, Walter, I went to confession and I noticed something weird.

"I am on line to enter the confessional as the priest calls the passing porter into the confessional. The priest then comes out, hurrying to leave the church. The porter stays in it.

"It's my turn to enter. I'm unsure if I should enter with the porter sitting in the priest's seat behind the screen. I enter anyway. The first thing I ask the porter is, 'Shall I begin with my confession?'

"'Yes,' he says, 'the priest left me a list of all sins which people tell him, and what corresponding penance I will have them do. It's tacked on the wall in front of me,' the porter says."

"I began saying my list of sins, ending by saying I got a blow job from my girlfriend.

"The porter pauses, he gets nervous. 'Blow job isn't on the list,' he says. He asks me to be patient as he checks on my penance.

"I wait for my penance.

"As an altar boy passes by. The porter stops the boy.

"The porter asks the boy, 'What does Father give you for a blow job?'

"The boy whispers to the porter.

"'He gives us two cookies and a glass of milk.'"

Chas notices Walter's complexion is red.

"Walter, you got to admit," Chas laughs, "I had you going there."

"You did, up to the porter in the confessional part," Walter laments. "All priests are stigmatized as a result of the few pedophiles, who disgrace the church, and priesthood.

"Jokes like that really hit home."

"Castration or death is my choice of punishment," Chas mocks, "for all child abusers."

"Let's change the subject, Timmy. Give us more drinks,

please."

After some small-talk which Chas uses to change Walter's depressed mood resulting from the joke, Chas attends to business again.

"Now, if you will excuse me, Walter, I need to make the rounds."

Walking toward the entrance door, Chas checks the men's room. He looks inside; nothing unusual is going on. He proceeds along the softly-lighted corridor, making eye contact with all who are congregating there; if someone appears out of place, he will notice, and escort them out.

"Please move out of the corridor; you're blocking traffic," Chas asks.

As soon as Nick hears him, he moves everyone to the bar area.

"Nick, you need to prevent this area from becoming a hang-out for the bashful types or deadbeats," Chas advises. "The cocktail waiters service this area infrequently. I want people where they are made to buy a drink or leave. No drink sales, no pay for the staff."

Two customers approach Chas. Both are medium height with pleasant looks.

"Hi, my name is Michael. This is my friend Bernard. We are making the rounds of the bars on 53rd Street. Everyone we meet tells us we must see the new hot bar, *Rounds*. Nick pointed you out to us before; I hope you don't mind."

"It's always nice to meet pleasant people," Chas greets. "Where are you two from, Michael?"

"Bernard is from the West Village. I'm from Brooklyn."

"Brooklyn," Chas scoffs." Unfortunately, you didn't know we don't allow bridge and tunnel people in *Rounds*. Nick should have checked your ID."

After looking at their ID, Chas looks at the two bewildered men as they look at each other in disbelief.

"I'll make an exception for you Michael," Chas laughs. "You

come from a neighborhood better than my old neighborhood where I lived in Brooklyn."

"You are kidding, right?" Michael said.

"Right," Chas laughs.

"We are a snobby establishment. Our customer preference is the Upper East Side queens. We are a club where the rich, famous, older set come to meet the young, handsome, wannabe set. Of course we want proper people like you two young handsome men. Please come back; I enjoyed talking with you guys.

"Excuse me, I see Nick wants me," Chas says.

"Nick, what do you want?"

"Last night after the customers were out, and the door locked, I had to push the waiters to hurry up and cash in their silver and singles. They want to talk with each other and leisurely enjoy their free house drink."

"Keep up the good work, Nick," Chas lauds.

A few hours later, Chas and Seymour are finishing their drinks at 1:30 in the morning. Chas decides to call it quits and go to his apartment.

"I'll see you tomorrow night, Mary," Chas jokes. "Try to behave."

The next afternoon, Seymour is on the telephone to the hustler, Pete, who he met at the meat rack.

"It's Seymour. We spoke at *Rounds*."

"I figured you'd call," Pete answers. "You want to see me? When?"

"How's three this afternoon?"

"Okay, what's your address, Seymour?"

"282 East 15th Street, Apartment 14-D."

"I'll see you then," Pete says.

Pete arrives at Seymour's on time.

"So, what shall it be, Seymour. Fuck or be fucked?"

"Mary, why do you think I asked if you had meat? Just use the right amount of lubricant, not too much so I can't feel it, or too little and it hurts."

"Let me get my clothes off. You're in your robe already. Take it off and lay on your back," Pete orders. "That's how you want it, right?"

"I love to look at who's fucking me," Seymour answers. "Especially a handsome, young stud, but first I'll suck that hunk of meat 'til it's hard."

In no time, Pete was hard. He put the lubricant on and inserted it gently into Seymour, who has his feet against Pete's shoulders.

"More, Mary," Seymour demands. "Oh! Good, that's it; keep it moving."

After a minute, Seymour's eyes roll in the back of his head and he comes with a loud groan. Pete pulls out and goes to the bathroom to clean himself. As he gets ready to leave, he asks Seymour to buy him a drink next time they meet.

"It's a deal," Seymour replies.

The following week as Chas checks out who is having dinner, he notices a peculiar sight at a table. He decides to check the two out.

A young woman in her twenties is sitting on the couch. Her feet are wearing four-inch-high heels which barely touch the floor. Skinny legs terminate in a thin butt. Her upper torso is average, except for large breasts. Black hair compliments a pretty face. She wears a one-piece black body suit. An eight-foot white boa is around her neck. The rest of the boa drapes on the seat and floor next to her.

Her companion is a distinguished gentleman in a suit and tie. Six feet tall, trim build and thick, curly gray hair. Seymour is sitting next to the woman and talking to the gentleman.

Chas stops at the table and waits for an introduction by Seymour.

"This is Chas; Chas, this is Bruce Nid," Seymour mentions. "This nice Jewish girl is Enid Levine. Enid is going to audition for us, as soon as Mickey takes a break.

"Bruce sells pianos on West 56th Street. He says we desperately need a new one—ours is old and requires much tuning. What else is new?"

Enid performs for forty-five minutes. All the songs are written by her, and she brings the house down. Customers love her campy tunes, especially *Sex with a Used Condom*. Enid is hired to work three nights a week.

"Mickey will do two nights," Seymour advises. "Rick was previously hired for the remaining two nights. We know customers want variety. They like different styles, and come to *Rounds* especially when the piano player that suits them is playing that night. Well, that takes the pressure off Mickey. We also have backup in case one can't perform for one reason or another."

Enid and Bruce leave, and Seymour looks at the mostly-affluent customers that pack *Rounds*.

"Chas, I have always known I am gay," Seymour whispers. "Until the Stonewall rebellion, life for me and other gays was second-class at best. As a result of the rebellion eleven years ago, major legislation was enacted preventing police harassment. Before the change, I had to wear my coat when working a club at night. I did it so when the cops raided my place I could escape out the back door... or I would freeze before getting transportation home.

"What a difference now. You, my friend and partner, are fortunate to get in with gays during this recent age of freedom. In the past, we lived as in the feudal times. Now, we refer to this period of time as Camelot.

"*Rounds*, before Stonewall, could not exist. These talented, affluent people could not be having a good time congregating in our bar in peace. We are finally free of the chains of oppression.

"I am happy I got to witness Camelot during my lifetime, and with such a good partner as you."

Seymour blew his nose, removes his glasses and wipes his eyes.

"Thanks," Chas mentions. "I am glad the timing worked out so we met during a favorable time in gay history. Being straight, I was not aware of what life for gays was like back then. Let me leave to do my thing. I want to check to ensure our fortunate customers are behaving."

* * *

It's the following week and *Rounds* is hosting a party. Ken keeps the promotion going with a Christmas in July party that's a big success. The club is tastefully decorated with Christmas ornaments. Every patron receives a small Christmas gift as they enter *Rounds*.

The following afternoon, Ken answers his home phone.

"That was a great party last night," Michael lauds.

"Yes, I did it again," Ken brags.

"I met women's shoe designers from Rome, Italy at the party," Michael recounts. "They offered me a job in their design division. I'm so excited. They are not lovers, and I'm pretty sure the one I like, likes me. It could be the real thing. Roman fags are probably hot lovers. You know how the Italian mind works?"

"Yes, unfortunately, I do know how the Italian mind of my partner works," Ken moans.

"Do you know what that creep, Chas, did? All of my pay consists of bounced checks my friends used to pay their restaurant tab. He said, I was warned not to accept checks. How do you say no to a friend, when they ask me after they have already dined? If I say no, they feel I don't trust them; if I say yes, I get stuck holding the bag.

I was counting on cash to pay my bills. The hustlers don't take checks. My drug dealer Joe doesn't accept checks.

Trying to collect from people who give bad checks is a bummer.

I'm learning I don't have as many friends as I thought. I'm spending most of my day chasing down people who don't want to be found by me. It sucks.

I am going to seek counsel from Sam Singer. He is a good friend of Ms. Thing, but I know he'll be fair with me. For now I have a dancer from *Cats*. He was at the party last night. He spent the night. He's hung like a horse—he fucked me all night, and I can hardly walk. I'll give him head before I send him on his way. Take care, Michael."

Hearing Ken on the phone, the dancer is nude, standing facing Ken, as he holds his cock in his hand, massaging it.

"Let's see if you can make me come with that big mouth of yours, Ken."

Ken drops to his knees and grabs the cock, kisses it, and licks the tip while moaning. He puts the shaft in his mouth and begins sucking and tonguing the tip as he moves his mouth on the shaft. The dancer's cock is rock hard; he grabs Ken's head holding it still, looks down at Ken and releases his cum into Ken's mouth, who swallows the cum and keeps the cock in his mouth until the cum stops. The dancer kneels down and the two tongue-kiss. They fall asleep on the floor.

The next afternoon, Sam meets Ken at the bagel deli across from *Rounds*. Sam gives his reply, after listening to Ken's emotional predicament.

"Ken, because Chas asked me, John and Herb to help you, we loaned you money to be a partner in *Rounds*. Being part of a company requires playing by the company rules. You refuse to play by those rules. My suggestion is you should leave this partnership."

"Thanks, Sam, I appreciate the time you gave me. I want to ask for more… forget it."

"I will keep it in mind," Ken replies.

Disappointed, he leaves the shop to try to collect on the bad checks.

During this time, Chas is in the basement office. Minutes later he hears Sam come down the steps singing his favorite verse about Chas, who gives him an envelope containing the weekly payback for him, John and Herb to divide.

"*The king is in the counting house, counting all the money.*"

"Hi, Sam," Chas greets.

He opens the locked office door to let his good friend in.

"I just had a talk with Ken in the bagel shop across the street," Sam explains. "He is disillusioned and unhappy. He thought owning a restaurant would give him power. Instead, he has no say in the method of operation.

"I said you have to play by the group's rules. You can suggest changes to the rules and try to convince the majority to see it your way. If he couldn't convince his partners to change things, he should take a buyout."

"Well, Ken certainly has hubris," Chas replies. "His pay is useless unless he can collect on bad checks he approved. Out of his pay he owes you and the boys a loan payback. If he can't repay, he wastes his pay.

"In this envelope is the weekly installment. Seymour and I are kicking in to help him pay it off.

"Ken puts no hours in at *Rounds* working as Seymour and I do. We only expect him to promote the store. He can do that from his apartment, in between getting high on drugs and getting fucked. He is not needed here during the day; however, at night he can promote by schmoozing the customers. He's liked by everyone. He would be a better host than Ms. Obnoxious Seymour, or me—because I'm straight and tough, they have to tolerate me.

"He walks in at dinner time, picks up the phone and receives his personal calls which he forwards to our business phone. When he is finished on the phone he leaves. If he wants to be a star, he should act like one. A star has to play the customers; they are not supposed to play the star.

"Regardless, the star position is filled at *Rounds*. The paying customers are the stars, no one else. Thanks for meeting with Ken, he trusts and respects you. I will repeat our conversation to Seymour tonight. We can figure what kind of offer to make Ken, if he comes to us. I'll see you next week. Say hello to Irma tonight, and thanks for the help."

As Sam and Chas talk in the office, Tony and Leon are busy orchestrating various deliveries which seem to arrive within a two-hour window in the morning.

The basement houses all the refrigeration for the beer and soda systems as well as for the meat, fish, and vegetables. The whole basement is devoid of fresh air, and has a definite stink of stale syrup from the post-mix soda-dispensing system until the street hatch, allowing items to slide down from the street. The liquor is kept in a locked room. Access to the liquor room is attained by the bartenders with the aid of a manager with a key.

Headroom due to pipes hung below the ceiling prevents people taller than five-feet-ten-inches tall from standing erect. Chas and Tony stand erect only in the office or liquor room, where there are no overhead plumbing lines.

Chas' daytime functions are reconciling daily receipts, writing checks to pay bills, and doing payroll. Maintaining cash is needed for change banks, and for two registers to function. He makes daily visits to the bank, and makes sure that what is supposed to happen *does* happen.

After three to four hours of day work, six days a week, he is off until 8 PM. He returns to *Rounds*, picks up Seymour and they go to dinner. Then they return to *Rounds* and work until 2 AM.

Tuesday and Thursday afternoon, he drives to New Jersey to spend time with his three teenage children. This style of living is far from the life he wants as a father and husband, but the restaurant bar business is providing a good living, even though it has long hours.

New York City is a one-hour drive to where the kids live with Mari. Even if he and Mari reconcile their differences, working at *Rounds* requires he live in New York City. He dismisses the idea of moving the family to the city. Mari wouldn't consider it, and it would also be unfair having the children start new lives in a tough new town. Compromise is the only answer. At least, he concludes, this arrangement is a thousand times better than living alone in Puerto Rico.

Today is Friday, and he will meet five old buddies for lunch. Their favorite restaurant is the grill at the *Smith and Wollensky* restaurant at the corner of 49th Street and Third Avenue.

Chas spent many years working with them, building skyscrapers.

Their special table is reserved by the manager every Friday at lunchtime. In appreciation for years of regular patronage, small bronze plaques with each name are nailed to the wall near each one's regular seat.

Drinking alcohol starts before they order lunch. As they drink, they amuse themselves occasionally by playing dollar poker using the serial number on their currency. They create a poker hand and bet on it, starting with singles and gradually going higher, sometimes to a fifty-dollar bill. The winner gets three-hundred dollars from a fifty-dollar ante and some of the winnings go to buy lunch. After the meal, the house buys them after-dinner drinks.

Somewhere in the vicinity of 3:30 PM, half-smashed, they leave the grill, go their merry ways. Most return to work, except Chas; he heads home to nap before going to work later. The same group meets Monday night. Each week at a different apartment, the food and drinks are hosted in turn. The hours for playing all sorts of poker are rigidly kept between 6 and 10 PM. The purpose of playing is to have fun, not to make a big score. The latest jokes are told, and laughter is heard throughout the game.

Chas is awakened from a nap he's taking after his Friday lunch with his buddies.

"Are you sleeping?" Seymour asks.

"Not anymore."

"How did it go with Sam?"

"Fine," Chas says. "He basically told Ken if he can't play by the corporation's rules, he should leave."

"So, Sam agrees with us. That is great," Seymour lauds. "I was concerned we'd have a fight on our hands."

"Of course he agrees with us," Chas affirms, "Sam, Herb and John are all self-made businessmen. We are running our company just as they would if they owned *Rounds*. If we ran the business Ken's way, we would be broke in three months. The money they are owed would be lost."

"Do you want to try the new restaurant across the street from us?" Seymour asks. "*The Brazilian Pavilion.*"

"Sure, we need a change. The food at *Rounds* is great, but unfortunately, we can't eat there without a hundred interruptions."

"I'll be at *Rounds* at my usual time, 6:30," Seymour says. "That way, I'll make sure the morons are doing their job correctly. Meet me at *Rounds* when you're ready to eat."

When Chas enters *Rounds* at eight o'clock, all of the dining room's fifty-six seats are filled. There is a forty-minute wait for a table. The cocktail group from the afternoon is now mingling with the after-work crowd at the bar and lounge.

Seymour is easy to find in spite of the packed bar. His favorite spot is against the wall in the area reserved for waiters to get drinks for customers. This location allows the owners to see the entire bar, and both registers.

Seymour has the staff convinced that Chas is someone to fear. The bartenders and waiters receive generous tips. Stealing, therefore, is not a major issue. Seeing all the faces of the people sitting at the bar also helps the owners spot potential trouble-makers.

When the staff sees the owners are present, they tend to be honest and work diligently. Either Seymour or Chas is always on duty.

"Ready to eat, Mary?" Seymour asks. "We can't eat here even if we wanted to."

They have another drink across the street while waiting for their dinner and talk.

"It's great all the tables are full," Seymour brags. "We created a great menu, good food, at a fair price and large portions. No fancy chef to dictate to us. Our hardworking Orientals listen when I explain to them how to fill a plate based on our generous portions. They regularly come to work, leaving their attitude home. What a pleasure to work with them."

After dinner, they return to *Rounds*. Chas is called over to where Brian, Tommy and Walter have finished dinner and are having coffee and cordials.

"Hey, big man, looks like you have a hit on your hands," Brian praises. "The food is absolutely fantastic."

"Let us buy you a drink," Walter said.

"Sure. Jason, give me a Black on the rocks. Thank you, guys," Chas says.

"Next time you're at lunch with your buddies, you could invite the owners of *Smith*'s over to sample your prime rib," Brian lauds. "Their specialty is steak and prime rib. Your rib is as good as theirs, and *Rounds* is not a five-star restaurant like they are."

"Thanks, I will pass the compliment on to Tony. He's doing a fantastic job with the kitchen," Chas says.

A customer interrupts and tells Chas he's wanted at the door by Nick. Chas excuses himself and goes to the door.

Waiting impatiently is a twenty-five-year-old raven-haired beauty. Immediately, he recognizes his ex-lover's statuesque body. They had an affair before he went to Puerto Rico.

"You are back in town, and I have to hear it from Sal's girlfriend, Joann, that bitch? Why wasn't I allowed to enter?" Carmen laughs. "Give me a hug, I miss you. Am I intruding? Do you have a bitch inside?"

"No, and this is not the place to discuss it. Take my hand and come inside," Chas says. He gently led the beautiful five-foot-four-inch, well-endowed woman through the crowd. She was wearing four-inch-high-heels, a mini-skirt and a sheer blouse.

All eyes are on Carmen as she and Chas walk to the dining room. There is little doubt in customer's minds now, after seeing Carmen, that Chas prefers women to men. Chas witnesses beautiful women with fags all the time in *Rounds*. The customers could think whatever makes them happy; he didn't care either way.

The dining room has a vacant table in a somewhat private corner. They sit down and begin catching up on the past three years. Carmen is dumbfounded. Sal never mentioned to Joann that *Rounds* is a gay men's bar.

With a sly grin on his face, he looks at Carmen.

"Do you see any bitches in here?" Chas quips. "Bitch."

"Oh, don't be angry with me," Carmen moans. "It's been so long since we were together. I miss our love affair. When I learned you were back, first I was happy. Then, you didn't call, I became sad and hurt. Remember, we wanted to get free of our spouses, so we could marry?"

After a short pause, she checks out the handsome men watching them. Her black eyes sparkle as she looks deeply into his.

"The mustache looks good on you," Carmen lauds.

"Thanks," Chas replies. "Would you like a drink or something to eat?"

"A rum and coke is all, thank you."

For the next hour, no one dares bother Chas as he and Carmen are deep in catch-up conversation.

Carmen had another son, her second. He is a year old. Chas mentions his divorce is imminent. He lives around the corner.

"My older son is going to be five soon and is very attached to his father," Carmen advises.

"Breaking up with John is unlikely because of my son's attachment to him. I never knew my real dad, and that troubles me some. I don't want my son to experience abandonment as I experienced it in my life."

Her statement is as if she drove a knife into his heart. Chas had strong feelings for her before he went away, and he recently thought of calling her to rekindle their affair. He feels disappointed. Marriage is no longer an option for them.

"Well, mister big-shot bar owner, what's next for us?" Carmen mocks. "Do I get to see where you live? You're not afraid to take me upstairs, for fear I'll find a woman's underwear? Or maybe, *your* female underwear.

"Who knows what's happened to you these last three years? Possibly the hot sun beating on your head while being around those Latin fags turned you gay."

Her statement, "Next for us" confuses him; from what she just said, it is over. At least marriage is. He'll take what she gives him and deal with the consequences for now.

"Funny you should say that, Carmen. I was wondering the same thing about my sexuality. Should we go upstairs, and check it out?"

"Yes!"

As they exit *Rounds*, Chas advises Nick of his destination so he can tell Seymour.

They take the short walk to Chas' apartment around the corner.

"What time is John expecting you home?" Chas said.

"He and his friends are out on the ocean. It takes about six hours just to get to where the giant tuna are. They fish until they catch something. Then it's six hours to return home. Usually overall he is gone for twenty-four hours. My mother is caring for the boys. She is expecting me to get them tomorrow morning. My milk will all be gone by then. I guess you are stuck with me for the night… unless that's a problem, my sweet?"

"No! No problem," Chas says.

They ride the elevator to his floor. Chas recalls how excited just looking at Carmen made him feel in the past. The feeling is back, only now it's more intense. He has all he could do to just put the key in the lock to his apartment, due to anxiety. Had he not had much liquor, he probably would have been a nervous wreck by now.

Because of the full mirror walls, the apartment looks bigger than it is. The blinds are left open on the windows and on the sliding glass door leading to the terrace. Since there is no building across from his, he has a commanding view of midtown Manhattan via the mirrors.

As soon as they enter the dark living room, the mirrored walls reflect the lights from the tall buildings in midtown. The master bedroom wall mirror creates the same effect, as if the entire wall has a mural of Manhattan painted on it.

As soon as the door is closed and locked, they kiss passionately. Each hurries undressing the other. Clothes are thrown indiscriminately on the plush, light-colored carpet.

The six-foot-three Chas holds the five-foot Carmen in his arms. With her feet off the carpet, they keep kissing as he carries her to his bed. With his left hand, he pulls back the top sheet. Still kissing her, he kneels on the bed, and lays her body and his between cool sheets. It has been a long time since he had her voluptuous naked body close to his.

He loves sucking on her firm breasts. Now he also enjoys the milk which she nurses her son with. There is one other place he would suck before entering her. It's where Carmen enjoys multiple orgasms, her sweet vagina.

"Oh, Chas honey, it feels so good when you eat me. Oh! That's *so* good, right there! I'm coming... I'm coming. Enter me *now*, please, baby, do it."

"Here it is, sexy lady. Um, you are nice and wet. Oh, this is what I used to dream of when I was alone on that fucking island.

Move that hot sweet ass of yours. That's it, keep going, here is a deposit especially for *you* baby. Uh! Uh! *Uhh!*"

The cool breeze coming through the open patio door and window feels good on their wet bodies, as the sweat is evaporating quickly from their skin. They take a short nap in the cool night air as they cuddle under the sheets to be warm.

Waking up and feeling her body touching his, makes him hard again. They begin lovemaking, this time slow and sweet with a lot of kissing and hugging.

The traffic noise wakes Chas up, and he looks at the sexy woman next to him, still asleep. Her long black hair against the white pillow frames her beautiful, sharp feminine facial features.

One breast is exposed as she sleeps among tangled sheets. He looks at the large dark skin around her nipple. He is hard again, and he softly kisses the nipple. He sucks and massages it with his wet tongue. She begins moaning and smiling with her eyes closed. Gently, he guides her over on her stomach. She says softly, "Ah, Oh." He raises her onto her knees and elbows. She looks very tantalizing as Chas looks at her profile in the mirror with her hair hanging down and her breast swaying as he spreads her legs apart. Kneeling behind her, he begins kissing her shapely ass. Spreading her cheeks, he sticks his tongue between them, giving him access to her sphincter. Massaging it with his tongue, she begins moaning. From his night table he takes a lubricant, smears his hard cock with it, and inserts it into her rectum. They experience intense orgasm.

"Baby, you wore me out," Carmen exclaims. "I hope John is too tired for sex when he comes home. I wish I didn't have to go. The milk I left my mother is running low. Fortunately, you didn't consume it all; that's all you are getting today. Put me in a cab; there is no traffic. I'll be at 13th Street in ten minutes, and my son can suck a real nipple."

When they arrive in the lobby, the doorman goes to get Carmen a cab.

Chas puts money in her delicate hand for cab fare. She has the phone numbers where he can be reached anytime. Chas feels unlucky as the cab shows up soon and she leaves. He didn't want her to leave him. In his apartment he takes his jeans and shirt off. Tired from all the lovemaking and booze, he closes the terrace door and window, pulls the blinds closed, and gets back in bed. Carmen's fragrance dominates the room. He enjoys it. He exchanges their pillows so he can smell her scent on her pillow. Now he will sleep peacefully, as if she were still in bed with him.

Early afternoon, the phone wakes Chas.

"Who was that beautiful woman?" Seymour exclaims. "You vanished too soon!"

"She is an old love affair I had years ago," Chas explains. "We went to my apartment to talk."

"Talk, my ass," Seymour derides. "You were the talk of *Rounds* last night. The queens kept asking me who she was. I gave a different story to everyone who asked. I was so creative, I was cracking myself up."

"Well, I always knew you were full of shit, Seymour; now you proved it."

"My crazy urologist has been after me to take him and his wife to *Rounds*," Seymour mocks. "He's a real closet queen. I tell him to come out of the closet, but he thinks it will destroy his business.

"He knows I have a straight partner, and would like you to join us. Maybe we can get him to finance the next place. He's very rich."

"That's what I like about you," Chas affirms. "You're always working the angles. What time are we meeting them?"

"Eight is good; that way we'll be finished in time to work," Seymour responds.

"Okay, see you at eight," Chas says.

Seymour and Chas are having drinks at the bar at ten to eight. Their guests arrive.

"Hello, Seymour," Dr. Franks says. "This is my wife, Harriet."

"My pleasure," Seymour greets. "This is my partner, Chas."

"Hello, Chas," Dr. Franks and Harriet greet.

"Hello, Harriet, Doctor," Chas replies.

At dinner, the doctor seems a little uncomfortable in a gay restaurant. Harriet enjoys being the only real female in *Rounds* and is making a subtle play for Chas.

It's one of those marriages of convenience. They traded a life of sexual incompatibility for one of financial wealth. Both are unhappy living a lie.

Chas is thinking they can have the dual lifestyle his gay friends enjoy, by keeping love and sex separate. Realizing it's wrong to offer advice when none is asked for, he keeps his thought to himself.

"Thank you for a wonderful evening," Harriet says.

Smiling at Chas, with that *please fuck me* look. She shakes his hand, leaving a small piece of paper with her phone number written on it.

Paul enters the bar as the Dr. and Harriet are leaving.

"Mary, what are you doing here so early?" Seymour derides. "You usually wait 'til three when the remaining boys drop their prices."

"I'm here to see my husband and buy him a drink," Paul brags. "We had a great time bird hunting at his club. We even slept over in his room the night before so we'd be fresh in the morning. Where is my honey?"

"When you find him," Seymour mocks, "don't talk like a sissy; he'll divorce you."

"Get real, Mary," Paul scolds.

Paul finds Chas at the waiter's station, watching both the bar and the waiter serving the piano crowd. As Paul gets there, the space becomes tight. Chas says they have to move so the waiters will have better access to the bartender.

"Hi, you're looking handsome, as usual," Chas says.

"I came to see you and thank you again for taking me hunting," Paul lauds. "I had a great time. I hope you did too."

"I had an excellent time," Chas says. "You're good company. You remind me of a guy that I did ironwork with, when I was a kid. We worked hard but Louie turned work into a game with his constant humorous dialogue. I'm a serious bastard. I need easy-going up-beat people in my life, ones with a good sense of humor like you. Laughter is healthy."

"Does that mean that you'll take me hunting again?" Paul asks.

"Of course, and we don't have to confine our relationship to just hunting." Chas asks, "Do you like to play poker?"

"Yeah, I love it," Paul said.

"Great, I play with my old contracting friends every Monday night," Chas advises. "We need a seventh player. You'd fit in perfectly with that humor that you're always dispensing. We keep it friendly, a lot of joking, drinking and eating. Meet me here Monday at 5:45, and I'll take you with me."

"It's a date," Paul said.

Paul leaves to cruise the meat rack area, hoping he'll meet a date for tonight. This is the place to be seen by incoming potential dates for the night. Italian guilt makes Chas feel guilty for leaving the business earlier than normal, the night Carmen showed up. Tonight, he will close the place. He and Seymour did this occasionally, to keep the staff on their toes. Other than their guaranteed presence every night, no other routine is done in strict order. Everyone is kept guessing and on their best behavior.

It's about 2:30 in the morning when Chas hears a woman's high-pitched loud voice:

"I'm sick and tired of you constantly dragging me to these fag bars," Madame mocks. "They don't like the smell of my pussy in this faggot-ridden den. It doesn't smell like fish, you fucking sissy Marys."

The crowd surrounding Whalen and his famous hand puppet Madame are hysterical, listening to Whalen the puppeteer. He moves Madame at the end of his arm in a lifelike manner. The sound comes from Whalen as he speaks, but all eyes are on the non talking wood painted face of Madame as if she speaks.

Chas eases through the crowd until he is next to Whalen. Here he is close to the puppet at the end of Whalen's arm.

Madame's hair is pulled tight and into a pony tail. She has a nose long enough that a small-size bird could perch on it.

"Welcome to *Rounds*, you two," Chas greets.

"Thanks, but we'd rather have a drink on the house," Madame said.

"Sure, Madame, anything for a celebrity from *Hollywood Squares*," Chas lauds. "I watch it just to see you, Madame."

On cue from Chas, the bartender gives a drink to Whalen and the same drink to Madame, making it two drinks for Whalen. It's a bargain to pay for great entertainment.

Madame looks at the drink, then looks at Chas.

"One drink won't get you into my pants big guy," Madame scoffs. "I only put out for straight men with lots of money, honey."

"Well, my dear Madame," Chas responds. "I am straight, I think, but not rich."

Madame is quiet as she looks at each person individually using her fixed stare.

"Oh, fuck it," Madame shouts. "Only this one time I will let a fucking faggot stick his shit-stained cock in my sweet-smelling pink pussy. Since the straight guy is poor and I'm dying for sex tonight. I'll dispense with my usual standards and try sex with a rich queen or two or… ?

"Does anyone at this bar meet my requirements?"

"Me. Me. Me." Everyone answers, except Chas, knowing its Whalen asking for sex.

Last call is announced by the bartenders. Whalen finishes the two drinks Chas bought him, and looks at his host Chas.

"You make a good straight man for Madame to play off of," Whalen praises, "you straight, handsome bar owner you."

The last customers leave feeling happy, thanks to the show put on by the famous TV couple. Chas joined the exodus.

"Come join us at the afterhours club we're going to, in the Village?" Timmy asks.

"Thanks, kid, I need my rest. Have a good time," Chas responds.

The next day, Seymour, Chas and his new lady friend Linda are having drinks at the owner's table.

Linda lives on First Avenue and 52nd Street. Bruce Nidd is an old acquaintance of Linda's and introduced her to Chas. Looks-wise, Linda is above average and liberal when it comes to sex. She conveys it to Chas the first time they meet.

"I enjoy sleeping around," Linda boasts.

She got his attention and company soon after.

A young, handsome continental man comes to the table and speaks to Seymour.

"I love your place. The décor is warm, comfortable and very elegant," Luciano lauds. "Who designed it?"

"Take a seat, Mary, and say hello to my partner, Chas, and his friend, Linda."

"Hello, I'm Luciano; pleasure to meet you."

"Hi, Luciano," Chas and Linda greet.

"Jerry Richland did the design," Seymour informs. "You don't know him; this is the first joint he's done."

"Luciano is a popular makeup artist," Seymour says. "Working for girlie magazines, he travels to exotic locations all over the world."

"That sounds exciting. What exactly do you do?" Linda asks.

"Their hair, makeup, and their complexion has to be just right for the exposure the photographer is trying to capture," Luciano explains. "Because of the liberal censorship laws, the pussy is photographed now. I have to make sure every hair on their pussy is in place, groomed well, and the color matches their hair."

"Take me on your next trip," Chas laughs. "I'll work for you for free."

Chas said it in a kidding manner; in his mind he liked the thought of going on such a trip.

"Would you all be my guest at a new club which opened uptown, called, *La Cage's?*" Luciano asks. "Everyone who works there is dressed in drag. The waiters, bartenders, singers and piano players, all appreciate the advice I give them on how to look like beautiful women.

"Turning average-looking men into beautiful women is a job for a professional—like me, of course; they love me for that."

"I spend my one night off on Monday with my lover, George," Seymour says. "Count me out."

"I have a prior engagement," Linda says. "Sorry, I'd love to see it."

Chas considers joining Lucciano, and show up late for his regular Monday night card game. Business comes first. Checking what other bars are doing is being prudent.

"I'll meet you here, Luciano, and we'll take a cab to *La Cage's,*" Chas mentions. "Is six okay?"

"Six is fine; I'll see you then."

La Cage is a takeoff of a popular movie. It's about a gay nightclub in Paris. The movie audiences loved it. All the service help are in drag, young men dressed to look like women.

Rounds has become a big success and is known throughout the gay community.

Seymour is known as the fag who made the mob clubs attractive to gays, before Stonewall. Now he is partners with two legitimate people. Ken is well known in the gay community. Chas is straight, unknown in New York's gay scene, yet he's with gays. The question in some gay's minds is *why*. Is he a mob guy like Seymour? Some gays prefer to fantasize that he is, such as Luciano.

He regrets he has to cancel his date with Paul. Watching Paul's antics with his straight friends will be a sight to see. Next week is around the corner; he will bring Paul to the game then.

"Something's come up, Paul; I won't meet you for cards this week," Chas explains. "We will do it the following week. I promise."

"No sweat," Paul answers.

Chas hands the phone to Mark as a taxi stops and beeps the horn. He leaves *Rounds* gets in the taxi, and he and Luciano continue to *La Cage's*.

They arrive at *La Cage's*.

"Thanks for coming, Lucciano," Fredric greets. "This must be Chas, an owner of *Rounds*. I am a partner in *La Cage's*. Chas, say hello to Seymour—we go back before Stonewall; I remember his clubs, they are still vivid memories.

"This is the best table in the house, reserved for special guests. Enjoy."

"Hi, may I get you and your guest a drink, Lucciano?" Marla Ladue asks.

"Yes, is champagne okay with you, Chas?"

"Fine, but only one bottle. I have to work later, and champagne makes me sleepy," Chas replied.

The dining room has two levels. Chas and Lucciano are seated on the upper level.

A careful appraisal of the area tells Chas the room is decorated in good taste. As Chas' eyes are roaming, he notices he is being appraised as well. A beautiful brunette sitting in the lower level is flexing her shoulders so her partially open blouse exposes more of her tits.

As she catches Chas' attention, she raises her glass in a salute. He responds and smiles at her. As dinner progresses, she makes sure he can see as much as possible without taking her blouse off. Chas flirts along with occasional smiles in return for her showing off gorgeous tits.

"What do you think, Lucciano? Is that a he or a she? Based on the size of the hands, my guess is it's a he."

"You're right, Chas, I don't think you want any part of her; she hasn't had the cock removed yet. If you have sex with her, she'd want her cock up your ass. That's not what you want, from what Seymour tells me about you."

After dinner, Chas and Lucciano retire to the piano lounge.

Sitting on top of the piano is a blonde in a white silk dress, with a slit up the side, showing off a shapely leg for a guy. She is wearing five-inch heels on her feet. A long pink boa tops off the striking ensemble, and a slit down the front of the dress shows substantial cleavage. She mimes to singing from a tape deck as her mouth moves in sync with the recorded singer.

The bosomy piano player wears a tuxedo, white jacket, black pants. A man's haircut, is combed tight to the scalp. He creates the look of a woman in male drag.

Chas finds a comfortable couch to sit on and orders a scotch.

His host Luciano is busy bragging to his many friends who he is with.

The brunette that flirted earlier with Chas came to sit next to him.

"Hi, I'm Maggie," she says.

She has a deeper voice than Chas. She shakes hands with him. He notices her hands are a bit bigger than his.

"My name is Chas. I am pleased to make your acquaintance, Maggie."

"I'm happy to meet you, and be able to speak with you finally. Since I began my operations, I find fags like you who swing both ways, like my female look. Here, feel these firm tits."

She opened her blouse more so Chas can feel her tits. She has no bra on, and didn't need one. As he felt the tits he paid her a compliment.

"Yes, they will put most women to shame," Chas lauds. "I see why you are proud of their size and firmness."

"See, I told you," Maggie affirms. "Bisexual guys like you, who swing with women sometimes, love to fuck me. When I'm on my knees, my hair hangs down like a bitch, and my tits hanging down will really turn you on while you watch them in a mirror as you fuck me in my ass. I have a long way to go before I'll have enough money for my pussy operation. That's actually a bonus. When you finish me, I stick my big cock in your ass to get us off again. Is that great sex or what?"

"Sounds great to me. There is only one problem," Chas informs. "You can't fuck me. I'm straight, a hundred percent, not fifty percent. Thanks for the offer anyway".

Chas finds Lucciano.

"Thanks for a great time. I'll see you soon."

"Yes, it was great, Chas. We must do it again."

Outside, he jumps into a cab and heads to Larry's house on East 57th Street, to join the card game which is in progress.

Recognizing Chas, the doorman says hello and calls the apartment to advise Larry that Chas is coming up.

"Well, it's about time," Larry scolds.

"Yeah," Ted brags. "We need you to get more money into the pot, so I have someone else to win from."

"I feel lucky tonight, my good friend," Chas boasts. "Don't be disappointed if I clean you out instead. You should know I turned down getting fucked by a partial sex change to come here."

"Hurry up and sit down, we're running out of time." Losers moan.

"It is eight o'clock. You deadbeats have two hours to fleece me," Chas warns. "Next week, I'm bringing number seven. That is a lucky number, Paul knows that. He thinks he's psychic, and comes to *Rounds* often. I like him a lot."

"Oh boy, we got to watch Chas to see if he deals with a limp wrist," Bill laughs.

"So you like this Paul a lot," Larry laughs. "How much is a lot?"

"Fuck you guys," Chas scolds. "Paul is okay, and that's more than I can say for all you homophobes. You will treat him like one of us. No, I take that back. Treat him like a man you respect, or deal with my wrath. Are we going to play cards or bullshit all night? I'm going to clean you creeps out."

The rule is, the game ends at ten o'clock. Losers will have to wait until next Monday night to recoup their losses. This rule was enacted to prevent losers from protracting the game until they get even or begin winning.

Chas and his friends are leaving at the end of the game.

"Good night, guys, and thanks for being such good losers."

"Wait and see what happens next week," Bill replies.

Chas heads to *Rounds*.

Monday night is the slowest night in the restaurant business. The club will get by without them for a few hours on a slow night. In ten minutes, he's at *Rounds*, says hello to Nick, and proceeds to the bar.

As usual, the bar is busy. He checks customers at the meat rack as well as the bar. All is good, so he goes into the dining room and sits down at his table. Rick is entertaining customers at the piano. Seymour is smart to take off on Monday night; it's the slowest night of the week.

Tired from dinner and the card game, he wants the night to go by quickly. The host tonight is Terry. Chas begins describing *La Cage's* to him when two guests appear at the host station.

Tennessee Williams, accompanied by Truman Capote come to the host station.

"We would like a quiet table for two," Truman says.

The back section is empty. Terry seats the two legends there. They will have an area to themselves. On occasion, a loud burst from Truman causes some staff to look at him. He is okay; he's just being himself, animated. He will throw his arm without the drink up constantly to emphasize his point. They conduct a quiet conversation. Terry goes to the bar to tell the lucky waiter to take another drink order, and be charming. If Tennessee likes the boy's service, he is prone to autograph the brim of his hat and present the hat as a gift along with a tip.

Chas makes a point to greet his famous patrons.

"Chas, good to see you," Truman says. "Where is that despicable old queen, Seymour, tonight?"

"He is off tonight, spending time with his lover," Chas explains. "He won't annoy you. You know from the last incident, I will not permit that behavior from anyone."

Seymour has a bad habit of insulting people, especially those he can't hold a candle to.

He had insulted Truman over the years when they'd met by chance in different bars.

"Chas, I appreciate what you did last time, getting Seymour away from me. Thank you," Truman quips. "She has a lover? God be with the unlucky person. I am happy knowing our evening won't be ruined by her. We can enjoy ourselves."

"Yes, now can we enjoy the view passing by, please?" Tennessee asks.

Chas hears the phone and sees Terry is too busy to get it.

"Excuse me, gentleman."

He gets to the host's station and answers the phone.

"*Rounds*; how may I help you?"

"You can help me when I get to your apartment tomorrow morning at 10 AM," Carmen teases. "Will you be available for more mother's milk?"

"I can't wait," Chas says. "Got to hang up, now, I am understaffed. Bye."

Chas thinks, What a pleasant way to end an exciting day. After closing, he goes home too excited to sleep. Finally, exhaustion prevails and he is sleeping.

10 AM the following morning couldn't come soon enough.

The doorman buzzes Chas' apartment.

"Carmen is here to see you."

"Send her up; thanks."

The door bell rings, and Chas opens the door. To his surprise, Carmen is carrying her one-year-old son.

"Come on in, you guys."

"Sorry about the baby, my mother couldn't babysit," Carmen explains. "I wanted to see you and had no choice but to bring Steve with me."

"It's time to feed him. If he doesn't take all my milk, you can have what's left."

"Sounds good to me," Chas responds.

Chas kisses her hello.

Carmen sits at the kitchen table, exposes a breast, and puts her nipple in Steve's mouth. He begins suckling on her beautiful full breast.

Carmen and Chas make small-talk as Steve suckles away. Chas has been excited since she told him she was coming to see him. Looking at Carmen's breasts gives him a firm erection, creating a bulge in his pants.

After what seems like forever, Steve finally finishes suckling.

"Let's put him and his blanket, on the couch, with a chair against it so he doesn't roll off," Carmen says. "He'll sleep for a few hours now with his tummy full."

She gets Steve settled, and walks to Chas and gives him a kiss.

"My, oh my, what's that poking my belly, Chas?" Carmen laughs. "It's trying to get out of your pants and into mine!"

"It's Harry, you met him last week," Chas quips. "When he knew you were coming to visit, he stiffened up. I can't get him to chill."

"I have just the cure for that in my bag."

She grabs a bunch of black frilly lace undergarments out of her bag.

"Meet me in the bedroom," she whispers.

Chas is glad to get his pants off, finally, now that his cock is perpendicular to his body. He sits on the edge of the bed facing the closed bathroom door. He's impatient as he waits; he recalls a movie in which Sophia Loren teases Marcello Mastroianni. Marcello is sitting on the bed, excitedly looking like a young boy who's getting laid for the first time. He is waiting for Sophia who is in the bathroom, changing into a sexy outfit. Marcello quietly claps his hands as he waits anxiously for her to join him in bed.

When Carmen comes out of the bathroom, her figure is barely contained by the sexy two-piece outfit.

As she walks to him, he gapes at her sexuality, and parts his legs. She comes to him and stands between his legs. His head is even with her breasts. He pushes her skimpy top over her gorgeous tits, takes one tit in each hand and fondles them.

"Oh baby, I love when you fondle my tits," Carmen cries. "Start sucking, baby, please get my nipples hard with that tongue of yours. Please!"

"Since you said please," Chas moans. "I will suck these beauties dry."

A little milk is left after Steve is finished suckling. Bland, he thinks. He isn't going to complain.

"Oh, I almost forgot," Carmen exclaims. "Wait, my sweet. I have a joint to share with you."

She comes back with a lit joint. Sitting on the edge of the bed, they smoke it.

"Now that I'm wet inside my pussy," Carmen advises, "a little stoned in my head, we can get it on, honey."

Two hours and two orgasms later, they shower together. Carmen gets dressed, and she and a sleeping Steve leave to return home.

"Love you," Carman says.

Chas buzzes the doorman to get his guests a cab.

His energy drained, his head full of marijuana, he shuts the phone off and goes back to sleep.

He wakes at 4 PM, picks up the phone and calls Mark at the bar.

"Is everything okay?"

"Yes, Seymour called looking for you a few minutes ago. He said your phone is off the hook. He's concerned for you."

"I'll call him right now. Thanks, Mark.

"Seymour, Mark said you tried to reach me. I had the phone off," Chas says. "How was your night off?"

"I had a fight with George last night," Seymour laments. "He wants me to buy him a car, so he can run around with his trampy bitch friends. I'm lucky he spends Monday night with me. With a car, I'll never see him. I'm so depressed. What should I do?"

"Mary, you can't control his life," Chas advises. "Trying to do that will make you crazier. You knew he was bisexual when you two first met. Buy him a car, and let the chips fall where they may. Who knows? He may wind up seeing more of you with the aid of his own car.

"His complaining how hard it is to get a cab from Queens to you will be a thing of the past."

"I guess you are right, Chas. Didn't you tell me you were trading in your Cougar?"

"I'm selling it privately. I'll do better that way."

"Great," Seymour lauds. "George likes your car; it's sporty, he told me once. Maybe if you're free Sunday, the three of us will go to his soccer game together. He always asks me to come see him perform. He can take a good look at your car then."

"I am free," Chas affirms. "It will be good to get out of the city on Sunday; it's dull in town. Most residents who live in Manhattan can afford to recreate outside the city."

On Sunday, Seymour, Chas and George drive in the Cougar to the soccer field.

"What do you think of the ride, George?" Chas asks.

"It's great, I like the get-up it has, too," George responds. "I'd like to drive it on the way home."

"How much money do you want for this junk box, Mary?" Seymour jokes.

"For you, my dear, a hundred over the book value will do fine," Chas jokes. "How does that grab you, soccer mom?"

They arrive at the stadium. George goes to the locker room, and Chas and Seymour take seats in the arena, which has many unoccupied seats.

"These seats are good. The higher you go, the better the view," Seymour says. "Thanks for driving us, and the advice you gave me. You are a good friend and partner, Chas."

"No problem, that's what true friends do," Chas mentions. "The dealer has my black 380SL with black interior. I can pick it up next week. You can have the Cougar then, okay, Mary?"

"Yes, that's good timing," Seymour agrees. "Now I won't have to listen about a car anymore."

Seymour watches George run on the field. He has a special look on his face. Chas never saw such warmth in Seymour's expression.

"I know you think I am weird... but sitting here," Seymour boasts, "I feel like a proud parent."

"I think you need to love and be loved," Chas advises. "What's weird about that? George seems to give you love in general, as well as during your short encounters."

"You are correct," Seymour says. "I'm so suspicious of people, that I can't see honesty in people. Except you—something about you makes me trust you."

"Thanks, dear."

George and his team win the game. The three leave the stadium with a happy George driving the car home.

"It handles nicely, Chas; I'm anxious to own it. Thanks, Seymour."

Seymour is getting out of the car in front of his building when he remembers something.

"I met this old queen," Seymour mentions. "I've known him a long time. He works at *Mr. Chow*'s restaurant. It's a few blocks from us. It's on East 57th Street. I haven't been there in years. Having bars in the Village made it inconvenient to go uptown. My friend said the food is still great, and expensive. We should give it a try?"

"Okay, we'll meet for drinks at *Rounds* and then go for dinner," Chas agrees.

Seymour and George are riding in the elevator, going to Seymour's apartment.

"Well, George," Seymour says. "Now you can be nice to me instead of fighting with me all the time over a car."

"You are reading my mind," George replies.

They step out of the elevator and enter the apartment. As the door closes, George grabs Seymour by the back of the neck, pulls his face against his, and shoves his tongue into Seymour's open mouth. As they each swallow the other's tongue, they disrobe each other. Seymour is on his knees trying to get as much of George's huge soft cock in his mouth, almost gagging at times. As he massages Georges cock with his mouth, it grows to its ten firm inches.

"Get in the bed on your knees, you little bitch," George demands. "First, I'm going to spank you."

"Oh no, please don't," Seymour begs." You're not going to tie my hands to the bed post, are you?"

"You're damn right I'm going to tie you, "George replies. "Get the rope and lube from the night table, you little size queen. I think a little pain is called for—only a little lube this time."

George ties Seymour's hands loosely to the post, more for effect; then spanks Seymour just enough to turn his little white ass pale pink.

"Yes, master, whatever pleases you," Seymour responds. "Please fuck me now, and hard your majesty."

George puts a little lube on his cock and a little on his finger, which he inserts in Seymour's rectum.

"My ass hurts from the spanking," Seymour says. "Give me my reward, your hard cock up my ass, please."

"Okay, my little fag," George replies. "Here is the first of ten inches, the second, and the third."

"Just give me it all, Seymour begs. "That's it, harder, *harder*—I want to feel your cock vibrate in me as you shoot your load."

George is ready to come.

"Here is my deposit in your vault," George groans.

"Oh, I'm coming," Seymour mutters.

George unties Seymour; they turn toward each other, embrace and kiss before falling asleep.

Chas goes to *Rounds* as soon as he drops Seymour and George off. In the basement office, he catches up with his previous day's chores. The change bags that the bartenders need tonight have to have the correct amount of silver and bills. The total of two-hundred-fifty dollars will be in each change bag.

The receipts will stay in their envelope, which is deposited into the safe in the locked masonry liquor room in the basement. It takes Chas two hours to complete his work.

He needs to find a manager he can trust to relieve him of this chore. Especially on weekend days. Saturday and Sunday mornings, he leaves the bar at close to 4 AM. *Rounds* reopens at twelve noon; banking needs to done by that time.

Chas goes upstairs to the bar; Ken is reviewing the ad he wants to use to promote Halloween.

Michael Giametta, the owner of the popular weekly gay periodical, *Michael's Thing*, is listening to what kind of ad Ken wants.

"Good to see you, Michael, Ken," Chas greets. "I thought only I worked on the Sabbath."

"Nice to see you, Chas," Michael replies. "Maybe we'll meet when I come for dinner this week."

"I look forward to it, Michael," Chas replies.

Ken tells his assistant what the invitation is to say concerning first, second, and third prize values. The invitation will be mailed to everyone on Ken's extensive list of associates.

Halloween is a major event in the gay community, where wearing costumes is popular. The Village with its large population of gays puts on a large Halloween parade down lower Broadway every year. The event is covered by the local TV channels.

Chas knows the Halloween party is going to be an exciting show. His friends who helped get *Rounds* off the ground will find it entertaining. He calls Sam, to tell him of the popular party.

"Sam *Rounds* is inviting you, Irma, Herb, John, and their wives for cocktails, dinner and a show you will enjoy on Halloween night.

"You guys will have a great time as you see the staff's creative costumes. It will be packed, so you need to tell me if you're coming, and if you are, how many tables to reserve."

"Great, Chas, Irma will make the calls to Fran and Florence," Sam says. "I will let you know. How's business? Is Ken behaving?"

"Business is great, Sam," Chas boasts. "Ken does great promotion from home, where he has space to work. He stays away from *Rounds* at night. He won't get in trouble with the deadbeats that way. He's afraid to say No to accepting checks, and he's finding out the truth about his so-called friends."

On Halloween afternoon, Chas sees the outfits his help adorned themselves in. He is proud of the effort they spent to look authentic.

One in particular caches his attention. Timmy, the service bartender, is dressed and looks like Jane Russell, in the controversial movie, "*The Outlaw*" by Howard Hughes. The movie is considered too sexually-explicit to be released until years later. The objectionable scene shows sexy bosomy Jane in a peasant skirt and low-cut blouse. She is dressed and gets into bed with her costar, Billy the Kid. She does it so her body warms his and stops his violent shivering from a gunshot wound. Chas falls in love with the sexy Ms. Russell after seeing the movie as a young boy.

Looking at Timmy brings back memories of the movie.

"Timmy," Chas mentions, "I doubt you've seen Jane Russell in *The Outlaw*. Looking at you and how much you look like her in that movie is amazing. Come from behind the bar; I want to give Jane a big kiss on the mouth. I've waited a long time. Jane, it will be a closed-mouth kiss. In the fifties, they didn't swap spit, like they do today. If you want to keep your job, remember that."

"Wait 'til we get our cameras," the staff said.

The customers sitting at the bar are excited at what they're going to witness. Macho Chas is going to kiss a fag on the mouth?

Chas waits a few seconds for the kids to get their cameras; then in his mind, he kisses the sexy character that gets into bed with Billy the Kid.

The applause almost causes Chas to blush.

"Thanks, Timmy," Chas jokes. "We'll have to try that again when we have privacy."

"Any time you say, Boss," Timmy laughs.

Saying that starts the bar patrons buzzing. A limousine stops outside, and Sam and company come in. The coatroom attendant is dressed as Robin Hood in tights which advertise his crotch.

"Nick keeps it simple, no costume; he wears only a mask."

"The mink coats will be taken by Chas," Robin mentions.

"Thanks for coming, guys. Follow me past the crowd," Chas greets. "I'll take the minks and put them in my office for safety."

Chas leads them to their table. After they get seated by the new host, Michael Davy, they are introduced to their waiter.

"Esteemed guests, this is your waitress, Ms. Dolly Parton," Michael said.

Michael did a professional job with his Wolf Man makeup. Chas has to look carefully to see through the hair to find the handsome host.

"What may I get you from the bar?" Dolly asks.

They order drinks and look around in amazement at the costumes.

"You were right, my friend, this is a professional display of talent," Sam laughs. "These kids are convincing as the characters they portray. Look at Little Bo Peep, your piano player, talking to Frankenstein, the cocktail waiter."

"I knew you'd feel this way," Chas agrees. "What better night than tonight to celebrate our friendship. This way, Seymour and I feel we are treating you all to dinner and a show."

"Chas, I'm getting a boner looking at that sexy broad," John informs. "Please tell me it's real."

"John, you have very good taste," Chas jokes. "Yes, she is *real*...ly a screaming faggot. I can get you a date. I'm told she is very gentle. You can't knock it unless you try it."

"You know, partner, I think working in the fag business has made you come out of the closet finally," John responds. "Whatever turns you on."

"My hairdresser and I were talking while I was getting my hair done," Fran says. "I mentioned John invested in *Rounds*, and he almost fainted. He loves this place. He comes here often."

Paul appears at Chas' table, dressed as the Countess of Monte-Crisco. (...yes, *Crisco*, because of its lubricating uses.)

Chas rises from his chair and puts an arm around his friend.

"Irma, Fran, Florence, Herb, John, Sam, I'd like you to meet my friend Paul."

"Good to meet you, Countess, pull up a chair and join us," Chas greets.

Seymour joins the group.

"Hello, all," Seymour greets.

"Where is your costume, Mary?" Paul scoffs.

"I am always in costume," Seymour grumbles. "Don't you like my wig, Mary? Who are you trying to fool in those tight pants and sissy blouse?"

"I only use Countess when I'm with fine people," Paul jokes. "Now that you joined us, I can say my real name, but first, excuse me, ladies. You may call me the Cunt of My Crisco. You know what you old queens used Crisco for, Mary. You came up with the idea, way back when you couldn't afford good lubricant at the pharmacy."

The women, Seymour and Paul are hysterical at Paul's rebuttal. Chas and the men found it amusing, too.

"This is your entire fault, Sam," Chas jokes. "It was your bright idea that I go to the University of Fruits and Nuts. Because I went there, on your advice, I'm spending most of my time these days with nutty fruits."

All the guests laugh.

Chas and Seymour take turns excusing themselves a couple of times. The business takes precedence over entertaining guests in the bar business. If Nick doesn't check IDs from people with masks on, they could have problems if the wrong type sneaks into *Rounds*.

"Nick, is everyone that gets in here being scrutinized, especially people with masks?" Chas asks.

"Yes, if they don't take off a mask," Nick affirms, "I won't let them in. All my requests have been complied with."

"Good job, kid," Chas says. "If you need help, just ask for it. I will send Seymour to assist you. She is good at scaring people away, and she knows every queen in the five boroughs. Please, don't hesitate to ask for help."

After the festivities are concluded, his friends are getting ready to leave.

"Well, thanks for such an entertaining evening," Irma lauds. "I had no idea the food is so good here."

The three women kiss Chas, Seymour and Paul on their

cheeks.

Chas retrieves the minks and helps the women on with their coats, and escorts them to their husbands, who are waiting at the limo.

"It was a pleasure having you as our guests," Chas remarks. "We wouldn't be here if it wasn't for the help Ken received from the three of you."

He walks back to the table where Seymour and Paul are talking.

"You're having Thanksgiving here, with me, my mother, and sister, aren't you, Chas?" Seymour asks.

"Yes, my kids will be with their mother who's taking them to be with her family," Chas replies. "The customers that come to *Rounds* are my adopted family now. Many gay people are ostracized from their family. Here they are always welcome at their adopted home. It's my honor to be with them on a family holiday. Paul, what's your plan for the holiday?"

"My mother knows I'm gay," Paul mentions. "It hasn't affected her love for me. I will be with her and my brother's family on that day."

Walter appears at the table.

"We are counting who will be spending Thanksgiving with us at *Rounds*," Chas informs. "What are you doing that day?"

"I go to my godson's home," Walter replies. "That is the plan so far. If it changes, you will know. Thanks for the invite, Chas."

"Nick needs you at the door." Jason says.

"Thanks."

"What's up, Nick?"

"Chas, this is Joe. He wants to bring his underage friend in, not to drink, just to eat and see all the costumes."

Chas looks at the well dressed pedophilia hoodlum. What gays call a "chicken" lover.

"Joe, he's too young to come in here," Chas mentions.

"You can make an exception for me," Joe brags. "You know who I'm with?"

"Yes I do," Chas replies. "But you don't know who I'm with, and we make no exceptions. Sorry; *you're* welcome, but no children."

Chas turns away, to return to his friends inside.

"You will hear more on this matter," Joe warns. "I promise."

As Chas turns to go back inside, Paul is leaving the club with a two guys done up as Marilyn Monroe and Jayne Mansfield. With his mischievous smile on his face, he looks at Chas.

"Look what I found. I'll see you later," Paul says.

"See ya," Chas responds.

Paul, Jayne and Marilyn get to Paul's apartment on Third Avenue and 55th Street.

The apartment is a small one-bedroom with wood louver window treatment to keep out the Third Avenue noise and natural light, giving the room a dingy effect. Paul has had Marilyn before but Jayne is new. Both are full-time hustlers.

"What can we work out here?" Paul quips. "Business will suck tonight with everyone partying in costume. This is your only time to make some money."

"Give us a hundred each," Jayne asks. "That's the lowest I will go."

"That's too much," Paul responds. "Plus there are two of you to one of me. You won't work that much. I'll go for seventy-five for each of you."

"Okay, but you come once," Marilyn says. "We leave after an hour. Is that okay with you Jayne?"

"Sure, the sooner the better. Based on this place, he probably can't afford us."

Paul is all smiles. They all undress. Paul gets the lube ready.

"Marilyn," Paul says. "I know you give good head. Suck me; when I'm hard, I'll fuck you while Jayne fucks me. Make sure you use the lube, Jayne. Wow! That's the size cock I like, Jayne; being an old size queen."

"I will, don't worry," Jayne replies. "Let's get going; we're wasting time."

Marilyn sucks Paul, and he gets hard. Marilyn is on his back. Paul inserts his cock in Marilyn while they tongue-kiss.

"I'm hard and lubed," Jayne says.

He mounts Paul and inserts his cock into Paul's ass. Paul and Jayne get their rhythm; as Paul comes back, Jayne pushes forward, giving more thrust to Paul's penetration into Marilyn. Paul lets out a satisfying groan as he shoots his wad in Marilyn. Jayne and Marilyn don't come; they are "working girls."

"Good work, boys; here is your money," Paul says. "We have to do this again."

"Yes, we do," Jayne replies. "For a hundred each or no deal. Bye."

"Bye, Paul," Marilyn says.

Paul jumps in the shower, proud of how he hustled the hustlers. A grin is on his face.

* * *

On Thanksgiving, because of all the reservations, two seatings are needed.

One seating is at 1 PM, one at 4 PM. The price for the full-course meal is kept modest. It's *Rounds'* way of saying Thanks to its loyal customers. The house more than makes up for the food bargain; liquor sales are high as a result of two full seatings.

Two weeks later, Seymour and Chas are at *Rounds*.

"Now that it's December, we need to decide where to spend Christmas week," Seymour mentions. "Our upscale customers go to warm climates in the winter. Business will drop off some. It's a good time to leave town."

"Whatever suits you," Chas replies. "You're the sun freak."

"Puerto Rico is my bet, the weather is guaranteed to be good," Seymour advises. "We can socialize with our friends, Ms. Bill and company."

"That's a good idea," Chas says. "I'd like to see the girls, especially my ex-wife, Denis. Are you taking George?"

"I'm not that much of an old fool," Seymour scoffs. "I will get hold of Ms. Rocco. Let her get us a hot credit card and first-class airline tickets. Don't worry about getting caught. The credit card company gets stuck for the airfare and hotel."

A few days later they are in a taxi heading to Kennedy airport.

"Will you look at this crappy weather," Seymour grumbles. "The temperature is thirty-five and raining. I hate this dampness and cold. Puerto Rico is a great good idea."

"Relax, were in a warm cab on the way to Kennedy," Chas responds. "In a few hours, we'll be in your paradise."

The plane lands, and in a few minutes they are outside in the heat getting a cab.

"What a difference from the weather in New York," Seymour lauds. "The heat feels good, doesn't it, Chas."

"Yes, the heat does feel good, compared to the cold we left behind."

The taxi leaves the airport on its short ride to the Condado section of San Juan.

"I think I'll stop and see Denis at the Atlantic beach hotel," Chas mentions. "He should be at the beach bar, if he's not turning a trick somewhere else. Do you want to join me?"

"No thanks, Mary, I'm anxious to get some color back," Seymour mutters. "Sun tanning is what I came here for, not to socialize with tacky queens. When you get to the hotel, ask the clerk what room we're in. Remember to use the name that's on the reservation."

The cab drops Chas off. He walks the short distance along the street adjacent to the Atlantic beach hotel. He uses the street entrance, which allows non-guests of the hotel access to the beach bar and beach without going through the hotel lobby.

The bar and surrounding deck is packed with vacationers soaking up sun and lots of booze. He feels the breeze and enjoys the sweet smell of the ocean once again. To the guests, this is paradise. It offers the promiscuous patrons opportunity to have sex with strangers. They show off a sexy body and good looks, hoping to attract a partner. When eye contact is made, a short conversation ensues and the pair goes to a room.

"What are you doing working at the bar?" Chas teases.

Denis is facing the opposite way.

"Oh, my God," Denis exclaims. "It's my ex-husband. What a pleasant surprise to see my honey again. I have missed you."

The people sitting near Chas turn toward him.

"I missed you too, dear. Have you been behaving?" Chas jokes. "I'm glad you're here as I arrived, instead of turning a trick. Seymour dropped me off on the way to *The Hilton*, so I could see you. We will be here until the 30th and then we leave. We need to be at *Rounds* for our New Years Eve celebration.

Hey, you are busy now; we'll talk later," Chas says. "You can fill me in on *Otello*'s and stuff."

"I'm counting on it, dear," Denis said.

Chas gets in the room at *The Hilton*.

Seymour is already in a lounge chair on the beach, coated in tanning oil, without his wig. A straw hat is appropriate on the beach under the merciless hot sun. His brief trunks could make him look continental if not for a hairy gray chest. Some continentals shave their chest to look sexy, covered in shiny suntan oil. His expensive gold Rolex is worn, not to keep time but to flaunt his wealth to a potential trick who may notice him.

Chas puts on his bathing suit, but the air-conditioning has the room too cold. Raising the thermostat, he gets into bed to get warm. An hour later, the phone rings, waking him up. He answers it.

"Hello."

"Are you coming down?" Seymour asks. "I need help, the widows keep coming over to me. I can't get any peace and sun."

"Yes, I'll be right down."

"You look older without your wig, Mary."

"Screw you, Mary," Seymour says. "How is Ms. Denis? The bar must be packed."

Seymour has a towel on the lounge chair, so it appears to be taken, discouraging unwanted women from sitting next to him and talking. Chas sits down instead.

"He is happy in his environment," Chas informs. "He runs a bar packed with good looking johns and tricks, a few steps up from the most popular beach in San Juan. He has a tips goldmine there. Two nights on the weekends he earns money at a so-called straight bar. How could he not do great?"

"You know," Seymour mentions, "you're a good-looking straight guy with some class; you could score big with the rich widows who come here to vacation and look for a man."

"I am not in the market for old fish." Chas replies.

"That's where you are wrong," Seymour explains. "All you would do is treat her nice. Give her a little sex a few times a week. She will buy you anything your heart desires."

"You are describing the life of a prostitute, Seymour. I'm not ready for that life, yet."

"Chas, that's the mistake people make. Love, you can't buy. Sex is always paid for, either with money or by bartering, using different things people want."

"I see where you are coming from," Chas replies. "I guess I'm disinterested in having sex with a woman who I don't find attractive."

"Who said anything about sex with an ugly woman," Seymour responds. "There are beautiful older widows out there. Their husbands die, leaving them well-off. Would the doctor's wife be acceptable, if she were a widow?"

"Yes, but you're forgetting one thing," Chas mentions. "Women give sex to get love in return. Men give love to get sex in return. I can't fake giving love. She is married, so it makes it out of the question. ...I'm getting a drink, you want me to bring you back one?"

"Yes, a very cold light beer."

"Here is your beer," Chas jokes. "This sun is frying what little brains I have left. I'm going upstairs. If you get hit on anymore, just be honest. Tell her you are more of a woman than she is. That will turn her off. If not, ask her if she has a young son you can date. That should clinch it.

I'll call Bill to find out where they want to eat. Do you have any preference?"

"As long as we stay in Condado, it will be fine," Seymour says. "I don't feel like schlepping to Old San Juan tonight."

"Great, I'll see what I can do," Chas says.

Chas goes to the phone to call.

"Bill, how are you? It's Chas. Seymour and I are in Condado. Would you guys like to come into town and have dinner with us?"

"Sounds good to me, Chas, we'll be in the lobby of *The Hilton* at eight o'clock. I'll call you if we have a change of plans. Look forward to seeing you, Chas. Bye."

A short while later, Seymour enters the room.

"That sun was great—just what my old bones needed. Did you get the crew to join us?" Seymour asks.

"Yes," Chas replies. "They will be here at eight. We better have a nap first—you know how bitchy you and I are without it."

After resting, the two men shower, dress, and go the lobby to wait for their dinner guests.

"Good to see you guys," Chas greets. "We're happy to see you three again."

Bill, Allen and Stanley each hug Seymour and Chas. With the pleasantries over, they get a table in the dining room. Drinks are ordered from the waiter, and shortly thereafter, Allen prepares a toast.

"To our good friends, Seymour and Chas, we sincerely wish them much success with their new popular club, *Rounds*,"

Stanley toasts.

Dinner conversation is friendly, and the food fine. After two hours, dinner is over. Allen, Bill and Stanley drive back to Old San Juan, while Seymour and Chas sit at the beach bar a while.

The week in Puerto Rico is relaxing. Now it is time to board a plane to New York.

As soon as they are on board, they order drinks from the first-class steward who knows Seymour from New York's gay bars.

"It's tough to leave the tropics in the winter and fly to the cold northeast," Seymour remarks.

"I agree," Chas says. "If we don't take care of *Rounds*, she can't take care of us, and *that* we wouldn't like."

On New Years Eve day, all the staff comes in early to help with the decorations. Within a matter of hours, the club's ambiance goes from seductive to cheerful. There are balloons floating along the entire ceiling. Hats and noisemakers are everywhere.

"Happy New Year, Seymour," Chas greets.

"The same to you, Mary," Seymour responds. "Many more."

After dinner, Chas, Seymour and their guests are celebrating at their table.

"Look, there's Barry Manilow," Linda exclaims. "I just love him."

Chas looks and instead of Barry Manilow, he sees the popular hustler, Irv, who does resemble the singer.

"I need ask him something, I'll be right back, Linda."

Chas goes to talk with Irv.

"My date is a little drunk," Chas explains. "Do me a favor, play the role of Barry, and ask her to dance. I will owe you."

"Sure, Chas, it will be my pleasure," Irv says.

Irv comes to table and stands next to Linda.

"Excuse me," Irv remarks. "Would you honor me with a dance? This song is special. I'd like to share it with an attractive woman."

Linda beams as they slow dance for a few minutes.

When Linda returns to the table after she danced with Barry, she is glowing.

Seymour leans toward Chas.

"You are a bigger prick than me," Seymour brags. "I'm proud of you, Mary. If she ever finds out, you will be cut off from pussy."

"That won't be the first time it happens, or the last time," Chas replies. "What a crowd, everyone is cheerful. Men are in suits, and their female guests in gowns. All are relaxed, wearing silly hats while blowing horns and shaking noisemakers. There is nothing else like this holiday—it makes people behave like children. It's good to see them happy."

The ball on Times Square dropped, ushering in a New Year. Kissing and hugging is finished. Chas, Linda, Seymour and George stay with the party. Tonight it would remain busy until closing at 4 AM, Chas needs a break from the partying. Seymour will hold down the *Rounds* 'til he returns.

"Let's go upstairs. There is something I want to give you, Linda," Chas asks. "You probably haven't had it before. It will be a nice way to begin the year."

"Whatever you say," Linda agrees. "Whatever you give me will be appreciated."

"That's what I'm counting on," Chas replies. "Let's get out of here."

As they walk he realizes she is a little drunk and relaxed. It's the way he needs her to feel. They enter his apartment.

"Honey," Linda advises, "I need to put my diaphragm in, to contain the blood from my period."

Linda has sex during menstruation. It's the only time she used a diaphragm with Chas.

"You won't need that thing, Linda; we're going a different route tonight."

"Great. After hearing how good it feels from Bruce, I wanted

The Hunting Club in Winter

to try it. Men I date won't do it to me. They think sticking their cock in my ass will get shit on their cock. Do you believe such nonsense? Wow, finally I'm going to get it up my ass by a smart man."

"Yeah, how stupid some men are," Chas said.

They got undressed quickly. Both are horny.

"Get on your knees bitch, turn this way, parallel to the wall so we both can watch me fucking you in the ass, in the mirror," Chas says. "Watching your tits hang down while you are on your knees turns me on. Feeling it go up your tight hole is big turn-on, too."

Chas applies lubricant to his cock and her sphincter.

"Yes, master, but will you please stick that big thing inside me already," Linda asks. "Ugh, easy baby, slowly—that feels so good. Fuck me until I come. Oh. Oh. *Oohhh*. What a fuck, that's better than a pussy fuck. Thank you for doing me that way."

"Half the thanks go to Jerry," Chas informs. "Thank you, Jerry, and Happy New Year."

"Thanks, Jerry," Linda said.

When they wake, Linda would not take No for an answer. She gets Chas hard. After sex, Chas take a short nap and is happy to see Linda is finished for the night.

All the sex made him physically tired but relaxed. He gets dressed and returns to *Rounds*.

"Where did you go?" Seymour said.

"I went to make a deposit."

"Yea! The first one for the New Year," Seymour jokes. "George and I are tired. While I have the energy I will make a deposit, too... in the sperm bank. Let's go, George."

After breakfast, Chas goes to *Rounds* to reconcile last night's sales. The figures are noted, and the cash put in a bank's drop bag and locked. The bag is deposited in the bank's night deposit. Normally, the drop would have happened last night. Now he could rest with the cash in the bank. Exhausted, he returns to his

Paul Spinelle and Camille

apartment to sleep. At night, it is snowing as Seymour and Chas enjoy cocktails before dinner. *Rounds* has a decent crowd in spite of the weather on New Year's night following the previous celebration.

"The great thing about having a business in this city is the people." Seymour scoffs. "Our patrons refuse to listen to the exaggerated weather men. They talk about wind chill factor, as if we went outside in the nude. We are supposed to stay indoors all winter? Thankfully, our customers will get to a bar in a blizzard. We don't need cars, we have private chauffeurs—they are known as cab drivers."

"We made it through the winter with only one week in January and one week in February spent in Puerto Rico," Chas mentions. "It is probably due to being tougher in our old age. St. Paddy's day is around the corner, and that means spring will follow soon after."

"You can start driving with the top down," Seymour mentions. "I won't be able to join you, my wig will blow off the way you like to speed."

"I worked out a solution for your wig, Seymour."

"You are going to share it with me, I am afraid?" Seymour quips.

"Certainly, Chas jokes. "We take a pink kerchief. Put it over your head and tie it at your throat. You will look like an old queen, who's also lost her mind. People will have twice the pity for me, believing you're gay and retarded too."

Seymour is hysterical with laughter. Finally, he catches his breath.

"Mary, how do you come up with this shit?" Seymour laughs. "You should go on stage."

"The next stage out of town, I suppose?" Chas quips.

"You're smart, Chas." Seymour said.

Paul sticks his head in the dining room.

"Hey, Paul," Chas lauds. "My old hunting buddy. Come over

here, I need to tell you something."

"Hello, Chas," Paul says.

"Hello, Seymour," Paul mocks.

"What's up, Chas?"

"I am going up to my club to get in some hunting. There will also be a game feast, with whatever was killed by hunters during the past months. Would you like to join me?"

"Absolutely! That will be great," Paul replies. "When are we going?"

"I'm off Wednesday," Chas says. "If it's pleasant out, we'll drop the top and bask in the sun as we drive there."

The club comprises five-hundred acres of mostly open rolling fields. A trout stream flows through a wooded section and settles into a large pond before continuing at a trickle. The buildings were built in the late 1800s, made of large stones taken from the original property. A stone shale roof maintains the old original rustic look. The building had originally been used as a private school for girls of wealth. It has a two-bedroom apartment that the female principal occupied. Two bedrooms in the second story area were for the female teachers. The large main lounge with a huge fireplace was originally one classroom for two grades. The original kitchen was converted into a gourmet kitchen. It adjoins the lounge, which is also a banquet room for special occasions.

As the Mercedes pulls onto the club property, they are greeted by Bob, the dog handler.

"Perfect timing, the birds are waiting. I put them out a half hour ago," Bob said.

Paul and Chas take their shotguns from Chas' room and go to meet Bob.

"We're ready, Bob," Chas mentions. "Remember the last time, Paul? When the bird first takes flight, don't get startled. Lost composure costs valuable seconds and the bird gets out of range."

"Want to bet I do better than you, Chas?" Paul brags.

"Don't be cocky," Chas quips. "Mary, don't shoot Bob or his dog."

"Paul you shoot to the left," Bob says. "Chas you shoot to the right. You both can shoot straight ahead if it goes straight. As soon as it gets up, I get down. Oh, wait 'til I'm clear; I hate bird-shot in my head."

As soon as they reach some good bird cover, the dog stops, his tail sticks out and he stands still.

Before Bob can get close enough, the birds' nerve gives out. The noisy flapping of wings as the bird takes flight tells Paul and Chas to take aim.

"Paul, it's your shot," Chas exclaims.

Bang… Bang.

Loose feathers and no bird in the air tells Paul he got the bird.

"Go get it, Jesse," Bob asks.

In seconds Jesse had the male pheasant in his mouth, carrying it to Bob.

"Good boy, good boy. Nice shooting, Paul," Bob said.

"You did good," Chas lauds.

Bob put out six birds. Chas shot two, Paul shot four and was very happy with himself.

"Good thing you didn't bet; I won," Paul brags.

"Congratulations," Chas said.

When the hunting is finished, Chas tips Bob.

"Bob, thanks for a great hunt," Chas mentions.

"It was my pleasure," Bob replies. "I'll have them cleaned and put in the cooler with your nametag on them.

"Can we keep on hunting without the dog and Bob? Paul asks. It's such a beautiful day, still. My juices are still going strong."

"Sure, but we won't have much success without a dog's keen nose," Chas advises.

With their shotguns, they begin walking in the fields. Chas

knows there is no chance they will walk up on a pheasant. It's a pleasant day and it makes Paul happy.

They come to a shallow pond, and each walks on separate sides of the pond.

A mallard duck flies overhead. Chas sees Paul shoulder his gun.

"Don't shoot!" Chas shouts.

"Bang... bang."

"I got him!" Paul shouts.

The dead bird falls into the pond.

"I told you *not* to shoot," Chas scolds. "Ducks are federally-protected. They're only hunted at certain times of the year. A special license, called a duck stamp, is required. What the hell! Didn't you kill enough today?"

"I am sorry. Here, take my gun," Paul moans. "I'll get a long branch to reach it, and get it out. No one will know."

"I hope no one sees you, Paul," Chas mocks. "I'll be thrown out of the club. Don't drown, you fucking asshole. Meet me in the lounge later. I need a drink to calm down."

Twenty minutes pass. Chas sees through the lounge window, Paul walking toward the lounge entrance. A cocky smile is on his face. He is carrying two birds, not one. Astonished, Chas goes to Paul.

"What the fuck did you do now, Mary?" Chas scolds.

"I had to wade out a little to reach the dead duck," Paul explains. "As I wade, I see the female duck out of the corner of my eye. She is hiding under some brush, at the pond's edge. I had the male in my hand. I took the branch and whack the female on the head. She dies on the spot. One thing I know about mallards: they mate for life. She can't survive without him."

"I don't believe my ears, but I do believe my eyes," Chas derides. "Without a gun, you manage to commit the same crime twice. Only you could pull this off. Actually, I have to laugh. It reminds me of the wacky comedians Oliver and Stanley. Give those birds to me; I will hide them in car's trunk before they're seen."

"Oliver and who?" Paul asks.

"Forget it," Chas quips. "Help yourself to the booze on the bar. And for God's sake, Paul, while I'm gone, don't kill anything else."

After putting the birds in his trunk, he returns to the clubhouse.

"Okay, let's relax, Paul," Chas suggests. "It's a big, comfortable room. The red leather sofas and recliners give the room a cozy atmosphere. The wood paneling is original and is over a hundred years old. We have few members. Most are fly fishermen. I always have this room to myself. I like it that way, except when my guest is The Killer. Well, we better take showers and get ready to eat later."

"This has been great," Paul exclaims. "I'm happy you took me hunting again."

There are twenty people, members and guests, later that night for the game feast.

"Enjoy the food," Chas says. "Paul, please don't ask if any of it is mallard. Just kidding! I'd better put the top up on the car for the ride home. It looks like rain."

"I have a good friend—he is a retired chef," Paul responds. "He will gladly cook the birds for me. The three of us can enjoy a meal at his apartment."

"Sure, Paul, I'll bring the wine. I'm going to the room for a moment."

During the meal, Paul tells the inquisitive guests sitting near him:

"This country hasn't seen the fantastic gowns I display at fashion shows in Rome," Paul jokes. "It's where I live most of the year. We are scheduled to show in Paris soon. My label, *La Rotunda E Senora*, will soon be famous. We don't use the skinny, sad, tall models that look anorexic. Our models are zaftig women—you know, big babes."

Some women guests actually believe Paul's bullshit story. They didn't know the word *zaftig* is "fat" in Yiddish, a slang form of Hebrew. A rotund woman in a gaudy dress even asks Paul when he is planning a show in the United States.

"Thanks to all you superb sportsmen for the game we enjoyed," Chas lauds. "Special thanks to our great chef, and his competent help. We have to get to the city tonight. Good night."

He and Paul make a hasty exit before the Anglo-Protestant women get wise to Paul's joke. Driving back to New York, Chas shares his thoughts with Paul.

"I enjoyed your company, in spite of the duck incident. We had a lot of laughs, and no one got hurt, except the ducks. That's what matters most. We'll do it again."

* * *

On a windy evening, early in April, Chas and Seymour are walking back to *Rounds* after dining at *The Mayfair* on First Avenue.

"We made it, partner," Seymour brags. "Our first anniversary will be here in a few weeks. Ken is working on the promotion. He is almost done with it."

"Coincidently, this will be his first note we have to cash, as part of the buyout deal we made with him last month," Chas replies. "He seems calmer, now that the deal was made. Don't you agree?"

"Absolutely, he is a good kid at heart," Seymour agrees. "We just have different methods of running a business."

"Now whatever deal he does in the future, he will be careful to structure his relationship so he is the boss," Chas says.

They arrive at *Rounds* and each goes to check a different part of the club. In the rear of the dining room is Vladimir Horowitz, the great concert pianist. He is with his tall companion, sitting side-by-side in their usual spot.

"Is everything satisfactory, Mr. Horowitz?" Chas asks.

"Chas, as always, the drinks are wet and the people pay me no mind," Vladimir responds. "I prefer it that way. It's one reason I love it here. The piano players are entertaining. Last, but not least, I like you, my elegant handsome host."

"Thank you, Mr. Horowitz. A compliment from such a discerning Maestro is special to me," Chas lauds.

On the opposite end of the dining room, John, the realtor, is treating a few hustlers to drinks, and a petty game of chance. Since only quarters are used to play the game, Chas let it continue. Gambling in bars is illegal… but he and his buddies do it at lunch almost every Friday.

"Chas, these kids are cleaning me out of money," John jokes.

"John, you have experience on your side," Chas teases. "They are better at cheating, though. The only thing I can do is stop the game."

"That won't be necessary," John jokes. "I'll get a few more drinks in them as soon as the waiter comes back with our order. We are having a good time; that's what counts. Plus, any winnings they accrue will go toward what I'm going to pay them later when we leave here. Don't mention to them that I'm very rich."

Chas became friendly with a few businessmen like John who come to *Rounds*, in the early afternoon. At *Rounds* they are safe from being seen by their straight coworkers in a gay bar.

Customers are designers from the decorator building a few blocks away. Sales clerks from *Bloomingdale's*; married men who are leading a double life, business owners like John, and unemployed executives, as in the case of Mike Ostfeld.

Mike and Chas hit it off from the start. Mike saw Chas as stodgy when they first met. He calls Chas "Sunshine", as a joke, since it is opposite to Chas' true demeanor.

Chas finishes his work in the office the following afternoon, and goes to the bar.

"Sunshine, it's so nice to see you," Mike exclaims.

"Good to see you, Mike. Aren't you supposed to be going on interviews or something? Instead you're hanging around a decadent famous fag bar full of hustlers and old johns."

"I was just telling these fine people and my friend at the end of the bar, John Johnson," Mike says. "You know him, don't you?"

"Of course I know John. Hi, John."

"Hi, Chas."

"So, here is what I've been telling my friend and this interested audience. Since you are reasonably close friends, and I am in need of employment, you will make an exception for me regarding prostitution."

Mike wears a smile on his rotund face.

"I think I am going to need a drink," Chas laughs. "Mark, a drink for me and the bar, please. We *are* close friends? With that huge gut you have, how could I possibly get close to you, to *be* a close friend?"

The patrons hearing the joking between the two become hilarious. Mike maintains his composure.

"*Rounds*, does not permit solicitation, for the purpose of prostitution," Mike jokes. "We, however, have a special friendship. You will allow me to sell my body, at *Rounds*."

"Mike, I will allow you to sell—body *parts*—only!" Chas jokes.

The group at the bar becomes hilarious.

Mike is pointing to his belt, indicating how his girth had gotten smaller.

"Look, I *am* losing weight. You can get close to me now."

"The only place you are losing weight is between your ears, my dear," Chas teases.

The entertainment, at Mike's expense is over and everyone, especially the affable Mike, is satisfied to be part of the enjoyment.

"Chas, there is a new Italian restaurant on 51st, near Third," Mike advises. "It is called *8½*. The walls have pictures of rotund nude woman. It's like in the movie by the same name. Let's eat there tonight."

"Sounds good to me, I'll meet you back here at eight and we'll go there," Chas says.

At dinner that night, the two men get serious and speak of their families.

"How's the divorce going, Mike?" Chas asks.

"My wife and her lawyer think I'm purposely out of work, to keep her settlement low," Mike replies. "My son and daughter know that's not true. No way will I avoid my responsibilities to her and the children. The kids accept that I'm gay, and that makes me happy, for now. What about you?"

"My ex and my teenage daughters can't seem to live in the same house any longer," Chas says. "I'm looking to hire a full-time housekeeper for my kids. Mari wants to move into an apartment nearby. My daughters blame Mari for our splitting up. A girlfriend explained to me, teenage daughters have a special attachment to their father. From what I gathered, they are practicing on me, the love they will give their future husbands, something to that effect. Those men will be lucky to marry my daughters, whomever they may be. That's enough about me. How's the job search going?"

"Not well," Mike replies. "I was advised that even though I don't have a job to report to, I should maintain a work-type schedule. I shower, shave and get dressed every morning as if I'm going to an office. Then I sit at my desk at home and work at getting résumés out. That routine gets me out of bed otherwise I'd lose my purpose."

"Mike, I have two Cuban cigars," Chas says. "David, the MCA executive who drinks in the afternoon at *Rounds*, gave them to me. He also gave me the pass to their corporate box at *The Garden*. It's great in the box, even though you're far from the

Rounds exterior

Rounds Lounge

action. The good feature is my daughter doesn't have to contend with the rude, vulgar fans. Dawn, the fourteen-year-old, has a crush on the forward for the Rangers, Ron Dugey. He wears no helmet on his head. I tease Dawn that he doesn't wear one because it would prevent his shoulder-length black hair from flowing in the breeze as he speeds along on the ice. Do you believe It.? Why does a girl likes hockey? It's such a belligerent sport. Now, I do two round-trips a night to New Jersey to take her to the games. Two and sometimes three nights a week, and I go to work on top of it all."

"I believe it," Mike lauds. "Because you are a devoted father, you're staying bonded with your children. That is love. Some divorced fathers forget that they have children. Chasing young women is all that is on their mind. Let's get out of here and light up the Cubans. We can enjoy them over brandy at *Rounds*."

When they get to *Rounds*, Chas inquires, "Nick, is everything going okay?"

"All is well, Boss. James Levine, and his brother Tom are here. Tom asked if you are in. De has tickets for you—some opera he said you wanted to see."

The first stop Chas and Mike made was the bar.

"Kelly, give Mike a brandy and I'll have a Johnny Black on ice. Thanks."

"Chas, did you ever think of asking the famous Maestro James Levine to give a performance at *Rounds*?" Mike says.

"You know we never impose on a customer. They come here for other reasons but mainly for the privacy the club and patrons extend to famous people."

"What is that horrible stink?" someone says.

An irate customer looks at Timmy, the bartender. The customer knows full well where it is coming from. Mike answers the question.

"It's the stink that real men give off, Mary, while enjoying a prize cigar, along with expensive cognac. Something you don't normally come into contact with in the usual fag bars you frequent. *Rounds*, is partly owned by my bisexual lover next to me. He enjoys a cigar occasionally with me in his bar. Would you deny him that brief enjoyment?"

"Come, my dear, let's share our smelly aroma with the rest of the bar," Chas says. "No one group will get the pleasure of the Cubans."

"Thanks for the booze and cigar, Sunshine," Mike says. "I am going to the piano. I'm sure Enid will have something to say about me smoking a cigar. Fuck her; she is an employee, right?"

"Right, a damn good employee," Chas warns. "Don't make me have to toss your ass out."

Chas walks over to James and Tom Levine, who are with friends.

"Excuse me, Tom," Chas says. "Nick said you wanted to see me."

"Hello, James," Chas says.

"Hi," James replies.

"Hi, Chas, here are the tickets we spoke about last week for the opera."

"Tom, this is appreciated," Chas lauds. "Thank James, too, please. I'll tell your waiter, Justin, the next round is on the house."

"Thank you, Chas. Anytime I can help, please feel free to let me know," Tom says.

Chas goes to Seymour at the bar.

"Mary, you owe me dinner; Tom delivered," Chas boasts.

A week later, Chas and Linda go to Lincoln Center to see their first opera.

"Was it what you expected?" Linda asks.

"Sort of; operas are simple stories," Chas informs. "How well the performers sing, and the orchestra plays is the main thing connoisseurs appreciate, I guess. You can only assume what is being said, unless you understand Italian. I don't, except for a few words my parents said when I was doing something wrong. It's the arias at the end which make the hair on the back of my neck stand up, that I like."

"Well, take me to your bed and I'll get something else to stand up," Linda says.

"I'll drop you off. I need to meet Seymour first, and then we'll catch up."

Tony with jacket being hugged by Ralph.
Keven in black sweater and guest celebrate anniversary.

Tracy, guest and Edwin Dom at celebration.

7

The following night, Seymour and Chas stand at the bar in *Rounds* wearing white shirts and ties instead of their open-collared silk shirts.

"Mary, congratulations," Chas boasts. "It's our first anniversary. It's been quite a challenge, to say the least. How fast the time went! We accomplished so much, it's mind-boggling."

"We can't just sit on our asses now," Seymour advises. "We need to look for another joint. God forbid, something goes wrong at *Rounds*. We need another place for insurance. In this business, we must be on the lookout for any stores which go on the market in our immediate area. If we don't grab them, our competitors will. They will be able to compete with *Rounds*, our bread and butter."

"I told you two," Ken boasts, "different colored satin jackets, with *Rounds* on the back would be a big hit. Fags love them."

"What's even better, Mary, is they are paying twenty dollars for them," Seymour mentions. "I told you they would. You wanted to give them for free."

"Hey, Sunshine, come join me and my guests I brought to celebrate your anniversary."

"Be right over, Mike."

Rounds

"Ken, you did a great job promoting. As always, thanks," Chas lauds. "Seymour you did well, too. See you later, girls."

"People, this is the main owner of *Rounds*, Chas," Mike says.

"Please call him Chas; I call him Sunshine, but no one else can," Mike says. "He tolerates me because he knows I love him. When he comes out of the closet, I will show him the ropes."

"I'm sure all you fine guests of Mike realize what ropes he's referring to. It's the ropes they use during S&M," Chas jokes.

The following week, at dinner, Seymour and Chas are chatting with John Shanker.

"You should feel out the landlord who owns our lease, Chas," John suggests. "See if the building is for sale."

"I am one step ahead of you, John," Chas says. "Bill, who I play cards with on Monday night and drink with at Friday lunch is on it. He is a broker and handles million-dollar deals for Helmsley. I suggest we let him handle the negotiations. He can ascertain if the asking price is kosher or not. As soon as he knows something, we will talk. Okay?"

"We have a good thing with *Rounds*," Seymour affirms. "The thing that kills stores are greedy landlords. When the lease comes up for renewal, he knows we're doing well, and up goes the rent. They want such an increase that they become our partner. To avoid that scenario, we need to be the landlord."

"In each of the attached buildings, there is a commercial space on the second floor, two residential apartments on the third floor and two on the fourth floor," Chas says. "We need to determine what the rents are. We can see if the rents, including us, can carry the mortgage, taxes, heat and hot water, insurance, maintenance, etc., etc."

"That's easy, the seller provides documents showing those figures," John said.

"The cash down is going to be the hard part for me. One ex-wife and three kids starting college soon is a big nut to crack," Chas says.

"Don't worry, Mary, I have enough cash for the two of us," Seymour says. "I will loan you what you need."

The following morning Chas receives a call.

"Chas, I spoke to your landlord," Bill says. "His senior partner is vacationing in Europe for the next two months. When he returns, we will know what's what. We will talk more at lunch on Friday."

That summer, Chas' kids are spending two weeks at the New Jersey shore. He rents a house on the beach, where the family used to go when the children were young. The recently-hired housekeeper loves the idea of spending time where she has less to do.

Chas is at the bar talking with a few patrons interested in his cowboy story.

"Hello, Chas, may I join you?" Paul says.

"Sure, Paul. Don't you look sexy in your skin-tight see-through tee-shirt."

"They fell off the back of a truck. Isn't it hot? I bought six. I would've gotten you some if I knew your size."

"Don't shit me, you cheap fuck," Chas quips. "You fags know sizes. Especially a size queen like you. Linda and I are talking about taking a trip tonight to visit my kids at the beach. I was thinking of inviting you, but now... I don't know." What do you say, Linda, should we take Ms. Big Spender with us?"

"How do you feel about spending the night with two women," Linda asks. "Chas, it will be a first for me."

"I'll bet," Chas said.

"For your information, Linda, my dear, I have slept in the same room with your lover boy," Paul derides. "The snoring is the pits. That's all I get out of him, unlike you, baby."

"Looks like I started a cat fight," Chas quips. "I'll just have to take the two of you girls. Linda has some great grass, Paul. You should kiss and make up if you want a puff later."

Paul grabs Linda, puts one arm around her waist, the other around her neck, then bends her backward, and as macho as he can, kisses her on the mouth.

"Bravo! Bravo!" nearby customers shout.

"Wow! What a kiss," Linda said.

Then the three, leave *Rounds*. It is 1:30 the following morning as the trio squeeze into Chas' roadster and head for the Lincoln tunnel. In the tunnel, the windows and vents are closed to keep out the tunnel fumes. Linda seizes the moment and lights a joint, and passes it around. When they finish the joint, Chas says as a joke:

"Boy, these country roads are not as bright as in Manhattan. I can't see as well out here."

Paul gets paranoid hearing Chas' remark thinking it is the truth.

"Oh! No! We're going to crash," Paul shouts. "My handsome face will be disfigured. I will have to have a closed-casket funeral."

Chas and Linda couldn't believe how stoned Paul had become, and how serious he was.

"Mary, what is your problem, I made a joke," Chas derides. "I can see fine. You think I'm crazy enough to drive if I couldn't see the road?"

The tears from laughter roll down his cheeks. Linda is holding her stomach, as she laughs loudly.

"Please, let's stop at the next motel," Paul implores.

"Okay, there is one, just up the road. I'll stop at it. We all need to rest."

Paul and Chas go into the office.

"How much is it for a double for one night," Chas asks.

"Its forty dollars a night for two queen-size beds in a room," The clerk said.

Paul quickly lays a twenty on the counter.

"Well, I guess you're afraid of the dark too," Chas scoffs. "You want to sleep with mommy and daddy? You are such a cheap fuck. Okay, we'll take the room with two queens. I'm traveling with two *queens*. Here is the rest of money."

He takes the key and gets Linda out of the car without saying much.

A surprised Linda sees all of them enter the same room. She is confused. Would this be a threesome, she grins?"

"Paul is staying with us?" Linda whispers. "What if he sneaks into our bed when we're sleeping?"

He won't. It won't be *my* ass he's after. He knows better," Chas jokes. "After seeing the way he kissed you earlier, I'd guess he's looking to try pusses, or your ass."

The three of them, are tired, slightly smashed, and stoned. Linda and Paul immediately check out the bathroom.

"There is no shampoo! The towels are so small!" Linda grumbles.

"They don't supply hair rinse, or conditioner, and no blow dryer. How will I do my hair in the morning?" Paul scoffs.

Hearing Linda complain is okay. However, listening to Paul with his masculine good looks talk like a woman is too much to bear. Chas falls on the bed laughing. As soon as he stops laughing, Paul or Linda complain about something else. Paul has a vanity hairdo that requires time, as a woman's hairdo does.

"I'm pleading with the two of you to stop talking female shit," Chas pleads. "My stomach is killing me from all the laughter."

Finally exhaustion causes them to get under the covers, Paul in his bed, Chas and Linda in theirs. The next morning, the three walk out the door. The old couple that was in the adjoining room are leaving, too. The woman looks at the threesome, with a disapproving expression on her face.

Paul, notices the look from the woman, and seizes, the opportunity to tease Linda.

"Hey, Chas, wasn't she just great," Paul laughs. "Boy, talk about endurance, she's got enough stamina for six guys like us."

Linda laughs and pretends to be embarrassed. She chases Paul to the locked car. Paul covers his face as she proceeds to hit him on the arms lightly.

"Traveling with the two of you reminds me of my young children," Chas says. "They constantly teased each other."

It was a great day to be at the beach. Chas' daughter, Christine comes to greet her father and his guests as they pulled up to the house.

"Hi, we are so glad you were all able to come," Christine greets. "Did you guys bring bathing suits?"

"No, it was a last minute decision." Linda says. "We'll pick some up at the shop down the road."

"Here's money, Linda," Chas said.

Paul took Linda's hand he was in a sissy joking mood.

"Shopping! I love to shop. Come dear," Paul said.

"Where are Charles and Dawn, Christine?" Chas asks.

"They took the stuff to the beach, earlier," Christine answers. "I'm going to join them now, Dad. We are at our usual location. Where the macadam ends, just walk straight to the lifeguard stand. See you soon."

Chas went upstairs to find his suit, put it on, and grab a cat nap. He is enjoying the quiet, when he hears Paul and Linda return.

"Look at the great kite I bought," Paul exclaims. "I always wanted to fly one. Where we lived as kids, my brother and I had no open space to fly a kite."

Later, the breeze off the water provides a good updraft for kite flying.

"Oh, I can't wait," Paul said.

"Like my suit, dear?" Linda asked.

"Like *my* suit, honey bunch?" Paul jokes.

"I love both suits," Chas remarks. "Don't make the mistake of putting the wrong ones on, girls. This is a family beach, Linda; you can't wear Paul's bottom and go topless. And you, sissy Mary, can't wear Linda's two-piece. Drag queens are not allowed on this beach."

"Don't worry your masculine head, my sweet," Paul jokes. "I

go out only at night in drag."

At the kid's blanket, Chas introduced his friends to Charles and Dawn.

"Guys, this is Linda and Paul."

"Hi, Linda. Hi, Paul."

"Hi, kids," Paul and Linda said.

Chas, Linda and Paul go to the surf and stand ankle-deep in the water.

"The water is freezing," Linda said.

"*Now* who's the sissy?" Paul said.

Paul proceeds to dive into a wave. Chas cradles Linda in his arms, and walks into the ocean until he is waist-deep.

"You are gaining weight, my dear," Chas says. "I can't hold you any longer."

Linda submerges as she hits the water after Chas lets go of her.

"Actually, the water is rather nice. Thanks, sweetie," Linda quips. "I'll remember this tonight."

Paul and Linda join the kids soaking up sun rays and applying suntan lotion. Chas likes the ocean, but sun-tanning is not for him.

"I'm heading to the house, and out of the sun," Chas says. "One of my favorite quotes comes from India. When the British ruled there, the natives had a saying: 'Only Mad Dogs and Englishmen go out in the Noon Day Sun.' It is about noon, so it's time for vodka on ice, with a couple of olives. See ya."

After a drink, Chas takes a needed nap. Everyone started returning from the beach, and he woke up.

"Come on, Chas, the breeze is strong," Paul and Linda said. "We are going to fly the kite."

"Okay," Chas says. "This should be fun to watch the two of you urbanites compete with suburban children."

"Dad, I'd like to join you," Christine said.

"Sure, sweetheart, just like old times."

Chas put his arm around his beautiful, tall daughter. Dawn

is a year older but shorter than her sister. It is a short walk to the beach. Christine and Chas sit on a bench on the small board-walk. From here they can see Paul and Linda kite flying. They are having a ball doing it. The temperature dropped and people wore sweaters now. The tide is high, and the waves crash noisily against the beach.

"How are you and Dawn getting along with Mom?" Chas asks.

"It's sad, we fight with Mom so much," Christine explains. "We blame her more than you for the divorce. Every issue we dis-cuss with Mom is prejudiced by our negative feelings toward her. It's not fair to her, but we can't seem to change our attitude."

"I'm told it's common for daughters to favor the father," Chas explains. "We both are responsible for a failed marriage. We had a very short courtship. We married when I was twenty-two, and Mom was twenty-one. We thought we were in love. We were relating to who we were then. We hardly knew each other. We were in lust, as well as love. You can't love someone you hardly know sweetheart. Time moves quickly. Before you know it, you have three children. Ten years have gone by. People first start to know each other then. Sometimes they don't like what they see.

"That's what happened to us. We tried to accept each other. Mom accepted me. I wouldn't accept her, unfortunately. The vows say, 'in sickness and in health.' People don't realize how demanding that statement is when they first accept it.

"Christine, you have been my buddy since you were six. That was nine years ago.

"We used to go for walks every night, after dinner, and you would ask me questions. I still treasure those talks, as much as I do this one.

"You have my word. I will never leave you or Dawn or Charles. As long as Mom needs my help, she will receive it."

Christine hugs her Dad.

"You're still the best Dad a girl could want," Christine says. "I love you very much."

They sat and stared at the ocean awhile. The sea has a soothing effect. The smell and sound of the waves relaxed father and daughter.

"Did you guys see how high we got the kite to go?" Linda asks.

"Boy, did I show those kids how to do kite flying," Paul said.

"Dad, I will find Dawn and Charles and bring them back," Christine said.

Chas, Linda, and Paul with the kite, walk back to the house. The streets run perpendicular to the ocean. The house is a short distance from the beach. At the house, Chas turns and looks at the beach. He remembers happy days gone by that he and his young family spent here.

"Hey, Paul," Chas jokes. "Tonight you will have only your kite for company in the bedroom. I hope you won't be too lonely."

"I will be fine, wise guy," Paul responds. "At least your daughters have the right stuff for me and Linda to use. We girls appreciate that stuff and bath towels, too.

The next morning, Chas and Dawn are the first ones in the kitchen having coffee.

"Thanks for what you told Christine, Dad," Dawn says. "She told me what you said. It will help us get along better with Mom. Now we feel we can enjoy the best time with you, and with Mom, too."

Later that morning it is time to leave.

"It was great spending time with you guys, but now it's back to the Big Apple," Chas says. "I'll see you next week. Be careful and listen to Grace. She is more than a housekeeper; she is the adult that is in charge."

Chas kisses his daughters, and shakes Charles' hand.

"Charles, we didn't get a chance to talk," Chas says. "You

were busy talking with the chicks, and I was hosting my friends. Next time we will. ...'til then, take care, pal."

"Same to you, Dad," Charles says.

"We had a great time. You guys are great hosts," Paul and Linda said.

They got in the car with the top down. Paul borrows the kerchief that is kept in the glove-box. Some women use it to keep the wind from messing their hair. He wears it as a male pirate would.

"You had me worried," Chas jokes. "I wasn't sure you would tie it the masculine way."

"If I didn't have a mustache," Paul replies, "I'd do it bitch style. Two women to one handsome you; wow."

* * *

It was just after Labor Day. Chas receives a call from his friend Bill.

"The landlord called, he wants eight-hundred-fifty-thousand," Bill says. "I said seven-hundred-thousand. He is sending me the paperwork, to substantiate his price. I'll review it, and let you know what I think the price should be. Now that the summer is over, we can renew our card game schedule, this Monday evening."

"So we are probably looking at eight-hundred-thousand dollars for the building," Chas replies. "I'll let Seymour know. And yeah, it will be great to play poker again. I'll see you Monday, Bill. Thanks."

Chas calls Seymour to tell him the news.

"I just spoke to Bill," Chas advises. "He is doing this on his own time, as a favor to me. He won't take a fee, only reimbursement for expenses. That saves us eighty-thousand-large in commissions. The owner won't be charged, and he can't tack it on to the price."

"That is great news, thanks," Seymour responds. "My friend Bob is a lawyer, and he won't charge us more than a couple grand to review the contract and attend the closing. Today I see my dentist, and have lunch with my sister and mother. I do both painful things together, so they're done for the week. Bye."

Marie and brother Chas at Circles opening.

8 S&S Realty, Inc., is the subchapter corporation which Seymour, Sam, John and Chas form for the building. A month later, title is closed on the building. The cash down-payment was negotiated down to a hundred-thousand dollars. The bank, however, required that two balloon payments be made to compensate for the low down-payment. The first balloon of fifty-thousand dollars is due in one year, another fifty-thousand the year after. They are in addition to the regular monthly notes. Seymour and Chas secure the *Rounds* lease and their future at that location. At *Rounds*, that night, Seymour and Chas toast each other.

"Now we are commercial landlords," Seymour said.

Their glasses, filled with wine, touch in celebration.

"Seymour, there is a club around the corner, just west of Second Avenue on 54th Street," Chas advises. "The owner wants to sell the forty-year lease. He's a singer, and small band leader. There is no money in that business now; it's all discothèques these days. As you preached not to long ago to me, we need another store."

"That's good news," Seymour says. "I'll meet you here at one, and we'll take a look at it."

"I'll let the broker know we are coming. He can bring the seller," Chas says.

The following afternoon, all parties meet at the club.

"Chas, Seymour, this is Kyle, the owner. Kyle, meet Chas and Seymour. They own *Rounds*," Rob said.

"Hi," Kyle says. "As you can see, it's a big room, four-thousand square feet. It has a high ceiling and it also has a cabaret license, which you need to have dancing. A forty-year lease is unheard of in this city."

Kyle shows all the space to Chas and Seymour.

"You two," Kyle says, "think about it and let Rob know if you're interested."

"Thanks for showing us your club," Chas says. "We will get back to Rob."

Chas and Seymour go to *Rounds* to discuss what they just saw.

"He has only a lease to sell," Chas says. "There is no good-will, or improvements worth keeping. The place is a dump. He's not going to get two-hundred-fifty-thousand for just a lease. Not from savvy bar owners. We will need at least two-fifty-large just to do the renovation. What do you think, Seymour?"

"We need to figure the two-fifty over fifteen years," Seymour responds. "Tack that number onto the rent. That number becomes our nut. If we feel comfortable with the nut, we do it, but give him no cash down. He can't have both."

"We are going to need investors, Seymour," Chas says.

"We'll ask Sam, John and Herb. They are happy with the payback they are getting with Ken's deal, right?"

"Yes. I will mention it to Sam when he comes for the note," Chas says. "What about promotion? Should we offer a free piece to Ken to do it? Promotion is the key to getting the place known. That's what got us such a great start at *Rounds*. Ken is responsible for that."

"Ken is going for tests," Seymour advises. "He may have the

'Gay Men' cancer, which is attacking young, sexually-active gay men. He calls me when he returns from the hospital visits, twice a week."

"I never heard of this cancer," Chas moans. "That's terrible news. I hope it's not fatal."

Within two months time, the investors are on-board. A corporation is formed. The property is ready for Jerry to do preliminary drawings. The first sketch Jerry does is attached to the liquor license application, for the Board's approval. With three prominent Jewish business men, and only one Italian bar owner with an existing license in good standing on the application, it is easily approved.

"Congratulations," Sam said. "We received notice from the Liquor Authority that we've been approved."

"Now the fun begins, Sam," Chas explains. "Finish the plans, price out the work, give out construction contracts, and push the project to completion. It's a good thing my sister, Marie, is coming to work here. She will take over all of my day work. I will devote days to building *Circles*, and nights to *Rounds*. Imagine if I were in a meaningful personal relationship."

"Seymour should be very thankful he has such a knowledgeable partner when it comes to construction," Sam said.

"I hope Seymour has half the ability that Ken has, as far as promotion is concerned," Chas warns. "If not, we're in big trouble."

"The boys and I are leaving it up to you," Sam says, "either to proceed or not. You call it."

"Well, I'm as greedy as the next guy," Chas says. "If all works well, I will be able to sock away enough for my old age. This club could put me in a great financial position if it is successful. If not then… ?"

"Nothing ventured, nothing gained." Sam advises. "There are no guarantees in business. We are taking a shot. Don't take it personally if it doesn't work. Just give it your best shot."

Five grueling months, filled with delays, changes to the plans, and cost overruns, are drawing to a close.

Seymour and Chas are talking about *Circles* over dinner.

"We will be ready to open in two weeks," Chas informs. "Two months late. November is a bad time to get a club off the ground. The holidays and all the nonsense with shopping for gifts depletes people's bar cash. The rent these last months has killed our purse. We can't wait 'til spring—five months and twenty-thousand more in rent. The boys are anxious to see money coming in. It's all been going out. How is the promotion going, Seymour?"

"We have full page ads in *Michael's Thing*," Seymour says, "and some other periodicals. Too bad that Ken is too sick to get involved. Even with promotional help, we are still facing a very devastating opponent. AIDS is an epidemic. They have no cure for it. Gay people are dying by the thousands weekly. Gays have a pall hanging over their heads. They don't know if they are sick and will die soon. Or is a close friend going to die? Getting excited over a new dance club is not in their focus."

"Seymour, you chose expensive items that required a long delivery time and changed the plans often," Chas derides. "The club would have opened last September. Construction cost saved: fifty-thousand bucks; rent saved: eight-thousand bucks; a total of fifty-eight-grand. Last fall people, went out."

"Hindsight, my friend," Seymour responds. "Both of us were juiced up. We do classy renovations to appease our egos. That's who we are. The alternative was to do an inexpensive, no-frills joint. Money and time would've been saved. Had our discerning customers hated it and didn't accept it, then what? Our response: we should've, could've."

"The boys have two-hundred-fifty-thousand invested," Chas mocks. "We have fifty-grand invested. You need to get your shit together, Mary. Get off your ass, get *Circles* known."

"Fuck you—it was no party for me," Seymour scolds.

"Schlepping with Jerry here and there looking for the *right* items? He was always arguing his point, and I had to prove I was right."

"Maybe so, but I know little about promoting a gay club in New York City," Chas quips. "You were the fucking star behind the famous *Sanctuary*. That is why I got involved with you. All we lose is fifty-grand apiece. If you blow the promotion, my friends lose almost ninety-grand each."

"First of all, they are not to be considered as friends in this situation," Seymour explains. "They are *investors*, seasoned businessmen, who are used to losing money on deals. I thought I taught you that when we first began looking at stores. We don't use our money; we use investor's money. That's good business."

"Yeah, but I got them into this fucking mess," Chas moans. "We should have found someone other than my good friends. In addition to losing money, I lose my self-respect."

"What have I just said?" Seymour repeats. "You did not get them into anything. We presented a proposition to make a profit larger than they could make on their own. They are responsible. It was solely their decision."

"I can't help it; I take things to heart," Chas moans.

"My friend, you're taking this too personally," Seymour advises. "It's making you crazy. We gave it our best shot. We gave them their money's worth and more. I didn't steal a dime from them, thanks to you. In the old days I would've raked them over the coals. They would've lost their money, not us."

In the winter months that followed, the club lay dormant. Chas stays frustrated. Seymour is useless at getting *Circles* going. He didn't even seem interested.

"The boys are nervous, Seymour, I need to do something," Chas says. "I'd rather make a mistake of commission than one of omission like you are making. Call that creep, ex-associate of yours, Marvin."

"He deals in trash from the Bronx, straight garbage," Seymour warns. "They don't belong in this neighborhood."

"I don't give a fuck about the neighborhood—we have no other option," Chas snarls. "We are behind with six month's rent and a mortgage. That's thirty-thousand, plus unpaid electric, another fifteen-thousand. Are you going to your safety deposit box and lend the club fifty-grand? I don't think so. Either we do something, or we give the landlord the keys back. Tell Marvin to promote it to nice kids. If he's as good as you say, he could do it. Have you a better idea?"

Marvin comes on-board. He persuades John Shanker, Chas' most supportive partner, that he will make a lot of money. His cut is high, but he stops the group's financial bleeding. Unfortunately, his clientele is only Bronx trash. Chas has no other option. Seymour and Chas failed to deliver. John, Sam, Herb take over. John and Chas call the operational shots with Marvin.

"Angry neighbors can't say," Marvin mentions. "We don't want poor African Americans and Puerto Ricans in our all-white neighborhood."

"We're in the frying pan," Chas says. "Marvin, can you get us out of the pan? If you can, great. If you turn up the heat, we go into the flames and die.

"The neighbors will call the fire department. They'll complain that the club's exceeding its certificate of occupancy."

On a warm Saturday night, Sam and Irma are standing outside *Circles* with Chas. They hear the siren from a fire truck heading toward them.

"Well, guys, the party's over." Chas said.

They watched the truck with flashing lights stop in front of *Circles*.

"Can I help you, Chief?" Chas says. I'm the owner of the club."

"Yes, let's see your Cabaret License and C.O," Chief says. "Shut the music and have everyone leave the premises for a short time. We will count them as they re-enter."

Chas takes the firemen inside and complies with their request. Four hundred or so angry and noisy patrons fill the normally quiet street. The Chief and his three men thoroughly make sure the exit doors are unlocked and are the proper width. The sprinkler system is adequate and functional.

"Okay, let them back in slowly and in single file," Chief says. We need to count them. Your C.O. allows four hundred people, including house staff."

"Four-hundred-nine people. You're okay sir. Sorry for the interruption," the Chief says. "Have a good night."

They get on the truck and return to the firehouse. The club resumes operation.

"This visit, precipitated by the neighbors, is just the beginning of more bad news to come. *City Hall*, with all its power, is determined to close us down," Chas mentions. "We have the options of getting rid of this group. Pay the nut until we get an acceptable crowd or sell the place? The vote is out Sam. You guys call it."

In four months of fights by rival groups, some overflow into the street. The police had to cordon off the street during one incident. It is reported in *The New York Times* the following morning.

Herb Fisher is on the phone to Chas after reading the paper.

"You know, I run a chain of stores," Herb informs. "I can't be connected with this publicity. You need to call an attorney who was powerful in the Lindsey administration. Here is his name and phone number. He carries a lot of weight with the Liquor Authority. He can tell us the best way to protect the license."

"I have my own competent liquor attorney," Chas replies, "but to make you feel secure, I will use your guy."

The liquor license is suspended for two years. A fine of four-thousand dollars imposed on *Rounds*. The fine is punishment toward Chas because he is on both licenses.

"That fucking moron of a shyster had Herb conned," Seymour grumbles. "With his egotistical bullshit, he sold the boys and us out. Experienced as you and I are, we should not be told what to do. Now the joint is in a holding pattern for two years."

With no license to sell liquor, there was one more venue they would try.

"My friend Mel, a disbarred lawyer, runs a topless bar for the family," Seymour remarks. "What do you think, Chas?"

"With a two-year suspension on liquor, we can't sell the place to a bar operator, Seymour. You taught me that," Chas mentions. "As long as he pays the rent, we may ride it out. We can sell it in two years. A license with a beautiful interior and a great lease—it can't be beat."

The place runs topless. It has no gaudy neon signs outside. The customers never cause problems, or hang outside the club. It sells nonalcoholic champagne at a great profit. Customers sit around the circular bar and stuff money under the brief garment the girls have to wear to be legal. Girls are not permitted to date customers or have sex on the premises.

Mel knows not to fuck with the golden cow. He runs the club legally. Having once been a legitimate attorney, he also knows the games the city could play.

The rent is paid. A few hundred dollars is given to Chas and Seymour monthly; too small an amount to split with the boys. They consider the money chump change for keeping watch on Mel's operation.

A subpoena is handed to Mel. He has to answer false charges made by undercover cops. They swear solicitation for prostitution has occurred on several dates at the club.

"I guess the tenants committee is upset," Seymour says. "There is a big article in the paper about alleged prostitution against Mel."

Two weeks later, the club is closed. All five men lose their investments.

Sam still comes to *Rounds* regularly; the first visit after the *Circles* closing, he and Chas are talking.

"It is too bad we lost money at *Circles*." Chas said.

"Chas, we are not concerned," Sam says. "Business is business, and good friends are hard to come by, my friend. Don't worry so much. I love ya; take care."

Two months later, Chas gets a phone call with news from Seymour.

"My lawyer Bob has a rich African king who wants real estate in America," Seymour explains. "We can get a million for the building. The fifty-thousand balloon is due soon. We gave our cash to the *Circles*. We should sell. After you pay me back what I loaned you, we'll each clear a hundred-thousand dollars profit. Not bad. The banks are paying double-digit interest. We put the money there. Collecting interest, what's so terrible?"

"It is terrible to me," Chas advises. The building will keep appreciating, and in a few years, it will be worth millions. You are out for the short gain. I'm twenty-three years younger than you. I'm looking for the long gain. I figured I could live above the bar, rent-free and rich in my old age. My being partners with you, Sam, John and Herb was smart. I brought the boys in for this reason. I'm glad I did. They will give you a profit for your share, and the fifty I owe you. They know the value of real estate in this city. The building will be kept as long as I want. Both they and myself will receive compensation from the bar and the building's tenants."

9

A few months later, Seymour and Chas are having dinner at *Rounds*.

"Chas, I talked with Ken. The chemotherapy makes him sick for days," Seymour mentions. "He will, however, get out a mailing for our third anniversary. He wears a wig to cover his bald head, but without eyebrows, he feels self-conscious. I doubt he'll attend the party."

The crowd that attended the anniversary party was, for the most part, the same basic group that attended the opening. They attended the first and second anniversaries too. In spite of AIDS, people didn't check for the virus. They knew no cure was in sight. They hoped they were okay.

"Given what gay life is like, during these trying times, it's great to see so many familiar faces," Chas said.

A stretch-limo pulls up in front of *Rounds*. Frank replaced Nick at the door, and advises Seymour.

"Your favorite customer is here: Ms. Joel, with eight boys, Mary," Frank laughs. "She wants her table."

"It's ready for her, as usual," Seymour said.

Joel is an elegant, suave, good-looking middle-age gentleman with curly black hair. He always wears a jacket and ascot when he comes to *Rounds*.

"Supposedly, he has a high-ranking job in New York State government, Chas," Seymour informs. "About every two weeks, she gives me a hard time for charging regular drink prices for the bitters and soda she drinks. Sure, it's much cheaper then alcohol. Where else could she send her scout to canvass a meat rack like *Rounds*? The scout brings a half dozen boys to his tables. Drinks and food come to a hefty amount on her tab. The kids in this bar are decent, safe, clean, wannabe actors, dancers, musicians—even scholars trying to make ends meet. We should charge her a 'Sur' tax."

"Look, Seymour, we have Bruce managing at nights now," Chas advises. "Let him handle Joel now.

"Joel is no match for Ms. Bruce. Bruce is just what *Rounds* needs. You are obnoxious, and I am straight. Bruce is elegant, a salesmen during the day. He knows how to tell someone off, and the person thinks he paid them a compliment. You and I send them out almost in tears.

"Because of my trenchant manor, I appear rude. I'm not," Chas explains. "As a result, my nickname with Uncle Mike is Sunshine. I don't believe my eyes."

Chas watches three straight buddies, in their business suits, work their way through the crowd. The men are Bill, Willie who is back from Pittsburgh, and Larry.

"Bill and I were on the phone this afternoon, and he mentioned that you are celebrating tonight," Willie says. "We thought of crashing this all-gay bash, and see how you earn the money you use in beating us at cards."

Chas' obvious straight company always stands out like sore thumbs, when they seldom come to *Rounds*.

"Let's grab a table and have some drinks," Chas greets.

He leads his party to the spy table. From here, he could keep one eye on customers, and an eye on his friends.

"May I take a drink order?" Roger asks.

"Yes, one very dry gin martini up, olive on the side, one Jack Daniels on the rocks, and two Jonny Walker Black on the rocks," Chas says.

"We came tonight so I could fill you in on a trip," Bill mentions. "I'm putting together a trip to Lake Powell, in Utah, before school lets out. We'll rent a house boat that sleeps eight guys. No women are allowed. Page, Arizona is where we get the boat. There, we buy food and booze to last seven days. Sleeping bunks are thick cushions. A sleeping bag and pillow are all we bring with our clothes. Dishes and utensils are included. It's not expensive, split eight ways."

"Imagine, Chas, seven days traveling on blue water, under sunny skies, and surrounded by sandstone cliffs two-hundred to three-hundred feet high," Larry lauds. "The water is still cold, but the catfish and stripers don't mind. We'll take rods to fish with."

"The lake is so long, we won't reach the far end during our week stay," Bill explains. "Each night we drive the pontoon craft up on the sandy beach or a cave's entrance and anchor it.

"There are caves cut deep into sandstone cliffs, which rise two-hundred feet straight up above the water level. The cassette player is put at the rear of the cave. The music sounds like we are in a symphonic hall.

"Before the dam flooded, this was a five-hundred-foot gorge cut by the Colorado River. Now it is a two-hundred-fifty-foot-deep lake. At cocktail time, we climb the ladder to the roof deck, and enjoy the view. The last time I was there, Jeff and I slept on the roof deck, watching the star show."

"Bruney will let me go if you go, Chas," Willie says. "She thinks you are a great guy for taking time to help me out when I was sick.

"Well let me think—*of course* I'll go," Chas exclaims. "I wouldn't miss this for all of Seymour's money. Count me in."

"Great! We know you are busy, so we'll see you Monday," Bill said.

The group finished their drinks, squeezed through the curious crowd and left the bar.

Months later, Chas and his cronies were enjoying Lake Powell, their kind of Paradise. It was all that Bill described. A whole week away from the pressures of work, with plenty of joking, fishing, card playing and drinking.

* * *

Thirteen months later, in May of 1983, a few weeks after *Rounds'* fourth anniversary, Chas receives a call from Seymour, at 2 PM.

"Ken died," Seymour says. "Jerry received the news from Ken's family. We are meeting Jerry at the temple tomorrow at 10 AM."

"Is Jerry doing the eulogy?" Chas asks.

"Shelley Winters is doing it," Seymour informs. "I always thought Ken was lying about his relationship with her. It looks as though he was telling the truth after all."

They are sitting in temple the following morning waiting for service to begin.

"Funerals are bad enough, but when parents bury a child, it's very disheartening," Chas whispers. "My sympathy goes out to those parents. How miserable they must feel, burying a child. God help them."

Then Shelley Winters gives a passionate eulogy. She loves Ken, and it was obvious from her emotional state. She barely got her words out of a throat tense with remorse; tears keep her hanky busy.

That night as he sits alone at his and Seymour's table, Chas reflects about Ken. Aside from his lack of business acumen, he was a good partner at what he promoted.

"May I join you?" Joe asks. "You said some time ago, I was welcome. I am without a kid tonight. I'd like to apologize for my anger back then."

"Sure, Joe, sit down. How have you been?" Chas greets.

"Pretty good. I've been away on business. You know what I mean?"

"Yes, I do know, Joe," Chas says. "You're looking as dapper as ever, always in a suit and tie. I wish more customers dressed as well as you. What are you drinking?"

"Just club soda. Thank you," Joe says.

"Roger, a club soda for my friend, and give me a refill, please." Chas says.

"You seem unhappy tonight Chas. Can I be of service?" Joe asks.

"Thanks. We buried Ken today. He was just a kid. AIDS destroyed him," Chas said.

"That's terrible. I liked Ken. I met him often, you know, Chas?"

Joe begins sobbing softly. He maintains his tough exterior, and then he leaves *Rounds*.

Later that night there is a small memorial area set up in the lounge. A table with Ken's picture, a lit candle and an area with flowers that friends sent is set aside in Ken's memory.

"It was good of Jerry to get Ken's picture from his parents," Chas says. "I didn't expect people to come here and bring condolence cards. We'll get the cards to his family, Bruce."

"Most people didn't have time to plan to go to temple," Bruce mentions. "His death happened so fast. He was very popular, everybody liked him. I'll make sure the cards get to his parents."

"Chas, Calvin and I came by to pay our respects," Steve Rubel says. "The community will miss him. Tell Seymour we said hello. When your lady-friend wants to dance, security will let you in to *Studio 54*."

"She went there without me," Chas says. "Why would security let her in, silly girl? I'll introduce her next time. Thanks,

Steve."

"Ken's a big loss to so many of us who have known him well," Calvin Klein said.

"Thanks, Steve, and thanks, Calvin," Chas said.

All night, a steady stream of friends and famous people made a point of coming to *Rounds* to say their farewell to Ken.

The following week, Marie returns to work.

"Hi, brother. Guess what happened to me in Rome?"

"You kissed the Pope's ass."

"No silly," Marie says. "In a restaurant, I overheard a conversation between five men, talking about *Rounds*. They were planning a business trip to New York. They come here when they're in town.

"I mentioned that I am the owner's sister. They were friendly, and picked up our check."

"I will keep an eye out for them, so I can repay them. Welcome home, Sis."

A month later, Seymour and Chas are sitting in the dining room at *Rounds*.

"In spite of the AIDS epidemic, we're lucky to still have most of our original customers," Seymour mentions. "As I look around, I see most of the same faces sitting at the same tables. It's as if we are running a private club not affected by AIDS. We have a lot to be thankful for."

"Speaking of regular customers," Bruce says, "Hello, Mr. Williams, Mr. Capote."

Bruce is eavesdropping from his host station next to the spy table.

"It is good to see you, Bruce," Tennessee says. "We would like to sit at six and seven. That way we both can see the piano, as we sit side-by-side. Philip is on tonight, yes?"

"Yes, and I will send him right over to you," Bruce said.

Then he escorts the two legends to their tables.

Seymour and Chas stand to shake both men's hands. Smiles

are exchanged, not words.

Most people, especially famous ones, dislike Seymour's causticity.

"Well, I might as well check out the meat rack," Seymour mutters. "See if Ms. Frank let any garbage in tonight."

"I have office work downstairs to approve for Marie," Chas says. "I'll see you later."

When Chas returns upstairs, he hears Truman's upset voice as he speaks to Seymour. He listens briefly. Seymour is berating Truman.

Going to the table, Chas whisper's in Seymour's ear.

"Mary, what the fuck are you doing?"

Then he turns to Truman.

"Excuse me, Truman, Tennessee; I need to talk to my partner on an urgent matter."

Seymour follows Chas into the kitchen.

"What are you worried about, Mary," Seymour grumbles. "I know how to talk to a queen. She thinks she is so smart because of her writing. Does being a bar owner make me stupid? The both of them couldn't have survived what I had to when I started in this business. Dealing with the mob, before Stonewall, took brains and balls, for a Jewish fag school teacher."

"That's not the point," Chas scolds. "You know better than to get into contentious discussions with select customers, especially famous ones. Their audience believes every word they say, whether it's good or bad. Do you want *Rounds* to look bad? Please go smooth things over and leave them alone."

Seymour goes back to the table and buys a round of drinks. He puts his hand on Truman's shoulder. He smiles and says a few words to Truman who smiles back. Seymour quietly leaves for the night.

"I'm glad you came upstairs when you did," Bruce mentions. "I was getting ready to get you."

"'It ain't easy, Mary,' as Seymour always says," Chas says.

Chas sees Kevin and Ralph, two lovers who have a successful

decorating business and have come in for dinner. Chas enjoys conversing with them.

"Ah, my favorite decorators are here," Chas greets.

"Hi Chas, we were out of town on a big job in Miami," Kevin mentions. "It's the reason we missed your fourth anniversary. Congratulations, we are so happy to have this great club. It's only a short walk from our apartment. We also like the variety of boys here. Especially since we have different tastes in boys."

"Yeah, that way, we don't fight over the same cookie," Ralph laughs.

After dinner, Kevin and Ralph go to the bar for drinks, and cruise, or just talk with their peers.

Chas is content that the policy at *Rounds* is strict. If Frank can't vouch for a newcomer, he would say so to the patron asking if it's safe to leave with them. It is no guarantee, but it helps prevent crime.

The following night, Frank advises Chas as he enters *Rounds*.

"Guess who is here to see our new piano player, Ms. Robert?" Frank boasts. "Rock Hudson and his party flew in from LA."

"Rock is in good hands with Bruce at the helm," Chas replies. "I will say hello, and make sure he and his party are comfortable."

He walks in and looks for Seymour. Was his partner going to behave with the big star?

"Seymour we have special company tonight," Chas brags.

"I saw her," Seymour mocks. "She's all gray, almost white-haired. Maybe it's the AIDS medication."

"I'm going to say hello, are you joining me?" Chas says.

"You go," Seymour mentions. "I caught his attention as he came in, and we smiled hello."

"Excuse me, gentlemen, is everything okay, Mr. Hudson?" Chas greets.

"Everything is great Chas," Rock lauds. "Robert has told me so much about how well you and Seymour treat him. *Rounds* is what Robert said it would be. I'm glad I was able to see it for myself. Robert has said some nice things about his straight boss too. I'm pleased to make your acquaintance."

"The honor is mine. Have a good time, gentlemen," Chas says.

Two weeks later, Bruce answers the host phone.

"*Rounds*. May I help you?"

"Yes," the desperate woman answers. "I am calling from the pay phone on the corner. Your doorman won't let me in. He claims I am not dressed properly. I explained I am meeting Tennessee Williams there for dinner. He doesn't believe me. He says he is not there. Please help me. This is frustrating, and I'm embarrassed, to say the least."

Bruce, who a half hour ago seated Tennessee himself, made a beeline to the door. Outside, walking toward *Rounds*, is a gray-haired woman. Her clothes are simple and in good taste.

"I'm sorry for the misunderstanding," Bruce explains. My man meant nothing personal. He deals with a lot of people with various stories. Please come in."

"Mr. Williams, here is your guest. I apologize," Bruce mentions. "Frank was downstairs getting change when you entered. He was not aware you were here. The next round of drinks is on me."

"That's okay Bruce," Tennessee said. "Frank makes me feel safe here. Thanks for the help."

A week later, Frank asks Chas to cover the door while he gets more change for the bartenders from downstairs. It's a typical Saturday night.

"Well, well, look at you Richard, all dressed up," Chas greets. "You didn't tell me you were taking me to a fancy joint for dinner tonight."

"You know by now, I spend one week a month sharing your apartment so I can visit my New York clients," Richard mentions. "I need to take them to top straight restaurants, suit-and-tie joints. They can't suspect I'm gay, or I'd love to bring them here."

"Did you fly or drive from Pennsylvania, Rich?" Chas asks.

"I flew. Join me for a drink. Oddly, my client is a Mormon teetotaler," Richard replies. "I couldn't drink alcohol in his presence."

"I never turn down a drink in my bar, Rich, you know that." Chas replies.

Richard owns a company that supplies boxes to cigarette, cigar, candy, cereal and such companies with their logo and all printing complete, ready for the product.

After three weeks at his plant, he spends one week in New York City. Seeing to customers, and *being* a customer, where the boys are. He reimburses Chas for the use of the spare bedroom in Chas' apartment.

Walter is talking with a Major League Baseball umpire, Dave Pallone. He spots Chas and Richard and brings his friend over to introduce him to them.

"Chas, Richard, meet a friend of mine, Dave," Walter says. "Dave, this is Chas and Richard."

"Hi," Dave says.

"Nice to meet you, Dave," Chas greets. Welcome to *Rounds*." Richard and Chas shake Dave's hand.

"Dave is going to be in town for a few weeks while the Mets are home," Walter mentions. "He will get us free seats to the game or games, Chas, Richard. Do you want to go see any?"

"That would be great, but it's got to be a day game." Chas said.

"Not me, Walter, but thanks. I sleep and call customers all day," Richard mentions. "My office never stops calling me when I'm out of town."

Dave is a handsome young man, six feet tall well built, with black hair.

"Dave, you don't fit the profile of most umps," Chas says.

"They are usually much older and some are overweight."

"Myself and a few others broke into the Majors during the baseball strike," Dave said. "I'm enjoying what I do. All my life, I wanted to be in the Majors."

"We wish you success, Dave, and I hope to see more of you." Chas said.

Walter and Chas picked a day, and Dave had tickets waiting for them at the Will-Call window.

"Looks as though we'll have a good day for a ballgame," Walter said.

They're waiting on the Will-Call line to get the tickets Dave left for them at Shea Stadium.

"I came for tickets left in Dave Pallone's name," Chas said

"Enjoy the game," the agent said.

"Sitting off first base is great until the foul balls come," Chas warns. "We better be careful, Walter."

"The manager that Dave has the most arguments with is Pete Rose," Walter recounts. "Dave mentioned he was one of the groups who went against the union when the owners were on strike with the players.

"Dave thinks he is also disliked because he is gay. That is a rough position for Dave. It always was Dave's dream to be a Major League umpire."

"Unfortunately, prejudice is more profound in sports," Chas says. "The macho factor and all that crap that goes with it."

"By the way, doesn't another child start college soon?" Walter asks.

"Funny you should mention that," Chas responds. "I took Dawn to start last week. We and other parents and their kids went through orientation at the University of Delaware. During one of the many rooms we went to, I became emotional listening to a professor's dissertation on child-parent relationships. He went on how the children now leave home to pursue their goal in life. I was forced to go to the hall to dry my eyes. A deep sense of loss came over me as I listened to what he was saying. When orientation was over, I was emotionally drained. Exhausted, I still had three hours to drive home alone after leaving my daughter there to start school."

"That is the price people pay when they love someone… the pain of separation," Walter said.

"Why is it so hot in September?" Chas scoffs. "Here is some money for more beers, Walt, when the guy comes again. I have to get rid of the previous ones I drank. I will be right back."

Chas returns to his seat and is advised of the score.

"You missed a three-run homer by the Reds. We're getting killed," Walter says. "How is your son, Charles, doing in college?"

"He is doing well," Chas says. "Next year he graduates with a BS in hotel and restaurant management. He can work at *Rounds* if he wants."

"What about the youngest—your buddy Christine, how is she doing?" Walter asks.

"Christine will start college next year," Chas laughs. "I hope the bar business holds up so I can get through the college tuitions."

"I think you are blessed with good children, Chas," Walter mentions. "Not having children is what I miss being gay. Many gay people tell me it's the one thing they miss, too."

"Let's get out of here, Walter; we are getting murdered," Chas says. "I'm a poor loser, and 'only mad dogs and Englishmen stay out in the noon day sun.'"

"Good idea; we will beat the traffic back to town," Walter said.

On the drive back, Chas fills Walter in on the latest in his social life.

"I met a woman at Arthur's restaurant recently," Chas mentions. "The singles club meets once a month at a different restaurant. The only problem is, she is Italian descent."

"So what's the problem? *You* are Italian descent," Walter laughs.

"What happens when you try to get a positive pole to touch another positive pole? They repel each other!" Chas says.

"Now, don't be prejudiced. Who knows, you may actually like each other," Walter said.

"I have a date with her tonight," Chas mentions. "She likes French food. I'll take her to *The Balcony* on 50th. The owners come to *Rounds* all the time. I'll return the business."

Later that afternoon, Chas receives a call from Camille, his date for tonight.

"Hi, are we still on for dinner?" Camille asks.

"Absolutely, I'm looking forward to seeing you again," Chas says. "When you come west on 53rd Street, the garage entrance to my building is on the right, just before the canopy to *Rounds*. My apartment is 14-F. Drive safe; see you later."

At 7:30 the doorman calls to tell Chas his guest is on her way up. The bell rings. Chas answers the door.

"I see you found me. Welcome. Come on in," Chas greets.

"Wow! What a view. You can see all of midtown in the mirrored wall without going out on the terrace," Camille said.

"Didn't your mother tell you to avoid men with lots of mirrors in their homes?" Chas quips.

"She warned me about a lot of stuff," Camille jokes. "Mirrors on the ceiling was the big warning. On-the-wall mirrors is okay."

"Not to worry," Chas laughs. "I have enough trouble sleeping, without staring at myself in a ceiling mirror. I do like to stare at women in ceiling mirrors, when I can coerce one into joining me in bed.

"Let me show you around. This is a guest room. I have a customer of *Rounds* staying with me one week a month. He compensates me handsomely from his generous expense account he controls as owner of his company. It cost much less than the hotel he used to stay at. He travels light; his clothes are left here.

197

Are you ready to eat?"

"Yes, I brought my French appetite, as you suggested I do."

They walk the five short blocks down Second Avenue. Chas notices she is as short as Carmen, five-foot-five. Camille has black hair, dark eyes, attractive face, good body, and full breasts.

"Here we are," Chas said.

They enter the restaurant.

"Welcome, please come this way, Chas and lady," Peter greets.

Peter is one of the owners. They sit down and Peter asks if they would like a drink.

"Camille, as I recall, you drink Merlot," Chas says.

"Good memory, Chas," Camille replies.

"The best Merlot from our cellar will be coming up for my special friend and such a beautiful woman," Peter lauds.

"Thanks, Peter," Chas replies.

"What brought you to the singles club that night?" Chas asks. "I didn't see you at previous dinners."

"My girlfriend, whom you met—Ann—is a member," Camille explains. "I recently broke off a long relationship with a married man. I needed to get back to the real world. I don't know how good the real world is. I'm so tired of living a lie. It was more a relationship of convenience for both of us. I have been going for my Masters degree at night for a lot of years. I have no time for marriage and a family. What about you?"

"I'm divorced after seventeen years of marriage," Chas mentions. "I have a boy and girl in college. The girl will be ready for college next year."

After reviewing the menu, Chas asks Camille.

"How is the wine?"

"Fine. Do you know what you want to eat?" Camille asks.

"Yes; if you're ready, let's order." Chas said.

After dinner, they walk toward *Rounds*.

"How would you like to see some of the handsomest men in

the world?" Chas asks.

"Sure, who do I need to know?" Camille laughs.

"Just me. Let's go in this bar," Chas quips.

"Frank, this is Camille," Chas says. "It's Frank's job to keep the undesirables out of my club."

"Pleased to meet you, Camille. Welcome to *Rounds*," Frank greets.

"Good to meet you, Frank," Camille says. "Did I hear you say, 'my club'?"

"Yes, you did. I thought you would have picked up by now—I'm gay?"

Shrewdly, the attractive Camille says, with a Mona Lisa smile, "I did pick it up. I was surprised you own a bar. You strike me more as a hairstylist." Camille laughs.

"You are one tough broad," Chas quips. "I see I can't shit you."

Chas takes her hand and leads the way through the dimly-lighted corridor to the bar area and into the dining room. As luck would have it, Paul sees them and blocks their path.

"Mary, what did I tell you about bringing fag hags to our place?" Paul jokes.

"Haven't I told you, don't call me Mary," Chas laughs. "And never do it when I'm with a straight woman… Mary."

"Camille, this is my dear friend, Paul Spinelli," Chas jokes. "He prays every night that I will come out of the closet so he can have his way with me. I *said* they would be handsome. I forgot to say they are fags, and in Paul's case, a *crazy* faggot."

Paul looks at Camille.

"He's such a brute, that's why we all love him, especially me," Paul teases. "When you get to know him, you and I, girl, will have a talk."

"Come, let's get away from here and sit in the dining room with sane folks," Chas said.

They sit at a table when she asks:

"You *are* straight? I hope."

"Yes, the last time I looked, I was," Chas mentions. "My middle name is *anomaly*. It's a long story how I got here. If you see me again, I'll tell you."

Camille is about to discover what a magnet attractive women are to gay men.

Luciano was the first to come to their table.

"Hi, Chas, what a beautiful woman you're with tonight," Luciano lauds. "May I join you?"

"Of course. Camille, this is Luciano, and behind him is Ralph, who will take our drink order," Chas says.

As Luciano and Camille get into a girls-only discussion, Chas excuses himself. He goes to join Seymour, who was in a pensive mood.

"Allen called from San Juan," Seymour mentions. "His lover, Peter, was murdered in their home in Brooklyn Heights. The maid found the body a few days after he had been killed. The police suspect the house boy, a drug addict. The funeral is day after tomorrow. Peter was such a gentle person… that is so sad. He and Allen were together more than twenty years."

"I will pick you up for the drive to the temple tomorrow," Chas said.

"I see you're with a new date. She is very attractive. What happened to Linda?"

"Linda is still in the picture, on a casual basis," Chas replies. "I don't know how far this will go. I see Paul has joined Luciano and Camille. I'd better get over there before the three women get carried away."

"Paul has invited me to go to see the Chippendales next week," Camille said.

"And how are you going to see a women's-only show, Paul?" Chas asks.

Paul is grinning as he looks at his latest partner in gimmicks, Luciano, who answers for him.

"It's simple, Chas," Luciano says. "I will do the makeup to create Ms. Paulina."

"I don't believe it, Camille," Chas laughs. "You are left alone with two queens for ten minutes, and already you're dating a fag. You were worried about *me*? *You're* the fag hag.

"You're invited too, Chas, but men can only stay for the first half of the show," Camille explains. "The second half is only for women."

"The last place I want to be is in a room full of hysterical woman throwing their phone-numbered panties at young, handsome, well-built gay men," Chas says. "Seeing a male friend of mine who will probably look sexier in drag than you, my dear Camille, will be priceless. No thanks to joining you to the male portion of the show. I do want to see Paulina when she first gets into drag. That mental picture will be indelibly etched in my mind for eternity. The next time he screws up hunting, I will call him *Paulina*."

"You are such a brute, Mary," Paul laughs.

"Camille, it's time to leave this den of perverts," Chas Jokes. "I'll walk you to your car. Girls, I will be back soon. Try to stay out of trouble while I'm gone."

"We look forward to seeing more of you, Camille," Luciano said.

"Yes, me too," Paul says. "We'll talk during the week to set our date to see the boys. I'm so excited to see how I look in drag."

They say goodnight, leave *Rounds*, and walk to the garage.

"Thanks for such a wonderful dinner, and entertainment with your friends," Camille mentions. "You really know how to surprise a girl. Will I see you again?"

"You can count on it," Chas said.

He opens the car door for Camille, plants a kiss on her cheek, and tells her to drive carefully.

They enjoy four dates over four weeks, and there is no attempt by Chas to hit on Camille.

At the end of the fifth date, she is frustrated and confused by Chas' passivity. Before he can pull in front of her door to drop her off for the night, and drive off:

"Park the car and come in," Camille demands.

"Okay we're inside; what's on your mind, my dear," Chas said.

He knows full well what's on her mind.

"Better than tell you, my *dear*, let me show you," Camille quips. "A picture is worth… take off those clothes!"

Her blouse and bra drop to the floor, exposing firm tits and hard nipples. Looking at her as she bends over to remove her panties, her tits hang down. Chas fondles them as they passionately kiss. Once in bed, she gets on top and straddles him. She grabs his cock with one hand and inserts it into her wet pussy. She supports her weight off him with her other arm. Chas watches her tits moving as she moves up and down on his cock.

"Which tit has the chocolate milk?" Chas asks.

"Suck both and find out for yourself, hotshot," Camille teases.

When sex is finished she says, "You had me going there. Most guys want to get in my pants on the first date. I wasn't sure if you are straight. Owning a gay bar—and not coming on to me—had me guessing after the second date."

"That was the general idea, Camille," Chas replies. "I don't like rejection, so I let the woman tell me when she is ready."

"Well, I decided that I wasn't going to take off wet panties and sleep alone again tonight," Camille scolds. "You *prick*. Somehow, I can't picture you being denied anything."

"I guess I'm reacting to when I was a teenager," Chas mentions. "All I got was bare tits under a sweater which stayed on during making out on some broad's living room couch. I'd use my knee to rub the pussy; the hand was not allowed on it. Blue balls would set in after a while. Just as well; I wasn't prepared with condoms. I would have been a teenage father if I had gotten what I wanted then."

"What can I make you for breakfast tomorrow?" Camille asks.

"Breakfast and great pussy—what a great deal this is!" Chas says. "I'll have black coffee and whatever you are having."

"I'm having *you* again while the coffee perks," Camille teases.

They're having breakfast and talking after a good night's sleep... interrupted occasionally by more sex.

"Paul has been after me to go to Atlantic City," Chas mentions. "He feels lucky. You had mentioned on one of our dates that you like to gamble. I said I would ask you, but only if he brings a date, too. One threesome with him is enough for me."

"I love Atlantic City," Camille says, "but what threesome are you referring to?"

"It was nothing to do with sex, only sharing a room, so the cheap fuck could save money," Chas remarks. "Well, thanks for breakfast, and the great sex. I need to get to the city. Bye."

"Call me tonight, and let me know when. Bye," Camille said.

That night at *Rounds*, Chas is listening to the new piano player, Suzan, with Mike.

"She's great, Sunshine, she reminds me of my old aunt Becky," Mike lauds. "She is thin, with graying blonde hair, too. Becky also wore the long, tight satin gowns. As a kid I thought gowns were sleeping attire. I wondered why Becky wore a nightgown out of the bedroom. Suzan's singing style is very fortyish, big-band stuff."

"Ms. Vicente doesn't like her, but then what *does* that creep like," Chas derides. "He is always dressed impeccable, stylish suit and expensive tie.

"He has been coming here since we opened, and never gives me or anyone else a compliment. He will say, the A.C. isn't cold enough, the drinks too small, the food no good, the boys too ugly, etc., etc.

"Floating Couches" Anniversary Party #2

"Back Lounge" Anniversary Party

"I finally said to him, 'Bitch, you only come here to give your mother a break, Mary.' He is the quintessential queen of all queens. Excuse me, Mike; I see Paul. I need to ask him something.

"Hey Mary—I mean Paulina—when are we going to A.C.? Camille is game to go," Chas teases.

"I don't care when we go," Paul responds. "I have to ask Billy-boy when he's off. I had fun being with Camille while I was in drag the other night.

"It was great at Chippendales. I almost came in my panties watching the so-called studs doing their gyrations and tearing off their shirts.

"The women, including Camille, were screaming obscenities. Some threw crumpled paper balls with their phone number on it for them to catch. I wanted to throw my apartment keys, with a note that I was in drag, to one particular blond hunk.

"See, I know those fags would rather have sex with Paul than Paulina or the pussies in the audience. Chas, I couldn't wear those fucking heels. I tried, but it was too much effort. They hurt, too. I wore a nice pair of flats instead.

This weekend should be good to do A.C. for Billy. You can take care of freeing him from work. He works for you."

"I will let her know we're on," Chas says. "I'll catch up with you later, if you don't leave with some trick."

"Michael, it's nice to see you again. How have you been?" Chas greets.

"I stopped by to let you know I took your advice." Michael mentions.

"What advice, Michael?" Chas asks.

"I couldn't decide to accept the programmer position in California," Michael says. "I will have to move out of my parents' house in Brooklyn. Living with my parents has kept me in the closet. Moving away will allow me to be free to be gay.

"It's a big move. I'm thirty-five, and have always lived at

home. I was scared before I spoke to you. You gave me the balls to do it, Chas.

"Thanks for taking an interest in me. *Rounds* and you have been a second home to me. I will miss you both."

"Your moving to San Jose will put you in reach of San Francisco," Chas informs. "I've been considering the idea of doing a *Rounds* operation there. The rancher friend I cowboy for has ranches in northern California, and Nevada. Having a bar in northern California will make it easier for me to play cowboy.

"Doing that is my only recreational passion, other than sex. See, you thought you would be rid of me, but that's not that easy to do. I will miss you, Michael. Only you and a small group of others do I regard as friends whom I enjoy spending time with at *Rounds*."

"As soon as I get settled, you will know how to reach me," Michael said.

"Safe trip," Chas said.

"Chas, Camille is on the phone," Frank says.

"I'll be right there, Frank."

"Hello dear," Chas says.

"Hello," Camille mentions. "You were supposed to call me about going to Atlantic City."

"I know I was," Chas replies. "First I had to find your girl-friend, Paulina. Then I had to listen to how the two of you carried on so disgracefully at the sight of male flesh. Absolutely disgusting behavior, and I thought men acted like animals. Women are a hundred times more obscene than men. I already know I can count on Paul to embarrass me, whether he's in drag or not. It's you I am concerned with now. What is a clean cut guy like myself to do? Oh, what to do, what to do?"

"Oh! Stop the shit! Your friend is a real trip," Camille laughs. "He looked better than me as a woman. I didn't stop laughing the whole time we were together."

"Paul is dating my bartender, Billy," Chas advises. "We

should take your car. It's big enough for four people. Will your bomb survive the trip?"

"Don't knock it, it's big and old. That's what turns me on," Camille laughs. "Just like you, big guy"

"I got to go, Camille. Herb Fisher and some people came in. Bye."

"Chas, where is Seymour. We brought him a gift," Herb greets. "This is my corporate financial officer, Josh, and you've met my secretary, Lisa."

"Hi Josh, Lisa; good to see you again. Come this way; will sit with Seymour," Chas says.

"Seymour, a female admirer has brought you a gift," Lisa greets.

"This is Josh, Seymour. He keeps the firm out of financial trouble," Herb said.

"It's a pleasure to make your acquaintance, Seymour," Josh greets.

"What are you people drinking?" Brian asks.

"Nothing, thank you," Herb mentions. "Seymour, Lisa remembered the last time you two met. She complimented the scarf you had on. You said she could buy you one. So she took your kidding to heart. Silly girl; I hope you like it."

The naïve, proud Lisa looks on.

"It's beautiful, Lisa," Seymour lauds. "I will think of you each time I wear it."

Seymour kisses Lisa on the cheek, causing her to blush like a six-year-old.

"We were in the neighborhood, taking clients to dinner, and dropped by," Herb mentions. "Business looks good. Keep up the good work. Bye."

Seymour and Chas talk business when they are alone.

"Richard Knox was telling me he is interested in being partners in San Francisco," Seymour informs. "Good, you'll need a working partner out there. We know this business is too much for one operator. You will have me here, and we'll have Richard there full-time when you're here at *Rounds*. All our bases will be covered."

10

It's April, 1985 and the two partners are having a drink at their crowded bar at *Rounds*.

"It's our sixth anniversary. Do you believe how fast the time is traveling?" Chas mentions. "My son Charles graduates college this June and my baby, Christine, just started college. He will be here to help you, Seymour, when I'm in San Francisco."

"It's two years since we buried Ken and still no cure in sight for AIDS," Seymour laments. "Slowly but surely, our original customers are disappearing because of it. When AIDS started it was called the young gay man's cancer. Not true, all age groups are affected now."

The next morning Chas calls Paul at home.

"Camille should be here at eleven, we're finally going to take that trip to Atlantic City that we talked about way back when. You two ready?"

"I just have to do my hair," Paul replies.

"So, are you telling me to come at 1 PM? Two hours should be enough time for that vanity style of yours," Chas jokes.

"Just ring my bell, wise guy, when you're downstairs," Paul says. "We'll come right down."

Camille picks the three men up. As soon as she gets on the turnpike for the two-and-a-half-hour drive, the men fall asleep.

When they arrive in Atlantic City, Camille wakes Chas and Billy, who didn't get much sleep the night before working. Paul partied most of the night.

"We are here," Camille shouts. "Wake up, it's time for gambling and fun. We can take the strollers that are pushed by bicycle drivers along the boardwalk to get to *The Golden Nugget* from here. There are two drivers waiting for customers. Let's go grab them. We'll take this one; Paul, you and Billy take that one."

"Okay," Chas replies. "What's the cost?"

"Ten dollars," His driver says.

"I'll give you twenty plus the ten," Chas whispers. "You have to beat my friends in the other stroller to the hotel."

"You got a deal," his driver says.

Then he pedals as fast as he can while avoiding the pedestrians that are desperately getting out of the way of both competing strollers. The other driver receives orders to follow the competition from Paul.

Looking over his shoulder at Paul, Chas goads Paul to a race.

"Hey, Mary, I have a twenty-dollar bill that says I get there first," Chas teases.

"Camille. open your eyes, you're missing all the fun," Chas laughs. "Watch out, kid! They're gaining on us! Faster, *faster!*"

"Paul is cheating. He is out of the stroller, running alongside it," Camille laughs.

"Foul. Mary, you're cheating; automatic forfeit," Chas scolds.

"No way, the rules didn't specify two people in a stroller," Paul laughs.

"Oh shit!" Chas' driver said.

The driver stops abruptly for a police officer with his arm extended and an angry look on his face.

"What are you jerks doing?" The officer scolds.

"It's my fault, officer; we were just having some fun," Chas says.

"Fun? You can get someone injured, and the drivers would lose their jobs, to say the least," the officer advises. "You, driver, I can give a speeding ticket to, and a citation for public endangerment. Don't you drivers ever let me see you doing this again! Go!"

At the hotel entrance we get out of the strollers.

"Here's thirty kid, we would've won the race," Chas lauds. "Thanks. It was fun, even though my honey was holding on for dear life."

"Oh, I was not," Camille laughs. "I was keeping from being knocked around. I was sure we would hit someone or something, so I closed my eyes."

"Paul, Camille and I play craps," Chas advises. "What do you and Billy play?"

"We play mostly the slots and a little flirting and cruising." Paul laughs.

"Not in my presence," Billy warns. "You're not going to cruise someone else, Mary. Get real."

"We need a time and place to meet up since we are going separate ways," Camille says. "Let's meet at that bar over there. It has comfortable lounge chairs."

"Two hours should do it," Chas says. "Can you two sex-fiends stay out of trouble that long?"

"Stop sounding like my mother," Paul jokes. "We came to have some fun. This is not *Rounds*."

"Just make sure both of you don't get caught by Security occupying a toilet stall," Chas warns. "This place has cameras everywhere. I don't want to have my service bartender not make work tomorrow because he's in jail."

"Are we going to gamble or listen to a lecture?" Camille said.

Each pair goes their own way.

"Boy, Chas is such a party pooper," Paul laughs. "Let find the men's room; I need you to do me. Don't worry, that is the only place where there are no cameras."

"Always thinking of yourself," Billy moans. "You do me, too."

"Sounds good," Paul confirms. "I'm excited. Here it is, let's check it out."

They go in and no one is in there; they go to the last stall. Billy sits on the toilet and Paul stands, bent over slightly, takes out his cock and Billy sucks it. Paul comes. They reverse positions and Paul sucks Billy. Both are relieved of the pain of sperm that had built up in their balls, known as "blue balls." They leave the stall just before three men come in to use the urinals. They can relax, now; they play the slots and flirt with the patrons and cocktail waitress who thinks they are handsome straight guys.

When they finish at the craps table, Camille and Chas sit in the lounge waiting for Paul and Billy as they have coffee.

"We made four-hundred-fifty dollars," Chas mentions. "It's enough to pay for the trip and dinner for the four of us."

"That is because you listened to me," Camille brags. "You have to leave the table while the dice are hot and you're ahead. It's hard to walk away when you're winning—greed takes over, and then you lose."

Paul and Bill join them.

"We did great. How did you guys do?" Paul said.

"We lost. That means you buy lunch, Paul," Chas jokes. "The winner always buys."

"Okay. No problem. I saw a McDonald's as we drove in to town," Paul teases.

"I was just testing you," Chas laughs. "We won too. I will treat all to lunch. Paul you can relax now."

After a pleasant time, they leave the hotel and Chas drives back home.

The following June, Charles graduates from Johnson and Wales University. Mari and his two daughters attend the ceremony with Chas.

Figuring he would follow in his father's footsteps, Charles receives a BS degree in restaurant /hotel management.

Watching the proceedings, Chas whispers to Mari:

"Watching Charles today has made me emotional," Chas says. "I have had a lump in my throat all morning. I feel as though my son is no longer my boy. Now he is his own man. The father-boy relationship is gone forever. I feel as if I am going to cry. I need to find a water fountain. Excuse me."

"What is wrong with Dad?" Christine asks.

"Your father is very proud of your brother's accomplishments," Mari mentions. "The emotional feeling is being contained in his body. Men try to hide emotion, seldom crying, subjecting their body to a lot of stress as feelings are suppressed. He'll be okay, don't worry; he only needs to drink some water."

After the ceremony the whole family takes pictures with the beaming, happy graduate.

Chas hugged his son.

"Good work, Son," Chas lauds. "I am very proud of you."

"Thanks, Dad, for all your support and help. I appreciate it a lot," Charles says.

The lunch is a welcome relief. Chas doesn't have to drive the three women to New Jersey. Dawn will handle the trip home, and drop Chas in Manhattan. The double scotch and food settles his head and stomach. The stress is over.

The following month, Chas and Charles are talking.

"Are you and Tracy all settled in your apartment in Fort Lee?" Chas said.

"We are all settled and ready to start working," Charles responds. "Tracy is with a travel agent, right in town, a few blocks from the apartment. She starts tomorrow. I'm ready to start tomorrow as well, Dad."

"Great," Chas replies. "Aunt Marie and I will see you in the morning and show you the ropes. Now the real education begins,

Son."

Bright and early the next morning, Charles began learning the business from his aunt.

A few nights later, Walter and Chas were having a drink at *Rounds*.

"Seymour has been acting strange, don't you agree?" Walter said.

"Absolutely," Chas affirms. "He knows better than to take the mike and try to sing. He clears the room when he does that. Let me get him off, I'll be back."

Chas put his arm around Seymour, takes the mike, and hands it to the piano player.

"Come, Seymour," Chas says. "The cook has a problem in the kitchen."

Once they are in the kitchen away from the customers:

"Seymour, we talked about this sort of behavior," Chas scolds. "Are you on a quest to destroy this business, as well as *Circles?*"

Chas is holding Seymour by the arm.

"You're drunk, Seymour. Let's get you to a cab," Chas demands. "We can go out the kitchen door. No one will see us."

"Don't tell me what to do," Seymour grumbles. "I taught you this business."

As he resists Chas' efforts to take him outside, Seymour grabs a small frying pan from the rack over the stove and hits Chas in the head. When Chas regains consciousness, Chan, the cook, helps him to his feet. Chan holds a cloth napkin to Chas' head to control the bleeding. Bruce, with the aid of Frank, are forcing an angry Seymour into a cab.

"Don't worry you didn't kill him. He's just knocked out," Bruce explains. "Go home. We'll call you later."

Chan says as he helps Chas to his feet:

"Hold towel on head. You need go to hospital."

Walter escorts Chas out the kitchen door, without realizing

Chan is behind him. Not knowing Walter, Chan keeps holding onto the cleaver. He would use it to protect Chas from further attacks. As Walter, Chan and Chas reach the curb to hail a cab, a cruising squad car happens by.

"Drop the axe, or we will shoot!" the police said.

The police officer exits the patrol car, with his hand on his revolver.

Bruce, with both arms raised, runs between the police and Chan.

"Don't shoot, don't shoot," Bruce implores. "It is not what it appears. He's our cook. He is helping us get our boss to the hospital."

"Okay. Tell him to go back in the kitchen. We'll take it from here," the officer said.

"It is okay. Chan," Bruce says. "Chas will be fine. Let's go back to work."

"Do you want to file a complaint against someone, sir?" the officer asked Chas.

"No," Chas replies. "I hit my head on a sharp corner of a steel shelf."

"Okay, whatever you say sir," the officer said.

"Would you drop us off at the hospital?" Walter says.

"Sure, get in," the officer says.

Chas gets his head stitched at the emergency room.

"You should have Camille wake you every two hours tonight to make sure you don't have a concussion," Walter said.

"No way," Chas remarks. "I'd rather have a concussion than be awakened every two hours. She's sleeping. I will sneak in and change my jacket and shirt. They're covered with blood. I'll be back to work. I need to talk to Seymour, and get this situation resolved. Thanks for hanging with me. I'll see you in *Rounds* as soon as I change. We need some drinks, Walter."

"I still wish you'd do what I said. A concussion is serious stuff," Walter affirms. "I'll see you when you come back."

Walter and Chas are having drinks when Seymour returns

Chas' call. Chas is handed the phone by Bruce.

"I'm so sorry for what I did," Seymour cries. "Are you alright?"

"I have a thick skull, my mother used to tell me," Chas replies. "How are *you*, is my big concern right now."

"Promise me you won't tell a soul?" Seymour laments.

"I promise," Chas says.

"I'm sick and so is George," Seymour cries. "It is driving me crazy. My drug doctor has both of us on anti-depression pills, but they haven't taken effect yet."

Chas is afraid to ask.

"Sick... with what?"

"AIDS," Seymour cries. "You can't tell anyone."

"Shit! Seymour, not you, too," Chas laments. "Ah, *fuck* me, what a fucking life! All this death—I promise I won't say a word. Stay home until you feel better mentally. I will stop by to see you tomorrow. Whatever you need, let me know. Our friendship is still intact. Don't worry, get some rest now."

"You know I would never hurt you," Seymour says. "I'm not myself. I never had a partner I trust like you before and a truly good friend."

"I know," Chas replies. "Get some rest, please."

Bruce returns to the host's station. Chas is temporarily in shock. Walter senses something is wrong with Chas.

"Sit down here let me help you," Walter mentions. "Take your drink and just relax. If you need me, I'm at the bar."

Walter leaves to give his friend privacy.

The next afternoon, after visiting Seymour, Chas has a talk with Charles.

"I will be spending a couple weeks a month in San Francisco, looking for a bar to buy," Chas explains. "Seymour, Richard, and I will be partners.

"Seymour will work part-time at night and be available to you by phone full-time. Bruce will be full-time. We hired a smart new black doorman, Tony Chambers. You and he will get along fine. He has a great personality, and the most class anydoor man has ever had.

"When I'm out of town, I'd like you to cover nights. That's where the owner needs to be. Dealing with the customers and making sure the help performs properly is most important.

"We will talk daily. I'm only a phone call away. Do you think you can handle that, Son?"

"No problem, Dad, don't worry about a thing," Charles mentions. "On a personal note, Tracy and I were talking last night about setting a date to marry, this coming spring. We have been dating since we met, the week we started at college, four years ago."

"That's great, Son. You two have a lot in common. Congratulations."

"What do you think of Tracy doing the day stuff, Dad?"

"Is she not happy with the travel agency work?" Chas asks.

"Not really," Charles says.

"Fine," Chas responds. "Bring her on-board. She'll be perfect handling the purveyors, and for the bookkeeping."

Charles and Tracy handle *Rounds* in an exemplary manor. Chas, Seymour, the customers, and the staff are happy with them. The following March, Camille and Chas are in the apartment in San Francisco. Chas brings the mail to Camille, who immediately opens the invitation envelope.

"We are invited to a wedding, Chas," Camille lauds. "Here is the invitation they sent us. Charles and Tracy are going to do it legally starting in May. Before you know it, your son and Tracy will make you a grandpa."

"That is just like a woman—they are not married yet and you have her giving birth." Chas replies.

"Let's get something straight right now," Camille warns. "I will not be called Grandma under any circumstances, no matter what we may do in the future. With the crazy hours they work, she made sure they found time to conceive."

"You're so vain, Grandma," Chas teases. "They have done a great job at *Rounds*, affording us time to spend in San Francisco. I'm very proud of the man my son has become."

"Will we be in New York, so we can go to the St. Patrick's parade?" Camille says. "I love to go to Fifth Avenue in early spring and watch it."

"St. Patrick's Day is in the middle of March. Maybe we'll be there. It's not *we*. I don't do parades or windows," Chas quips. "I have to deal with drunks all year. I'm not traveling to see drunks get rowdy and vomit in the streets."

At *Rounds*, after returning to New York, Chas is greeted by Tony at the door.

"Welcome, Chas. How was California?" Tony greets.

"You can't beat San Francisco," Chas mentions. "They get no snow, but lots of rain, and it was their rainy season. Ten miles north of the city, it's warm, sunny weather. We visited with friends who retired there. See you later; it's cocktail time."

At the bar is Dr. Gonzales.

"Hi, Doc; it's good to see you," Chas greets.

"Same here. Did you find a place yet?" Eduardo said.

"We are making progress," Chas mentions. "I have my broker concentrating in the Castro district. It's where the greatest numbers of gays live, and go barhopping. It is similar to Greenwich Village."

In the dining room, he receives a hug from Bruce.

"Good to see you kid," Bruce greets. "It's another busy night at *Rounds*. You can see your table is taken by a gentleman with a beard. I can't place where I've seen him. The beard is concealing his identity. Sit at number two and I'll bring a drink to you."

"Thanks," Chas said.

He recognized the celebrity, even with his beard. Chas plays a game of cat and mouse to amuse himself.

"Hello George," Chas quips. "Why the beard? Are you trying out for part in '*Fiddler on the Roof*'?"

"No, *Fiddler* is not in production, you know that," George remarks. "My friends are at the piano. They came to hear Rick. They are his friends."

"Rick is a good performer," Chas informs. "Lots of people come to put money in his jar. You know, like Billy Joel sings in *Piano Man*. Too bad you didn't bring your banjo; I caught your performance on the Carson show. You entertained me, and the live audience along with Johnny and Ed. If you played here, I'd provide you your own tip jar. It would fill up fast, Mr. Se… George."

"Thanks, you're very kind, but the banjo is just a hobby," George says.

"Bruce, get George a drink, please—on me. Thanks for talking with me, George. Excuse me; I see my partner."

"Thank you, I enjoyed the conversation and the drink," George says. "You were complimentary. It was nice hearing what you said."

Chas finds Seymour in the lounge, engaged in a discussion with John, the realtor.

"I was wondering where I would find you," Chas greets. "I'm glad to see you in such good company, Mary."

"The cowboy returns from the west. Find a store yet?" Seymour said.

"Not yet. Hello, John," Chas mentions. "Castro is a hot area; owners know it.

"If we approach an owner, the price goes out of range. We would do the same if *Rounds* is approached, without us putting it up for sale. Correct?

"I have a hungry realtor beating the brush for us. We need to be patient."

"I miss schmoozing with Marie, but Tracy is doing as good a job," Seymour mumbles. "They call me only when they don't know how to solve a situation. Charles is so nice to me—not like his father, the brute."

"Seymour was telling me, you two are looking for investors for California?" John says.

"Seymour is always looking for investors. It's his game, an old habit that I can't break him of," Chas replies. "We will keep you in mind if we do take non-operating partners in, John."

* * *

The weather for the wedding of Charles and Tracy, in the church Tracy had been baptized in, is perfect. Sam, Irma, Camille, and Chas are outside the church, after the ceremony.

"Look how Dawn and Christine have grown into such beautiful young women," Sam lauds. "It seems as if it was yesterday, when Charles was in high school and worked for me during the summer recess, while the girls were in camp."

"Thanks for coming up here," Chas lauds. "You and Irma are family to me. Camille and I will be sitting with you, Larry, and Florence at the reception. Mari has her family to sit with.

Being divorced makes me feel a little uncomfortable at family occasions."

"Get used to it," Irma advises. "Chas, this is only the beginning. Hopefully Mari will accept that you are no longer her husband, but you will always be the Father of her children."

While the kids are on their honeymoon, Chas covers the operation at *Rounds*.

The following Monday afternoon, Seymour calls Chas.

"How was the wedding?" Seymour says.

"It went off as planned, a little uncomfortable for Camille," Chas replies.

"Are you and Camille available to join George and me for dinner tonight?" Seymour mentions. "We are going to *Mr. Chow's*. You mentioned that Camille took cooking classes in Chinese food. She would love the food there, she being a gourmet."

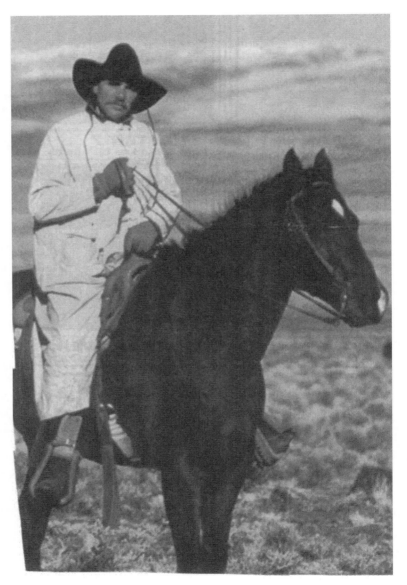

Chas "Drover" on cattle drive

View from "Drag position"

"Sure," Chas replies. "We don't have anything planned. We'll see you at eight?"

"Eight it is," Seymour says.

At seven that night, Chas goes back to *Rounds* to wait for Camille.

"Tony, didn't I see you at a wedding recently?" Chas teases.

"You sure did. Senior, junior and Tracy looked very happy," Tony says. "Paul is looking for you."

Chas finds Paul at his favorite spot—the meat rack.

"Chas, I just got a great deal on a trip to Egypt. You have to come too," Paul exclaims. "We can ride Arabian horses in the desert sand. Ride camels. Climb the pyramids. I always wanted to go to where I'll spend my next life."

"I'd love to," Chas replies. "Paul, I know I would enjoy every crazy minute with you. I just have too much on my plate right now. When are you going. This is sudden, isn't it?"

"Next week," Paul mentions. "You know that old queen, Sidney, who has a travel agency? She got us a great deal. It's only good if we go now. We're going together. She has the hots for me, but he knows it's a lost cause. I like them young and good-looking, like me, Mary."

Paul is wearing his usual grin as he speaks.

"You will have a great time, Paul; you always do, no matter who you're with or where you are," Chas jokes. "Bring me back a pinch of sand and try to stay out of trouble. Some people like sex with anyone they can get their cock into. Living in the desert with no women and just animals, your little tight ass is going to be a big temptation for them. Bring plenty of lubricated condoms for them to use with you."

"Don't worry about me, Mary," Paul laughs. "I am particular who I spread my cheeks for. For starters, first I see the money, and then they get the honey."

"Well, I may not see you before you go, so here is a hug," Chas lauds. "Join me in a toast to your successful trip."

Their glasses touched.

"Have a safe and enjoyable time, Paul."

Camille arrives at the bar.

"Hi, Paul; hi, dear," Camille greets.

"We have been invited to dinner with Seymour and George at an exceptional Chinese restaurant," Chas remarks. "You, being schooled in cooking Chinese, will find this place exceptional. Is it okay with you? Paul, you may join us if you like."

"Great, I heard about that restaurant from my cooking teacher," Camille said.

"I'll pass," Paul mentions. "Seymour and I don't see eye-to-eye, and I'm not crazy for expensive Chinese food."

When Chas and Camille get to *Mr. Chow*'s, Seymour and George are seated.

"George, this is Camille," Chas greets. "Camille, this is George, and you know Seymour, Camille."

"Glad you could make it, Camille," Seymour says. "With your background in Chinese cooking, you will appreciate this food."

"Bruce tells me you hired a new piano player, Seymour," Chas mentions. "We are going back after dinner to see her perform."

"Her name is Berry Blair," Seymour mutters. "She's been around the block a few times, and the crowd loves her street style. Let me know what you think."

After dinner, Camille and Chas go to *Rounds*. At the piano is John, the realtor.

"You're spending all your real-estate commissions here; thank you," Chas jokes. "How is she?"

"Hey, Chas, Camille," John lauds. "Boy, this one I like the best of all the ones you have had."

"Berry, this is the other half of *Rounds*," John says. "The straight one: Chas."

"I'm pleased to make your acquaintance," Berry responds.

"Good luck Berry; good to have you aboard," Chas greets.

"How did you like the food at *Mr. Chow*'s, Camille?" Bruce asked.

"Very good, but I can do better," Camille laughs.

"Edwin, this is Chas and Camille," Bruce mentions. "Chas this is a new waiter/host I hired. He has a lot of experience. He is originally from Brussels. Now we will add a little continental flair to our service, thanks to Edwin."

"Thanks for the introduction, Bruce," Edwin says. "May I get drinks for you, Chas?"

"Yes, please, a rusty nail and a Merlot. Thanks," Chas mentions. "Looks like you picked a winner to replace you when we get a San Francisco joint, Bruce.

"Junior will be back from his honeymoon next week. He will take my place here until I return, then he goes back to the day shift.

"My rancher friend, Bob, has asked me to help push his herd of fifteen-hundred beeves from Ravendale, California to Gerlach, Nevada. It is a six-day drive on horseback.

"You know I said yes—I love doing that. I probably was a cowboy in my past life, Paul says. After the drive, I will spend time with my realtor to see what's available for our bar.

"Bruce, we don't allow hats to be worn in here, so who is the dude with the straw cowboy hat, at the meat rack? Tony would not allow it unless he is special."

"That is Ebare," Bruce answers. "He does Liz Taylor's hair and other famous people in Los Angeles. He is special in our patron's eyes. The hat is his signature; he always wears it. Tony makes an exception for the famous."

"See ya, Bruce," Chas informs. "I'm going to wear *my* hat, where real cowboys wear their cowboy hats, soon, in a rustic old western mansion."

Camille and Chas leave *Rounds* and go to the apartment.

"Are you really going on a cattle drive—or to gamble, drink

and chase hookers in Reno Nevada?" Camille quips.

"Who put that crazy idea in your head?" Chas replies.

"The travel agent called, and left a message for you to call him," Camille mentions. "Something about not getting you a direct flight to Reno, as you requested."

"So that's it," Chas teases. "Reno is the closest airport to the ranch, and I will still have a ninety-mile drive north after I land in Reno. Why don't you come with me and see for yourself, Camille?"

"I'm not crazy," Camille exclaims. "You expect me to sleep on the ground, in a tent in a sleeping bag.

"Relieve myself out in the open, behind a bush. No showers, only two changes of clothes. Sit in the saddle for ten hours a day, with only a short lunch break consisting of an orange and a ham sandwich.

"Breakfast is at 4 AM. Then get hot food served in a metal dish I balance on my lap while sitting on a bale of straw to eat it."

"Well, it's the price you have to pay if you don't trust me, Camille," Chas teases. "Besides, why would I chase hookers when you satisfy me so well? Come to bed and show me what I mean."

The next week, Chas is happy to see his son back at work.

"I hope you guys had a good time, on your honeymoon, Son," Chas greets. "Were the accommodations what you expected?"

"It was great, Dad," Charles replies. "All the years we dated in college, we never took such a nice trip. We couldn't afford to. Now we can—we both work, and make a good living, thanks to you."

"You deserve it," Chas lauds. "You guys worked hard to get here. I'm flying out tomorrow. One and a half weeks pushing beeves, and two weeks looking for a bar. I'll call every chance I can. Take care of yourself, Son."

Tony Chambers, Kelly, Tracy, and Charles Jr. New Years Eve, 1988.

The flight to Reno took five hours and two double scotches on the rocks. When he landed, it was 3 PM west coast time. Chas picks his luggage full of cowboy gear at the carousel and heads for the rental car pickup area.

He has an hour-and-a-half ride north on US 395, an old one-lane highway. He was smart to grab a nap on the plane. Fighting the boredom on the high, lonely desert road is difficult enough completely sober. As he drives, he admires the terrain, with all the different fauna. He recalls a time he rode point on a drive, in this part of the desert. He learned to avoid long, narrow sections of green willows about six feet in height; they grow along narrow creeks with little water in them. Getting the beeves through is no problem, but horse and most riders have a tough time getting through. His job as the point rider was to lead the herd around these obstructions. He's enjoying daydreaming during the dull ride.

Chas pulls into a crowded parking area at the *Spanish Springs Ranch* banquet hall and goes inside. He wonders why so many cars are here; usually a few pickups at most are there. The main room is thirty-feet high, fifty-feet wide, by one-hundred-feet long. Huge windows let the desert colors in with all their majesty. Large paintings of the old west with bucking broncos, and wild steers resisting three ropes attached to three struggling ponies and their exhausted riders are a few of the paintings which adorn the stone walls.

The wood plank floor accentuates the sound of boot heels walking on it. The two main fireplaces could each accommodate a six-foot man standing upright. Plush leather furniture, coffee tables, and end tables with expensive crystal lamps cater to the guests' comfort. The massive oak dining table sits twenty-four people. Along the solid stone wall is an authentic hundred-year-old refurbished saloon bar with a matching back-bar filled with any liquor a guest could want. He feels good to be back.

As soon as he sees Chas enter the huge guest room, Bob

Roby says to the group:

"Here is the man. You thought I was joking about my New York City top hand," Bob lauds.

Chas is stunned.

"What's going on," Chas says. "Who are all these people?"

"We decided to promote the ranch for guests," Bob explains. "My late son, Bo, wanted it that way. Bo was why I got into ranching a few years ago. Sadly, he was killed, as you know, in a car accident.

"The ad we took in *The Wall Street Journal* paid off. These twelve men and woman, from cities all over the country, are paying seven-hundred-fifty dollars so they can experience a real cattle drive. I told them you've come out here for years to help push my beeves.

"You speak city language that they can understand. My regular hands don't get their point across too well to city folks."

"Folks," Chas greets. "It will be my pleasure to teach you what I know."

"I didn't intend to surprise you, Chas," Bob remarks. "This is Phil, my new P.R. man, who handled the whole thing. I'm too busy with my modular-home business. He takes care of the guests' regular needs here at the ranch."

"Pleased to meet you, Phil. Whatever you need of me, just ask me," Chas said.

Chas looks at the wannabe cowboy guests as Phil talks.

There were two gray-haired women—one a school teacher, the other a surgical nurse. One woman with black hair is an executive. The other younger woman is a skinny blonde attorney. The eight men are mostly middle-aged. By their attire, Chas figures they all have ridden before. Whether they could handle ten hours of tough terrain on a horse, time will tell.

"Thanks, Bob assures me you'd help, Chas. For start, these people are pleasure riders. I warned them this is a working cattle ranch, not a dude ranch."

They understand it will be long hours in the saddle. What I'd like you to do is draw a diagram on the board in the lounge after dinner, indicating the various positions drovers have to maintain when moving a herd. You can imagine the disaster if the herd is not controlled because they don't keep their positions."

"I'll make drovers out of them by drive's end, Phil," Chas says.

After dinner, Chas stands up and addresses the crowd.

"I'd like you all to join me in thanking the cook and staff for a great meal," Chas lauds.

The clapping is unanimous.

"There are a few simple customs we follow in buckaroo country, when in camp on the trail," Chas mentions. "One: always thank the cook. Two: bring dirty dish, cup and silverware to the wash tub. Three: horses are not permitted in the camp area. Four: don't run a horse unnecessarily. Finally: avoid vulgar language and excessive alcohol.

"The simplest way to describe what we will attempt to do is what I will draw on the board.

"A diagram will make it clear.

"This three-sided box is filled with circles; these represent cattle.

"On the left and right side of the box are the letters F, three on each side, which represents riders on horses. These are the flank riders who keep the cattle contained on each side.

"The rear of the box has four Ds. These are the drag riders who keep the cattle motivated to move forward.

"In front of the flank riders, on each side, is an S for two swing riders. They are far enough in front so they can guide the flank riders to move left or right. The swing riders follow the point man, P, or trail boss, who is the navigator, and determines the path the herd will take.

"Cattle that break out of the box are guided back by a flank rider. Flank riders need to go into whatever brush the cattle get into, and push them out.

"The last and most helpful note I can give you is, cattle are afraid of a rider on horseback. They will always point their butt toward the rider. So, get behind a cow to move it where you want it to go.

"That's it. I'll answer any questions at the bar. These long talks require a drink of scotch to wet my parched throat. Thanks for your attention, and enjoy the drive."

At the bar, Chas is greeted by most of the guests, who ask questions, which he answers.

Early the next morning, the cook shouts, "*Roll out,*" as Chas drinks his coffee with some of the hands. He helps rouse the guests. He tells the guests what they need to do.

"After breakfast, folks, bring your packed gear and leave it on the porch," Chas explains. "The hands will load it on the wagon. In the barn, you will be given a horse, fitted to you, along with a saddle and headstall. When you're in the saddle, ride to the herd and go to a drover. He will assign you a position. If anyone does not want a position now, you may ride alongside and enjoy the ride and scenery. The drovers and the rest of us will control the herd."

All the guests are ready, and anxiously waiting to hear those famous words… with everyone in place, the trail boss holds his hat high and shouts, "*Get 'em up! Move 'em out!*" Twelve excited guests, paid hands, and Chas, whistle, slap their chaps and shout, "*Hi Ya! Get! Get!*" The reluctant cows, calves and steers raise a huge cloud of dust from the high desert floor, as they begin the sixty-mile trek to Nevada.

An hour into the drive, Vinton pulls alongside Chas.

"Hi buddy," Vinton greets. "I missed you at breakfast. Tina needed my help with Christopher this morning. I wanted to join you so we could catch up on what's been going on."

"Good to see you, Vinton," Chas greets. "Yeah, the first morning is the craziest—especially with guests dumped on me at the last minute."

"I'll see you later. I'm riding swing. Keep the dudes in order, and show them what I taught you, *pardner*," Vinton says.

Most of the guests did well. Occasionally, one would ask Chas, "How much further is it to our first break?" or, "How much longer will it be 'til we are over those mountains?"

"Well, let's see," Chas teases, "do you want me to give the answer in cowboy distance and cowboy time? It's shorter in cowboy measurement than real measurement."

"Real time and real distance," they say.

"Out here we only speak cowboy," Chas jokes. "Because I like you, I'll tell you in real time and distance."

After a while, the guests knew better than to ask. The panorama on the trip is breathtaking. The weather changes by the hour on some days. Calm turns to wind, wind turns to snow, and snow turned to rain; rain ends and the sun shows bright. The terrain goes from flat to rocky and hilly. Cold mornings turn into hot afternoons.

The guests perform well at being Drovers; the older woman gets maternal when a calf can't keep up with its mother.

"Oh, poor thing. We are going too fast—we should slow down, Chas," Phyllis said.

"Not to worry," Chas assures. "When we stop, the little one will find the right cow and they will 'mother up'."

Six and a half days later the fifteen-hundred beeves settle in the pasture adjacent to *Soldier Meadow Ranch*, outside of Gerlach, Nevada.

"After the horses are cared for, let's get cleaned up, Vinton. I'm buying drinks, with ice this time—neat is not for me," Chas says.

"Tina will join us tonight for dinner," Vinton mentions. "Tomorrow she'll drive us back to *Spanish Springs*. Too bad you can't stay with us awhile, but business is business, I guess."

"We'll see what happens when I get to San Francisco, and meet the realtor," Chas mentions. "Maybe I can stay awhile.

While I'm out here, I'd love to spend time working cattle with you. We're done with the horses. I am going up to the house for a shower, shave and clean clothes. I'll wait for you and Tina in the lounge. I can almost taste that drink—don't take too long, pal."

The next day, Tina drives them back to *Spanish Springs*.

"It was so nice to see you again, Chas," Tina says. "Please come see us soon."

"I promise. Take care now. Bye."

At the ranch Chas gets in his rental car and drives to San Francisco.

* * *

In the apartment that night, he calls Camille.

"I'm back in the San Francisco. How are you?" Chas greets.

"Fine. I miss you. How was the drive?" Camille asks.

"Okay, except for babysitting a bunch of dudes that Bob sprung on us," Chas remarks. "Dave hasn't come up with a store yet so I have a seat on the 8 AM to Newark tomorrow morning. I'll see you. I want to call Charles to hear how he's making out. Bye."

"Charles, it's Dad, how's it going?" Chas asks.

"Good, Dad. Business is good, and everyone is doing their job," Chas says. "Stanley called last night with bad news. Denis died of AIDS; I guess you knew he was sick.

"Allen is hospitalized; he has little time to live. Stanley left numbers of family members of both men you can call if you want to send condolences."

"I was afraid this day was coming when I would get these calls," Chas moans." I'm not in a frame of mind to check out if anything is available, bar-wise, and Dave hasn't come up with anything. I will see you tomorrow night. Take care, Charles."

ROUNDS

RESTAURANT • PIANO BAR

Cordially Invites You
to our
"8th" Anniversary Party
Tuesday, April 21st, 1987
Free
Buffet • Champagne
6-8 p.m. • Invitation Only
Champagne Toast at Midnight
Entertainment

Proper Attire Please   *303 E. 53rd Street*
Telephone: (212) 593-0807   *New York, N.Y. 10022*

The following evening, Tony sees the car service pull in front, and the trunk pop open. He helps Chas, with his bag full of western apparel.

"Welcome home, cowboy," Tony greets.

Then he hugged Chas.

"Thanks, Tony, it's good to be back," Chas mentions. "Camille is working late tonight, so I figured I'd eat in my favorite restaurant."

After sharing pleasantries with the help, Bruce, and a few customers, Chas has a quick meal and leaves. He isn't interested in socializing. Tomorrow he will make a few calls to his dear friend's surviving family.

That morning in the apartment, Chas is up early enough to have coffee with Camille before she goes to work.

"I got bad news last night," Chas remarks. "One of my dear friends died of AIDS and one is close to dying from the same killer. I will be making plans today to go to the funeral. You need not join me. I know this is your busiest time at work."

"Oh, honey, that is so terrible," Camille laments. "I feel sorry for you. Is there anything I can do to help you?"

"Thanks, Camille, but this is a private sorrow that I have to handle alone," Chas replies. "It's kind of you to offer. I don't know my schedule. When I do, you will know, sweetie. Have a good day, and don't worry about me. Bye."

Chas opens the paper note he scribbled the phone numbers on that Charles gave him over the phone. He dials the number for Denis' mother. Someone answered the phone.

"Hello."

"Hello, my name is Chas," Chas whispers. "I'm an old friend of Denis Larson. Are you his mother?"

"No, I'm his Aunt May. My sister is sleeping," May informs. "She doesn't sleep well at night since Denis died. May I help you?"

"Yes, but first, please accept my sincere condolences," Chas responds. "I'd like to attend the funeral."

"That is so thoughtful," May says. "There will be brief service at the Methodist church in town tomorrow. And the funeral is behind the church."

"I'm not familiar with the town," Chas replies. "I'll be flying in from New York City."

"Oh dear," May remarks. "Hold the phone, I will put my son on. He will give you directions. Don't go away."

"Hi, Chas," Jason says. "Fly into Cumberland, West Virginia. Take Rt. 20, south for thirty miles to the town of Limestone. Left at the traffic light for three miles, and the church is on the left side of the road. Service is at 11 AM. Anything else I can help you with?"

"No, Jason, thank you and your mother," Chas replies. "I will see you tomorrow. Bye."

Chas calls his travel agent to have him take care of the necessary arrangements. The florists he uses will send the appropriate flowers.

The following day, Chas was in a rental car heading to pay last respects to his friend.

As he drives the hilly one-lane road through a poor rural area, his mind wanders to all the happy moments he and Denis had spent together. Denis' gift of humor would no longer bring a smile to the pensive Chas. He has a sinking feeling of sadness in his stomach as he realizes his friend is gone.

The church is small; only a few friends of the family and the family are there. Chas is one of a few people that are friends of Denis.

After a brief service and burial, Chas is on his way home. He grabs a cab at the airport in New York, and shortly arrives at *Rounds*.

"You and Paul must be psychic," Tony laughs. "He popped in twenty minutes ago, all excited. He found a bar in the Village he wants to tell you about, Señor."

"I'm not in the mood," Chas moans, "but I better go in and

hear what he has to say."

Chas comes up behind Paul and puts his arm around Paul's neck.

"What's up, buddy?" Chas greets. "Good to have you back. How was your trip?"

"Great, I'll tell you about that later," Paul exclaims. "I am going into the restaurant business. My friend who cooked the pheasants for us found a closed restaurant in the Village. We'll be partners, but he will run the place, being he has been in the business all his life. I will be like you are here.

I want you to see the place before I start the alteration. It will be called *Pharos*, with Egyptian décor."

"Is this the brainstorm you got riding a camel through the hot desert, Paul?" Chas scoffs. "Were you without proper head protection?"

"We had a great time in Egypt. I'd live there if it were realistic," Paul lauds. "Instead, I'll bring Egypt to New York."

"Is your menu going to be Egyptian?" Chas asks.

"One or two dishes will be; the rest, American," Paul lauds. "The décor will be like the Egyptian palace when Moses led the Jews out of Egypt."

"Paul, gimmicks don't make a restaurant successful," Chas warns. "Savvy customers are not fooled with décor. You need good food at the right price."

"I know all that. We know what we're doing," Paul mocks. "I have the key to the place. Can you take a ride now?"

"I guess I'll have to," Chas teases. Let's go; I need cheering up, and what better person than you to do it for me."

During the taxi ride to see the restaurant, Paul asks:

"So, Marlboro Man, how was the drive?" Paul quips. "Any luck with a bar in the Castro?"

"The drive was great," Chas replies. "The bar is taking time; it will happen."

They are in the space. Chas walks around, looking at everything. He is making an appraisal of what the store will require in renovation and décor.

"Nice layout, don't you agree?" Paul lauds. "The layout is perfect and the street gets a lot of walk-bys."

"Don't overdo the renovation. This is the Village, Paul," Chas warns. "You're not uptown, my friend. Keep it simple, I warn you. I learned my lesson the hard way with *Circles*."

They jump into a cab to return to *Rounds*. Paul is explaining how great he feels at being able to do his own restaurant and bar.

* * *

Two months later: In *Rounds*, Bruce tells Chas that Bill is on the phone.

"Hello, Bill," Chas greets. "How's the weather in Puerto Rico?"

"I'm in Brooklyn," Bill laments. "I brought Alley... ah... home in a coffin. Everytime I talk about him I break down; I'm sorry. I know you want to attend the temple and the funeral. It will be tomorrow at the same place, on Atlantic Avenue, where we buried Peter. Ten o'clock. I need to hang up now Chas. Sorry; see you tomorrow."

The next day, Bill, Stanley, and Chas pay their respects to Allen's mother and other relatives. After the service, the somber mood between the three friends is difficult to break. Chas said they should join him at *Rounds*.

"Thanks, Chas," Bill and Stanley say. "But we're anxious to go home where we can deal with our sorrow privately. Tell Seymour we said hello. We have a flight out late this afternoon. Take care."

Four months later, Chas and Camille go to the grand opening of *Pharos*. Paul is beaming as he greets his friends. He kisses Camille on the cheek and gives Chas a hug.

"Thanks for coming," Paul greets. "Let's sit here. Guess what

Jon has cooked up especially for us? The pheasants we shot two weeks ago at the club."

"Okay," Chas lauds. "I always wanted to taste one that is cooked by a professional. Grab a waiter so I can order drinks and spend some money here, Paul."

"My compliments to the chef," Camille lauds. "And your decorator Jerry, where he finds things to accompany a theme is amazing!"

Jon presents the best pheasant meal. After coffee, they are ready to leave.

"Speaking of themes and Jerry Richland's ability, Camille," Chas informs, "we need to get to *Rounds* so I can earn my salary. Paul, you did a good job. Congratulations; we'll see you later."

At *Rounds*, Walter and Richard are sitting at a table, talking and smiling.

"Here are my two favorite drinking partners," Chas greets. "What's up, guys?"

"Walter has been accepted into the seminary, and will be leaving for awhile," Richard said.

"Walter, that's what you wanted," Chas lauds. "Yes, we'll miss you while you're there. But when you get out, we will be able to get together. It will be like old times, except you'll have to lay off the boys for a while."

"I'll be here until after the Christmas holidays," Walter jokes. "You still have time to tease me. God bless you, Chas. You bring a smile to my solemn face these trying days."

"On the bright side, my son said I will be a grandfather next April," Chas exclaims with pride. "Camille will probably be a grandmother if we get married in January as planned."

"No! I won't be a grandma," Camille laughs.

"That is good news, you guys," Walter says. "God takes people with one hand and he brings new life with the other hand."

11 The following January, on a night when a heavy snowfall brought most of the city to a standstill, a stretch-limo with Chas, Camille, her mother, Charles, Paul, and Willie pull up to *The Tavern On The Green* restaurant, adjacent to Central Park, in New York City.

"Wow, look how beautiful the trees covered with snow and all the lights on the branches look," Camille lauds. "It is so quiet with so little traffic, due to the snow. The city has an air of serenity because it's free of the traffic noise. It smells so clean. *Silent night, holy...* "

"I hope you don't intend to sing carols," Chas derides.

"Let's get inside, Camille, I'm getting cold," her mother said.

At their table, Willie raises his glass of champagne to make a toast.

"After all the years we worked together in the construction business," Willie jokes, "I'm happy to be present when my good friend Chas finally does something right: he marries Camille. I wish a happy life to you both."

The following week, Seymour returns from vacation in Puerto Rico, and he and Chas met at *Rounds* for dinner.

"Well, look at you," Chas lauds. "That's some tan you have,

my dear."

"The weather was great, as usual," Seymour replies. "Sorry I was not able to attend your wedding, or the funeral for Allen."

"I received a call from the broker. He finally has a store for us to look at," Chas mentions. "I told him I would wait 'til you came home to see if you wanted to make the trip to San Francisco."

"No, thanks; that is too long a flight," Seymour replies. "Take Ms. Richard, and the two of you decide."

The following week, Chas is waiting at *Rounds* at 2 PM, for Richard to pick him up to go to the airport for their flight to San Francisco. One of the regular day-crowd patrons of designers and sales clerks at Bloomingdales speaks to Chas.

"You must be so excited to be a grandpa soon," Geoff mentions. "We all love Tracy, and we're very anxious about the birth."

"To tell the truth, I was excited when my firstborn was due," Chas remarks. "Now it's my Son's turn to be excited. I'll save my excitement for the birth, not before. Don't let me dampen your enthusiasm. Here is my ride; nice meeting you, Geoff. We'll meet again. Bye."

They arrive in San Francisco. Dave, the realtor, takes them to see the bar.

Both Chas and Richard are impressed with the location, the size, and the condition of the Castro premises. They close the deal and head back to contact Jerry and Bruce. At the airport lounge, congratulations are in order.

"Here's to a successful venture," Chas and Richard say to each other.

Their glasses touched.

Two weeks later, at the *Rounds* cocktail hour, Mike Ostfeld comes in.

"Sunshine, the drinks are on me," Mike lauds. "*Readers Digest* hired me as VP of sales, and they are moving me to San Francisco."

"What a relief, Mike," Chas jokes. "We here at the bar were

wondering if you're going to ask me if you could peddle your body parts at *Rounds*. I'd have to agree, since I suggested that idea. The consensus was to let you do it, so you could afford to buy us drinks. It's great news, my friend. You deserve the best. Congratulations."

Later, Bruce came on duty.

"Jerry and I are set to go and start the design for Castro," Bruce mentions. "We can stay with my friend in Sausalito, and I'll rent a car. I told Edwin to come in tonight so the two of us can tell him what you expect of him in taking over my responsibilities. Okay?"

"That is fine, Bruce; good planning," Chas replies.

The following week, Chas and Camille are in their apartment in the Marina section of San Francisco which overlooks the Golden Gate Bridge.

"I need to see Jerry and Bruce later, to go over some designs that Jerry has," Chas says. "Do you want to join me?"

"No, I made a lunch date with Connie, but thanks for asking," Camille relates. "She misses your buddy Bill, now that he's dead. He smoked and drank excessively."

"You're telling me," Chas remarks. "At lunch every Friday, he drank us all under the table, and did the same at Monday card games. There was always a cigarette in his mouth. He had a great sense of humor. I miss him, too. Give Connie my regards."

As soon as Chas pulled into Dr. David's driveway in Sausalito, Bruce comes to greet him.

"Hi, Boss," Bruce says. "Come on in and say hello to my host. David, this is Chas; Chas, this is David."

"It is good to meet you, David, and thanks for putting my staff up," Chas said.

"No problem. I enjoy the company," David said.

Jerry begins explaining his drawing to Chas.

"This is the layout of the space," Jerry explains. "Here in the center is the huge oval bar. Aside from the bar seating, there is ample standing room, and still room for tables for two people along the wall. In the back area we put the piano lounge, similar to how *Rounds* is set up. Now this is what I'm really excited about. We should name the place *Crawford's*. On the walls, we hang Hurrel headshot photos from the Hollywood studios, taken in the late forties, of famous actors and actresses.

"Especially the Joan Crawford cropped photo, showing only her eyes and mouth. We'll make the photo our logo. The queens will love it.

"I want to spruce up the place with some nice wood, wall covering, a little marble and brass. The lighting is okay, as long as we put in dimmers to complement the mood."

"Jerry, that is cool, and we don't spend a fortune," Chas lauds. "Richard and Seymour will be pleased, along with me, with what you have done. What do you think, Bruce?"

"Being close to the project while Jerry worked on it," Bruce mentions, "I have been in total agreement all along."

"That's good, Bruce, because Seymour, Richard and I made you a full partner in the corporation," Chas lauds. "No financial investment will be required on your part."

"I am at a loss for words," Bruce says. "Here is a hug to convey my appreciation, kid. Does anyone have a tissue?"

"David, if you can recommend contractors that you can vouch for," Chas asks, "it will be a big help getting the place built."

"I know just the people to contact," David replies. "I'll start calling today."

The following week, Chas receives a call from Kelly, the current day bartender.

"Chas, it's Kelly. How are you enjoying California? I'm not disturbing you, am I?"

"No, what is the problem?" Chas says.

"There is no problem," Kelly remarks. "Geoff has a question to ask you. He wasn't aware you were not here. Can he speak to you?"

"Sure, put him on the phone," Chas replies.

"Hi, Chas," Geoff says. "Sorry to call like this, but we need your approval. Me and a bunch of the afternoon's girls' club want to throw a surprise baby shower for Tracy and your granddaughter, Nicole, who's due in April.

We would like to have it at *Rounds* from 1 PM 'til 3 PM. We will cater the food. Since the day crowd is mainly us girls, we will have it by invitation only. A door sign will say Private Party. The group will be about twenty-five people."

"Sure, you can do it," Chas remarks. "I will let my son know. It's so sweet of you guys. Nicole will have twenty-five godmothers. What an entrance that will be."

Mid-March, Chas and Camille traveled to New York to await the birth of Nicole and *Rounds'* eighth anniversary party. On the plane, Camille is reading a magazine. An article she reads seems to pertain to Chas.

"Read this article on Dysthimia. It's a form of low-grade depression, which I think you may have," Camille informs. "It is a recent discovery. There is medication to relieve it."

Chas will check to see if he has it after he is settled in New York.

"Welcome home, Señor," Tony greets.

"Thanks, Tony. How have you been?"

"I can't complain," Tony jokes. "Who will listen to a black man who dresses as well as I do? Who has an important job in a famous Upper East Side club?"

"Glad to hear that. Thanks to you, I rest easier at night," Chas says. "Think I will go socialize."

Inside he finds Paul at Billy's bartending station. He goes over to the two lovers.

"Hi, Boss," Billy says. "Want a drink?"

"Absolutely, and give our honey, Mary, one too."

"Paul, why are you so glum?" Chas teases. "Did you misplace

a dollar bill you can't find?"

"Let's go sit down," Paul says.

They go to a quiet table and sit down side-by-side on the cushion section.

"I have this lump in my arm pit," Paul laments. "The doctor thinks its AIDS. He wants to do more tests this week. I was telling Billy when you came in. I want him to get tested as well. He prefers to wait for my results."

Chas is dumbfounded. He stares at the ceiling, then gulps down his scotch and waves at the waiter to bring him and Paul another round.

"Shit, that sucks," Chas replies. "What do you need me to do for you, Paul? I have a lot of free time."

"Nothing, thanks," Paul mentions. "I'll move in with my mother in New Jersey. From what I know, there is new medication that requires intravenous application. She can help with the nursing. I'll need her to do that stuff. I hate needles. I don't want to be alone in my apartment on Third Avenue. It's too noisy there; I won't get any sleep."

"Give me your mother's address and phone number, and expect to see me as often as you can tolerate visitors," Chas remarks. "Give me a hug, you fuck."

After a long hug the two go to the bar to try and socialize with people they know.

A few days later, Paul's brother brings his truck to the city. He, Chas and Paul load Paul's clothes and personal items. Everything is brought to Paul's mother's house in Ringwood, New Jersey.

"When are you going to the doctor?" Camille scolds. "You mope around all day."

"Having Willie kill himself in his garage with the motor running makes me feel as though I missed an important sign he was trying to convey to me or Bruny," Chas laments. "I can't believe this happened. I thought he was all right, taking his medicine. What a shame, what a damn shame. Boy, will I miss him."

"Okay, Eduardo gave me a number of someone he recommends. I'll go see him tomorrow."

Chas is diagnosed as being depressed, and put on anti-depression medication along with cognitive therapy.

Two weeks later, Geoff and friends hold their surprise shower for an unsuspecting Tracy.

"You guys are such sweethearts, look at these beautiful and expensive presents," Tracy lauds. "Nicole won't need much more than what's here. I'm so touched, I can hardly speak."

She takes a tissue to her nose.

After the party, Charles and the waiter load his pickup truck with all the gifts, then he and Tracy drive home.

Three weeks later: After Tracy's natural childbirth, Charles goes home for some much-needed sleep. Tracy is asleep in her hospital bed.

Chas arrives at the hospital a short time after the birth.

"Grandpa," the nurse greets. "You may take Nicole and sit in Tracy's room."

"She is so small, Nurse," Chas lauds. "She fits on my two hands."

He sits quietly in the room with mother and granddaughter, both sound asleep. He sits, looking at his beautiful first grandchild.

"How are you doing, Grandpa?" The nurse says as she re-enters the room.

"Fine, thanks," Chas answers.

"I will take her now," the nurse says, "and put her in the nursery, where other relatives can see her."

As Chas is leaving, he greets Mari and his in-laws who arrived at the hospital.

"Mother and child are fine," Chas brags. "The nurse just took Nicole from me. She is so good-looking. I see a lot of me in her. Enjoy the view! See ya."

A big grin is on his face.

"Yeah, right," Mari laughs.

Three weeks later, *Rounds* celebrates its eighth anniversary.

"I'm glad to be here," Seymour whispers. "I see some original guests from opening day."

"It wouldn't be a celebration without your presence, my dear," Chas lauds.

"This will probably be the last time I attend our anniversary," Seymour laments. "Chas, you have been my dear friend and partner. Thank you.

"We opened *Rounds* at the height of Camelot. Now our original Camelot customers are quickly disappearing. Because of the AIDS pandemic, forty-thousand talented people have died so far in this city.

Camelot has gotten lost because of this terrible disease. It will take a generation before New York and the world see people comparable to those who have already died. More still will perish from AIDS. I'm glad we shared Camelot together. You made it extra special."

12

A month later in Saint Vincent Hospital, Jerry and Chas are at Seymour's bedside.

"I'm dying, but what bothers me the most is," Seymour bemoans, "I'm embarrassed that my mother has to bury one of her children. Parents shouldn't bury children.

"Jerry, in the eulogy, I want you to say that I went from a grade-school teacher to a perfume salesman and on to a star in the nightclub scene in New York. Everywhere I went, people knew me. I reached my goal to be famous."

Hearing and seeing his emaciated partner and friend of twelve years is twisting Chas' gut. Seymour had become like a father to him. Mostly, he was his constant companion. Not having Seymour in his life is going to require a major adjustment for him.

One week later in a synagogue in Queens, New York, a closed casket with Seymour's body is in front of the bema. The synagogue is packed with people who knew Seymour, as well as friends and relatives of his family.

Jerry says what Seymour asked of him, plus what he feels personally, deep from his anguished heart. Outside after the service, Chas and Jerry hug and go to his mother and sister to pay their respects.

The following week, Chas and Camille are on a plane to San Francisco.

"Mileage rewards are great—we easily get bumped to first class, with minimal extra expense," Chas lauds. "It's the only way to travel, especially for a tall guy like me."

"The alcohol can't wash away the sorrow of losing Seymour and the others," Camille advises. "You only feel more depressed afterwards. Alcohol prevents the medicine from working. Focus on the positive, not the negative. We are going to the opening party of your new club. You have a beautiful new granddaughter, and I love you."

"I know, but Paul is sick and he will die," Chas bemoans. "There is no end in sight. In the back of my mind, I wonder who will be the next casualty."

"The way the government is ignoring AIDS, it is as though they want the gay and intravenous drug users to perish. Government won't have to deal with them anymore.

"As Seymour used to say, 'It ain't easy, Mary'."

"Okay, already; take a nap," Camille scolds. "I will drive when we go to *Crawford's* to meet Bruce and check on how things are progressing. The opening will be a big success; you'll see."

Camille drives the rental car from the airport to *Crawford's* to check the status.

"Bruce, the place looks great," Chas lauds.

"Thanks. We had good contractors and Jerry's design is fantastic," Bruce lauds. "We received positive reviews from the periodicals. The mailing list we used had access to the most concise amount of quality people."

"Good. I'm only sorry Seymour won't be here," Chas mentions. "Richard is due in later. We'll see you tonight."

That night, at the packed *Crawford's*, the customers are in awe over Jerry's work.

"Nice crowd, Rich," Chas boasts. "If we maintain this

response, we will be doing real well."

"I guess I will be bicoastal, like you two," Richard mentions, "spending time in New York, and in San Francisco. The airlines will love both of us."

"In the future," Chas mentions, "I'm going to spend some of my weekdays rounding up beeves for the move to the summer range at Bob's ranch, and some of my weekends in this bar drinking some of the profits."

"While you are playing cowboy," Richard replies, "I will check on Edwin and Charles at *Rounds* in case they need help."

"Thanks. When I get back, I want to see how Paul is doing," Chas remarks. "He tells me over the phone that he is taking a drug that they think will halt this insidious disease. I will believe it when I see it. I hope he's right."

For the next week, Chas enjoys being with Vinton and the other working hands, gathering cattle, putting them in one area, and coming up with a total count.

He and Camille leave California and return to New York.

As usual, Tony Chambers' friendly personality is at the door to great him at *Rounds*.

"Good to see you, Chas. How was San Francisco?"

"Fine, Tony. *Crawford's* is doing real well, thank God," Chas replies. "I got to play cowboy again in the mountains. Those cowboys are dedicated to taking care of the cattle. They put in long, hard hours for low wages. You got to love your work to do that".

"You love *your* work, right, Tony?" Chas asks.

"Yes, however, the customers aren't the caliber we used to cater to in the past. Most are dead," Tony laments. "I have to relax our standards a bit."

"You're doing a great job Tony," Chas praises. "I'm going to have a drink. Can I send you a soda?"

"No thanks," Tony says.

Chas goes to his son.

"How are my granddaughter, her mother and father?"

"Everyone is fine, Dad. You look well. How's Paul doing?" Charles says.

"I will see him tomorrow at his mom's house," Chas mentions. "Business looks good, Edwin makes a nice impression. His continental flair adds class to the place."

"He is a big help with Tracy at home. He helps with some of the day stuff, too," Charles mentions. "I help with the night work, too. We are a good team."

"I am glad you have it under control," Chas remarks. "These customers are not what we started with. It's a whole different clientele now. I won't be spending that much time here, unless you ask me."

"I understand, Dad," Charles says. We have it covered and I certainly will keep you apprised of what goes on."

"I know I can count on you to do a good job. Thanks, Son," Chas said.

The following afternoon, Chas is in Paul's room at his mother's home.

"Boy, you have a lot of medicine here. This should kill any virus, Paul," Chas quips.

"AIDS is a tough virus," Paul responds. "Anything I can get my hands on, I use. What have I got to lose?"

"Your *life*. Don't cut it short," Chas pleads. "Who knows how soon a cure may surface? You want to be around when it does."

"I do what I do, so I feel as if I'm doing something," Paul explains. "If I sit and wait, I'll go crazy."

"Don't say those things. Something will come down soon," Chas mentions. "Keep your chin up, Paul, okay?"

Chas has nothing else he can think of saying to his desperate and discouraged friend.

"Okay, Mary, you look tired. Get some rest," Chas whispers. "I'll see you next week."

For the next eight months, Chas and Camille spend two weeks in San Francisco and two weeks in New York. They spend time at *Rounds*, seeing his family, and visiting Paul. He and Camille visit her family and her friends.

As Chas is visiting, Paul gets the shotgun he used to hunt with Chas, and hands it to him.

"I want you to take care of my gun 'til I return. You can give it back to me then," Paul laughs. "We can hunt birds again. …And I promise I won't shoot mallards again."

To keep his emotions in check, Chas answers.

"Mary, what if you come back as a retriever?" Chas teases.

"Then you won't need any gun," Paul jokes. "I will grab the birds on the ground before they can fly."

A week later, Chas receives a call from Paul's brother Rob, telling him the name of the hospital where Paul has been taken.

Chas quickly gets to the hospital and enters Paul's room. He is greeted by Rob.

"Thanks for coming, Chas," Rob greets. "I know how close you two are. He's sedated, his eyes are open, he can hear a little, and can just about respond.

"Look at how uncanny this is," Rob mentions. "Look what's on the TV—*The Egyptian*. I found it flipping channels."

Chas turns and there on TV, with his white beard and red robe, is Charlton Heston. Chas turns and looks at the skeleton of a once well-built, handsome Paul. He takes Paul's hand, and gets his mouth close to Paul's ear.

"Mary, I've been thinking of our last talk," Chas teases. "Don't come back as a retriever—you grabbing the birds before I shoot them will piss me off. You will love this idea. Come back as a small lapdog. You will sit on my lap and watch TV with me. I will scratch your belly, and you will lick my face and mouth. The best part is, we can sleep in the same bed, but still no sex."

Paul squeezes Chas' hand.

"A lapdog it will be," Paul whispers. "See you later."

"I'm counting on that, Mary," Chas says.

Chas returns from the hospital, but he couldn't go to *Rounds* in the state of mind he is in. Instead he goes to his apartment, fills a glass with ice and Johnny Black, and sits on his terrace to get drunk. Camille is not home, so he doesn't have to deal with her objection.

Two days later, at the funeral parlor, Chas and Camille approach the closed casket. On top of the casket is a picture of a healthy, handsome Paul, smiling, and wearing white pants and white short-sleeve shirt.

"This is what he was afraid of," Chas laments. "He didn't want a closed coffin where mourners couldn't see how handsome he is."

After the church service and the funeral, Chas and Camille are driving to their apartment.

"I'm glad we are scheduled to fly out early tomorrow," Chas mentions. "This city holds too many sad memories. Being here is making me more depressed."

The next day, they are at the modest ranch house in Standish, California. The house sits on three acres that are kept green by Pete, the care taker, and cleaned by his wife, Emma. The remaining fifteen acres are fenced-in to allow the horses freedom to graze and run. The caretaker greets them.

"Glad to see ya," Pete greets. "Did y'all have a good trip?"

"Yes, thanks," Chas replies. "How are Red and the bay horse doing?"

"Fine, just fine," Pete says. "The missus left that stew you like on the stove, anytime you get hungry."

"Oh honey, I forgot to tell you," Camille informs. "Tina and a bunch of the girls are going to a bridal shower tonight, over in Red Bluff. There will lots of food and booze. You know how the cowgirls love their beer. We are staying over. It is too long a ride at night in the condition we'll be in. I'll see you tomorrow afternoon."

That night after dinner, the phone rings.

"Hello," Chas says.

"Hi, Chas, glad you're back," Vinton greets. "I just got a call from Bob. He and his pilot flew the plane checking for beeves in the Sierras that might've escaped our drive last fall. They spotted about ten who managed to survive the winter. He wants me and you, if you're up to it, to push them out and down to the ranch. They are scrawny and need to fatten up."

"I'm up to it, but Red is not in shape," Chas mentions. "What horse is, after not using their muscles for the last four months? You taught me that."

"What we'll do is trailer the horses to the sixty-seven-hundred-foot level," Vinton says. "Bob said the fire road is clear to that point, and that's where the beeves are. It will be good exercise for the horses. It's almost April. They need to start buildin' up. They won't need shoes—the snow is at least a foot or more in the wooded areas."

"Can we wait past sunrise to leave?" Chas asks. "It's still cold here at forty-seven-hundred-feet altitude."

"Sure, we ain't got much work to do, just a few hours," Vinton replies. "Those beeves will be glad to see us come get them. I'll pick you and Red up at eight. Is that late enough?"

"Eight is fine. See you tomorrow," Chas says.

The fire Chas built in the fireplace is going well. He mixes scotch and scotch liquor creating a "rusty nail" in an eight-ounce glass, filled to the top with ice. The leather recliner is comfortable. He relaxes, staring at the flames dancing in the fireplace. The wood burning gives off a pleasant aroma and warmth. He begins reflecting on the past.

This is the life I desperately wanted thirteen years ago. Back then, I hated life in New York City. I went to Puerto Rico, and hated it. Then back to New York to cash in during great earning years, when Camelot was alive. I love the people I worked with and espe-

cially the ones I knew personally. Everyone's dead now. With them, I felt alive and whole. Playing cowboy just isn't the same now. God help me.

When he wakes, he is feeling cold; the fire is out and his glass empty. The room smells of cold ashes. He crawls into bed with his clothes on, too lazy to take them off.

He changes clothes as soon as he wakes up in the morning, showers and dresses; he gets into jeans and a flannel shirt, and wool high-socks before wrestling with his boots next. They are made of durable elephant hide on the bottom and ostrich on top. The top is red; the bottom black. Spurs are strapped to his boots. He puts on chink-styled chaps with their split ends at the bottom that extend halfway down his boot.

This is *Vaquero* style, copied from the original Mexican cowboys. Its style is preferred by northern California cowboys known as Buckaroos.

He chooses a large purple silk neckerchief, called "wild rag," from the other colors in his drawer. It's worn after it's folded first into a triangle, then folded into a four-inch-long shape and raps around the neck, a knot tied in front.

His hat is shaped with the crown round and flat on top. The wide brim is flat to keep as much sun off the face and neck as possible. The brim tilts slightly down, allowing heavy rain to run off the hat and away from the neck.

An insulated vest under a canvas jacket and leather work gloves top off his gear.

As soon as Chas leaves the house, Red smells him, long before he enters the corral. He whinnies to let Chas know he is anxious to receive the grain he gets before a hard day's ride. As the saddle is placed on Red after he'd been fed and brushed, Vinton's dust cloud tells Chas he didn't finish saddling Red a minute too soon.

Vinton jumps out of the dusty pickup truck and comes over to Chas.

"You ready, *pard*?"

"You bet," Chas says.

Vinton leads the big sorrel to the open back of the trailer. Red and Kido, Vinton's horse, know each other and whinny to each other. Chas closes the trailer gate after the horses are in and secure. The fresh manure stinks, filling the air, blotting out the fresh smell of the budding fauna. The crisp air feels good as it fills Chas' lungs and helps clear his head of last night's drink.

"Let's go get some beeves," Vinton exclaims.

They head up the mountain. Chas is normally pensive, but this time his face tells his friend that his mind is sad and off in thought somewhere else.

"Is everything okay, Chas?"

"I'm just tired, Vinton. I'll be fine, not to worry," Chas says.

At the end of the fire road, Vinton shuts the truck off. They get out of the truck and take the horses out of the trailer. Replacing the halters with bridals and reins, they mount up.

"The air smells great with all the tall evergreen trees," Vinton mentions. "Let's get ridin'. I'll take the woods, and you ride along the ridge. That way, we'll get good coverage. Once we pick out the main cow, we'll turn her toward home. The rest will follow her."

"Okay," Chas said.

He climbs into the saddle and turns Red toward the ridge. The saturated ground makes Red sink slightly, making it harder for him to lift his legs out of the glue-like mud. They get to the ridge, and Chas signals Red to turn with a light touch of spur and a little neck rein for him to head in the proper direction, south.

"Good boy," Chas whispers.

Knowing Chas calm tone reassures Red that all is okay.

They have gone seventy yards when Chas spots the lead cow running in the other direction.

"Vinton, there she is, going north," Chas shouts.

Chas, not hearing a reply from Vinton, gives a hard spur to Red indicating he wants him to turn quickly. Red complies but has to back up a little to avoid a large branch in front of his head.

His hind legs get too close to the edge of the ridge. The muddy earth gives way; horse and rider fall backwards down the slope.

Chas is thrown out of the saddle and slides, on his back, down ten feet of slippery muddy ridge. Red is on his back ,sliding down the slope, too—kicking his legs, trying to regain his footing.

Red's total weight of fifteen-hundred pounds is concentrated on the small saddle horn's three inches of area, exerting a force against Chas' ribs of three-hundred-pounds per square inch, as horse and rider collide. Two ribs break, puncturing Chas' lung.

Red quickly rolls off Chas at the bottom of the ridge. He stands patiently with his reins touching the ground and nudges Chas to get up.

Vinton dismounts and is horrified at seeing the "wreck." He quickly slides down the muddy slope toward his friend. He kneels in the mud next to Chas' still body.

Scared at what he sees, he gently puts one hand under his friend's head and raises it slightly out of the mud.

"Chas, Chas—you okay?" Vinton shouts.

With no reply, Vinton checks for pulse and breath. There is no pulse or breath. He removes his glove from his free hand with his teeth. With his clean hand he wipes the mud off Chas' face and closes his friend's eyes. Vinton sobs at the side of his buddy.

The last thing Chas saw and heard in his mind as he suffocated was Seymour saying to him:

"What, are you crazy, Mary? You want to die with your boots on?"

The End

Made in the USA
Columbia, SC
30 January 2021

31725495R00146